POMPEII:

A Conspiracy Among Friends

Robert Colton

This is a work of fiction. All of the characters and events in this story are fictional or used fictitiously.

Pompeii: A Conspiracy Among Friends
Copyright © 2013 Robert Colton
All rights reserved.
ISBN: 148959096X
ISBN-13: 978-1489590961
Published by Seventh Zone Press
Saint Louis, Missouri
Printed in the USA
Cover photo by erburenustudio
Cover design by Robert Colton

10 9 8 7 6 5 4 3 2 1
First Printing June 2013

For more information:
www.robertcolton.com
Twitter @GaiusMarcellus
Facebook: Marcellus Sempronius Gracchus

IN MEMORY OF
BRETT RADLE

Beware that you do not lose the substance by grasping at the shadow

-Aesop

Also By Robert Colton

Rome to Alexandria:
A Collection of Short Stories

Pompeii:
A Tale of Murder in Ancient Rome

A LIST OF VICTIMS, WITNESSES, BYSTANDERS, SUSPECTS, MURDERERS, AND AMATEUR SLEUTHS:

POMPEII

Gaius Sempronius Gracchus Marcellus: a young noble falsely accused of killing his father, masquerading as a slave named Demetrius.

Tay: Marcellus's servant, masquerading as a young noble named Octavius Regulus, in possession of Demetrius.

Cornelia: the most enchanting woman in Pompeii, a broker of secrets, a master at deception.

Julia Felix: the most formidable woman in Pompeii, calculating and charming.

Gavia: the most frustrating woman in Pompeii, a seller of tonics and magic, served with a bit of scorn.

Zenobia: the most feared woman in Pompeii, no secrets are kept from her.

Curtius: a pleasant tavern keeper.

Staphylus: client of Octavius Regulus, a friendly brute.

Jucundus: friend of Octavius, a pleasant banker.

Albius Varro: advocate and frequent guest.

Lutatius: a nervous guest.

Admiral Proculus: despite his reputation, a congenial chap who likes the ladies.

A CAUSE FOR CONCERN

Actius Anicetus: the son of Actia, one of Rome's favorite pantomimes, a curious fellow with much to be curious about.

Celer: Actia's most earnest admirer.

Fannius: a freedman of M. Regulus, and resident of Actia's home.

Phillipus: descendant of imperial freedmen, acting in the best interest of Pompeii, elder brother to Polybius.

Polybius: descendant of imperial freedmen, acting in the best interest of Pompeii, younger brother to Phillipus.

Maius: Pompeii's elite, by merit of wealth.

Pansa: Pompeii's elite, by nature of political concerns.

SOURCE OF SUSPICION

Actia: former servant of Lollia Paulina and once the companion of Agrippina.

Numidius Sandelius Messius Balbus: awarded with a vacated office, the experience was less than rewarding.

Publius Vedius Siricus: awarded with a vacated office, which wasn't the reward he deserved.

Sextus Pompeius Proculus: awarded the office of Special Prefect with judicial power. Represented by his freedman, Eutychis.

Quintus Poppaeus: the uncle of Emperor Nero's wife. Represented by his freedman, Eros.

Marcus Licinius Crassus Frugi the Younger: former brother-in-law to Claudia Antonia, represented by his freedman, Ianvarius.

Claudia Antonia: daughter of the Deified Emperor Claudius, which leaves her at a disadvantage.

Valens: a local politician temporarily living with his son, in the house once owned by his late adopted father, a firm believer that some secrets are best kept among family.

Satrius Valens: son of the before mentioned Valens, proof that every generation has something to hide.

GONE, BUT NOT FORGOTTEN
Decimus Lucretius Valens: Before he crossed the River Styx, he owned a troupe of gladiators. Unlike his adopted son and grandson, he was determined to share a piece of information.

Livineius Regulus: sponsored the games which broke out into a riot, living comfortably as an exile.

Gavianus & Grosphus: his son and adopted son, the city magistrates fated with blame.

Lollia Paulina: formerly married to Publius Memmius Regulus and then Emperor Caligula. Killed by the designs of Agrippina, the last wife of Emperor Claudius.

HELPFUL SERVANTS
Xeus: an elderly slave assigned to Actia's door.

Porpurio: the gods made up for his undeveloped mind with a giant's body.

Samson: property of Cornelia, a tall good-natured man from beyond the Nile.

Ursa: property of Cornelia, a plump woman from Gaul, an expert on stews.

Hesiod: property of Cornelia, a swarthy fellow from Byzantium.

Corax & Ajax: servants belonging to Octavius, handsome young teenagers with much to whisper about.

Primus: property of the Pompeian council, proficient in collecting taxes and bribes.

A SOURCE OF INCOME
Porcia: ginger hair, freckled skin, sold for 500 pieces of bronze.

Servia: black hair, olive skin, harsh, prices vary.

Sosia: blonde hair, alabaster skin, seductive, pricey but worth it.

Delia: dark hair, doe eyes, full-figured, priced right.

Lucia: light brown hair, emerald eyes, fees negotiable.

Gaia: black hair, petite, a gift from the Far East, singular skills at reasonable prices.

Mucia: inquiries welcome.

ROMAN CITIZENS OFTEN REFERRED TO

Arria: the most beautiful stepmother a young man could want.

Appius: Arria's son, a bit of a quandary.

Petronius: Consul of Rome, dear friend to Marcellus, witty and well-connected.

Appian: a noted historian, recipient of many letters.

AND THOSE WHO REMAINED IN EGYPT, STILL

Eumolpus: Marcellus's chaperone, conniving and dishonest.

Young Milo: valet to Marcellus, smarter than he's given credit for.

A LIST OF GODS PRAYED TO AND CURSED AT

Roman Deities

Jupiter: King of the Gods, can't be expected to answer every plea.

Fortuna: The Goddess of fate, generous with other peoples' coins.

Bacchus: God of wine and mystery, a good deity to invoke when having a good time.

Morpheus: God of dreams, he has a vivid imagination.

Hercules: a demigod, and patron to the people of Pompeii.

Venus: Goddess of Love, which means she has a twisted sense of humor.

Laverna: Goddess of Thieves and Cheats, a busy deity, indeed.

Janus: God of Beginnings and Transitions. Of course, conclusions also entertain him.

Neptune: God of the Sea, had he brought about a rough sea, fewer prayers, and curses would have been invoked.

Charon: the ferryman, very busy taking the dead across the River Styx.

EGYPTIAN DEITIES

Ra: God of the Sun, bringer of Order to Chaos, sometimes.

Osiris: God of the Dead, enjoys irony.

Seth: God of Chaos, husband to Nephthys, proficient at his tasks.

Anubis: Protector of the Dead, nephew to Osiris, busy.

Geb: The Great Cackler, God of Snakes, father of Osiris, his laughter causes earthquakes.

Nephthys: Goddess of Transitions, mother of Anubis, on good terms with her sister.

Isis: Goddess of Fertility, among other things. Sister to Nephthys.

To My Dear Appian:

I pray this letter finds you well, as am I. I have just settled aboard a rather spacious boat preparing to depart from Rome and deliver me to where my own ship awaits us in Ostia. I must confess that I miss you and your wife already.

I wish that I had been able to spend more time with you during my stay, but my hostess kept my attention. As I indicated at dinner the night before, I was shocked to see how frail my friend Plotinia has become.

Reaching the advanced age that I have has certainly been a favor of the gods, and yet the pain of watching dear friends edge to and across the River Styx has been a harsh trade.

I hope that dear Plotinia recovers from her malady soon. Despite the insistence of my own physician that I'm too old for travel, it will prove a good reason to return to Rome for another visit.

I so enjoyed our brief time together, and I must apologize for what might have seemed befuddlement on my part. In truth, I was simply distracted by the endless interjections of Tay and my daughter as I tried to answer the questions you asked.

Your curiosity on the subject of Pompeii's recovery after the great quake did, of course, delight me. Ever the historian, recounting an episode of the past that I took part in is far more enjoyable than reciting a passage of my own works on Alexander or Agrippa. However, the days just after the quake proved to be a rather touchy subject with my companions. As Tay attempted to redirect our conversation, I became frustrated with him. Of course, that was until he gave up and I began to rattle on.

My own voice startled me; my descriptions of the prostitutes we had inherited from Popidius, and the explanation of how Tay had them rented out by a dependent, caused me to blush. And then came the unstoppable names erupting from my mouth: Actius, Julia Felix, and Cornelia, and then the mention of a love triangle, this made me realize why Tay had tried to change the topic. I stumbled over my words while my wife stared at me and my daughter continually cleared her throat; thank the gods that Tay made one more attempt to redirect the story.

He omitted a great many important details and focused mostly on our follies. My dear wife laughed at all the right puns, but I'm sure she was as irritated with me as I was embarrassed by myself. Yet I must remember, those so-called friends who attended the dinner held in your honor have all heard, in part, the stories of my masquerading as a slave. They still crowd my suppers at my house in Rome and flock to visit me at my estate in Liternum. Think what they will of me, I have always disagreed with my old friend Pliny's uncle when he wrote: "It is generally much more shameful to lose a good reputation than never to have acquired it."

Well, without shaming my companion or family in front of their friends, I must share with you the true account of those trying times. And I shall not leave out a single detail to spare my dignity.

The days just after the ground waged war on the poor citizens of Pompeii proved as challenging as the disaster. Fear and uncertainty embraced the populus. Acts of kindness and injustice played out. Tay and I witnessed the behavior of both the best and worst of the city's elite and the shunned.

Chapter One:
The Actor's Mask

丹丹丹丹丹丹丹丹

"Vesuvius?" an unfamiliar voice asked from over my shoulder. I smiled and nodded at the fellow who had wandered out to the courtyard. He looked carefully at the mural I was painting. Studying the figures descending from the local mountain, he pointed to a dashing man who was charging ahead of the rest, holding a drawn sword, and remarked, "Spartacus!" The stranger chuckled, eyeing me up and down. He hadn't failed to notice that the painted hero leading his fellow rebels bore a striking resemblance to the artist.

I had spent less than half of Februarius masquerading as a slave, yet those few days had opened my eyes to what life was like for people who were viewed as mere property. I could see how a man might decide to defy his fate and inspire others to follow him. I was more surprised by the fact that history recalled only a few such revolts. It took a man with pride and courage to flout what both the gods and civilization had decreed.

There were few Spartacus's in the world. I was a prime example of how few. Like the Slave Revolt's leader, I had defied my fate, but out of cowardly behavior rather than courage. When falsely accused of killing my father, I had fled from Rome. After stumbling into Pompeii, the custodian of a dead woman's newborn, my own slave staged *his* revolt. He introduced himself as a prosperous Roman, the friend of a Consul, no less, and he passed me off as *his* valet. Well, I suppose it was rather insulting to the long-dead Spartacus that I had painted my own features onto the figure leading his fellow rebels down the side of Vesuvius.

Standing beside me, the man's eyes followed the slope of the mountain down to the approaching army. I had chosen to portray the events somewhat differently than recorded. My Spartacus would confront his enemy head on, rather than a sneak attack from the other side of the mountain. As a historian, I have always preferred fact over romance, but as an artist, the boldest image is superior to the accurate.

The stranger surveying my work was a man in his mid-forties; he had dark, but greying hair, and a build that indicated an athletic youth that had been exchanged for a life of luxury. He wore a loose-fitting tunic, dyed in yellow, and clean, delicate sandals that suggested a handful of slaves had delivered him upon a sedan chair.

"How talented you are," he remarked with a genuine tone of approval.

Not only had I traded my freedom when fleeing from Rome, I had left my voice behind as well. My loyal companion, who had never really played the role of servant all that well, had deemed me too *honest* to keep up with the lies he had told upon our arrival in Pompeii. So, he introduced me to our original host as his mute servant.

Keeping true to the character of *Demetrius, the silent valet of Octavius Regulus,* I was left to remove the little wax tablets that hung from my neck and carve out the words, "Thank you."

The man's brow furled as he watched me, then his forehead smoothed, and he gave a slight nod as he realized that I *was* mute.

He spoke with a local accent, which gave his Latin words a rather Greek flourish, "Fine work, fine work, indeed."

"Celer?" I recognized the voice of a man named Decimus Satrius Lucretius Valens calling from the atrium. He was a guest of *Regulus's*.

My companion had become quite involved with the politically influential of the town, which were in the early stages of rebuilding after the terrible quake. This was a rather odd farce; Tay was too young to hold office, a native of Alexandria and, at least according to a long lost document, my property. All the same, the gods seemed to enjoy our little performance, thus, the actor's masks would stay on.

Valens joined us in the courtyard. Ignoring me, a mere slave, he reached out for the hand of the man he'd called Celer. "This must be urgent business, have you found out something?"

"I have received a message from Actius. He will be here as soon as possible."

Valens had worn the politician's face when he greeted Celer, a warm smile and wide eyes. After Celer spoke, the smile became less warm, and the eyes narrowed a bit. "Well, so be it, maybe he can get to the heart of the matter. The town council has more pressing matters…"

"You say that, but remember, Actius is a friend of Nero's." Celer's words may have been less of a reminder and more of a threat. "I think that her death should be explained before he arrives–" and the end of his statement was clearly meant to be a threat, "–less questions for *everyone.*"

In the few days that I had observed Valens, I had formulated a positive opinion of the man. He was a steady politician, mild-mannered and calm. He struck me as honest, at least as honest as any man elected to office might be. The fellow was in his forties and possessed the wisdom of a man who had taken the right course more often than not. He was respected, successful, and known for his sensible leadership. I suspected that veiled threats were not what motivated this man.

"Celer, *this time,* there is no conspiracy. Actia was killed in the quake. Whoever might claim to have seen her was mistaken. I need not remind you of your loyalties. By sending word to Actius that she was murdered, you are the one asking for more questions."

Celer pressed his lips together, perhaps searching for another threat. Instead, he slowly exhaled and said, "All the same, he will be here soon. Regardless if I remain silent, he will have questions."

A true politician, Valens replied, "And we will answer them as well as we can." The man's tone changed, and it was now he who made the veiled threat, "Know your place, let the rumors *die.*"

Valens excused himself and returned to his host's study. Celer waited a moment, frowning at the man's back, before he told me, "You are much better off without a tongue, you'll never find yourself trapped by a lie."

***

Tay snapped his fingers and beckoned me to his study. His numerous guests, all men of political importance, had departed.

Either Corax or Ajax was removing a tray of picked-over food. The two young Greek servants were nearly identical in appearance. We waited in silence until the mess was cleared and we were left alone.

Tay sat behind his elegant writing table, wearing a wig of little black ringlets to conceal his own growing hair. When we first met in Alexandria, nearly four years before, he had kept his head shaven and worn kohl around his eyes. Then, at the age of sixteen, he had appeared as a full-grown, handsome young man, while I, only six months younger, had still looked like an awkward youth.

The white linen robes, the shaven head, and the lined eyes had all been a sort of costume for Tay. I hadn't been observant enough to realize that his square jaw and aquiline nose hinted toward a Roman ancestry. Nor could I fathom the reason for the deception.

With the change in character, Tay looked perfectly natural in the new costume. His white tunic, with a dark crimson border, was reminiscent of a toga. He wore a tasteful, jeweled signet ring and no other jewelry. Soon, the wig would be discarded for his own natural black hair. No one would have guessed that he was once an Egyptian slave, whose owner was on the run.

"Well, that couldn't have worked out better if I had planned it. Just as I was seeing my guests to the door, a letter arrived from *my* dear friend Petronius." Tay pointed at the scroll on his writing table.

Petronius, who was a favorite of the Emperor Nero's, was, in fact, *my* friend. After arriving in Pompeii and assuming his false identity, Tay had boldly mentioned to anyone who might listen that he was friends with the former Consul. Via this connection, he had also fostered the implication of a relationship with Nero himself.

I resisted the urge to snatch the piece of parchment from the desk. Petronius's scribe had copied the few letters we had received in hieroglyphics, leaving me dependent on Tay to translate.

"What does he have to say?" I whispered, eager for information about the life I had fled from.

Tay gave me a condescending frown. "Mostly politics, you would be bored. The wheels are set in motion. *The Gold One* is very worried about the welfare of our sad city. His wife's uncle has sent pleas for money, men, and fresh supplies. Which is rather kind of Poppaeus, considering that he left Pompeii immediately after the quake." His voice took on a playfully frustrated tone, no doubt mocking one of his departed guests, "He's across the bay in Misenum where they have clean water." Tay's frown became less humorous. "I can tell by your glazed-over eyes that I have lost you."

I shrugged. I was concerned for the well-being of my fellow Pompeians but relatively powerless to do much about it. Besides, the mere mention of Nero and his family irritated me, for it was *he* that I was hiding from.

Tay's posture became less relaxed, while his voice took a jovial tone, this was my hint that I wouldn't care for his next piece of news. "Petronius did have a question he wanted me to ask you, he thought it might be rather amusing if you chose the epithet for *your* grave marker." He couldn't help but flash me his wicked grin.

While on the run, we had camped in a barn outside of Pompeii with two others hiding from their own secrets, Marcus and Helen.

A couple of hired thugs had killed Helen, leaving us with her newborn baby. Tay was left to battle the two henchmen. The barn caught fire and burned to the ground with the assassins inside.

The local magistrates had surmised that my bones were among the grisly carnage found. Petronius had dispatched his own men to collect these remains, playing up the theory. I was appalled by the thought that a nameless brute would rest beside my illustrious family. But then I considered the crimes my bloodline had committed and decided that Tay and Petronius might be correct. The bones of another man resting in place of Gaius Sempronius Gracchus Marcellus was preferable to the alternative.

Prepared for an argument or a plea to the gods for justice, Tay was surprised when I calmly told him, "*If not in this life, then perhaps the next.*"

A resurrection might still be possible. If not, I would make the most of the life I had just started. This was a wise attitude for a nineteen-year-old, and particularly insightful as it was mine. For I must now admit, my life had been a peculiar strand of many poor choices balanced by a few excellent decisions.

Tay contemplated my words, what meaning he took from them, I could not guess. Nor did I ask, a little mystery might serve us well. He let a quiet moment pass as we both thought about the events that had brought us to Pompeii.

"Who was Valens speaking to earlier?" Tay asked, changing the subject as he gingerly worked a finger under the wig he wore.

I whispered my reply, realizing that my tone had risen due to distraction, "His name was Celer. He told Valens that a man named Actius would be in Pompeii soon. He mentioned a woman's death and that there would be questions."

"What type of questions?" asked Tay, attempting to sound only vaguely interested in what the two men had discussed. We had just solved the murder of a local magistrate, the murder of the dead man's mistress, and the attempted poisoning of a dubious oracle, all of which we had concluded merely two days before.

My companion would never admit to it, but he had enjoyed the sleuthing. I had not; in the process of answering our questions, we had traded the life of an innocent man for our safety. Less troubling, but just as problematic, we had let a guilty man accidentally poison himself, stolen a baby, and made an enemy out of the local High Priest of Isis, a man capable of murder.

"Valens said something about a woman being seen after the quake, but this was an error. She had been killed during the disaster. He implied Celer had made a mistake by sharing this incorrect news with Actius...and some reference to all this as *not* being a conspiracy..." I hesitated before adding the words, "*this time.*"

"That's all?"

I whispered, "That's all."

My friend looked rather disappointed. Tay pressed his lips together and mulled over the little drama that I had witnessed before remarking, "Cornelia wouldn't be happy with such scant information."

This time I pressed my lips together and sighed. It was time for me to head off to the Oracle of Nephthys's cave for the evening rituals. Luckily, I was only admiring her, not spying for the woman.

The beautiful Cornelia – describing the woman is far easier than defining her. Less than ten years my senior, she was just in her prime. Long coils of lustrous walnut hair framed a small face the shape of a strawberry. Her eyes were dark brown and glistened brightly as if reflecting the rays of a well-fueled brazier. Petite and shapely, she was every dressmaker's dream. A discarded grain sack draped over her and tied by a leather cord under her bosom would have somehow managed to appear elegant on Cornelia.

I had been captivated with Cornelia since the moment my eyes fell upon her. She had mused that men fell in love with womens' faces rather than their hearts. I believe she had made an accurate pronouncement. Her beauty blinded me to her suspicious character. On the few occasions when I saw past the mask, I was left with unpleasant thoughts. However, I had to remind myself, someone had attacked the woman's slave, destroyed her property, and even tried to poison her just days after Pompeii had suffered a disastrous quake. Perhaps my expectations weren't realistic.

She was a mystery on two fronts. On a professional level, she proved masterful at deception. On a personal plane, she was little more than a shadow and vague innuendo. I knew as much about her as I did the mechanics of a siege engine.

Cornelia portrayed the part of a veiled translator who whispered the words of the Egyptian Goddess Nephthys. Her accomplice was a robust Nubian man who somehow made for a convincing female oracle. Dressed in gowns, wigs, and crowns, Samson became the embodiment of a mystical deity.

The fine ladies, and the not-so-fine women, of Pompeii sought the goddess's guidance, with the occasional male visitor as well. Daily rites were held at dawn and dusk, with private audiences granted every three days to the devotees. In exchange for an offering, a question could be put to the Oracle, in the hopes that Nephthys would respond through her mortal vessel.

In answer to the query, Samson spoke gibberish in a sultry, effeminate voice. Cornelia, wearing a semi-transparent, white veil clasped to her head by a simple gold diadem, would *speak* the Oracle's words in an eerie, breathy, high-pitched whisper.

Her answers were a combination of common sense, well wishes, logical warnings, and if the devotee was fortunate enough, a sound piece of information based on Cornelia's tireless spying and eavesdropping on the locals. Regardless of the value of the offering, the two put on a damn fine show.

Removed from her costume, Cornelia was a rather guarded person. I knew that she had trained in the nearby town of Cumae with the Sibyl. Either the Sibyl was a legitimate seer, or her skill level was just superior to Cornelia's abilities. The beautiful woman had abandoned her hopes of one day taking the current soothsayer's role and started her own franchise.

She had also mentioned being in love and having been hurt. I couldn't imagine the type of character who would have toyed with Cornelia and actually obtained the upper hand. Only a fool would have let her slip away once she had given him her heart.

I had no idea where she came from, what kind of family might tolerate her career, or even her social status. I was inclined to think she was freeborn, but her lack of a guardian gave me pause. Attractive, well-spoken, even able to read, she could have passed herself off, much like my own servant had, as a noble. I hadn't the nerve to ask her all of my questions, nor did it matter. She relished being a mystery.

Cornelia was the only person in Pompeii who knew our secret. We trusted her for the sole reason that, while she knew my identity, we also knew hers. It was an uneasy truce for Tay. Furthermore, I was prone to following my companion's instruction, unless redirected by a lovely lady. As far as Tay was concerned, he had accurately surmised on the day he had first witnessed her behavior in the forum that she was trouble.

For the time being, Cornelia had been our houseguest, occupying the decadent room that had once been Popidius's. When she wasn't walking among the locals listening to their chatter, or repeating the gossip in her cave just outside of town, I had hoped to continue my pursuit of a quiet moment alone with her, to share one more kiss.

Leaving Tay to his dubious business, I passed through our open vestibule doors, exchanging a quick nod with Mucia. The oddest of the prostitutes we'd inherited from Popidius, Mucia was a young hermaphrodite who easily passed as a door-boy when Ajax and Corax were assigned to other tasks.

Once on the uneven sidewalk, I glanced this way and that way, to see who might also be on the street. I had no cause for alarm or excitement. Other than the army of workmen repairing the damage to the house across the narrow avenue, I was alone to hurry off to the Oracle's cave.

In order to arrive at the same time as the principal cast, who traveled by drawn wagon, I had to leave nearly half an hour before them on foot. Of course, this early departure also kept, or spared, me from making the journey at the side of another temptation, a devotee named Julia.

The home that we had inherited from the unfortunate Popidius sat across the street from the residence of Julia Felix. An enchanting beauty herself, Julia was a wealthy woman who had interpreted the recent quake as a good reason to remodel her home.

The old saying goes: *There is nothing less attractive than a wealthy woman.* I understood the sentiment, even if I disagreed. I respected Julia's independence and desire to enjoy the power that her wealth offered her. My first impression had been that of a spoiled woman, removed from the world's day-to-day troubles. But I had revised my opinion of her. She traded her youth for duty; she had put her father's needs before hers. Now that he was Pluto's ward, her own life had begun.

Julia had been generous to the local Isis cult. Her coins had bought her the sycophantic obedience of the High Priest, Tiburs. The same man had attempted to kill Cornelia, as the new soothsayer was siphoning off some of Isis's profit. Tay had played a nasty trick on the priest and offered Julia the same jug of poisoned wine meant to introduce Cornelia to Osiris, god of the dead.

Tiburs, fretful that the bearer of so much generosity might come to harm, had slapped the cup of wine out of Julia's hand. Of course, the liquid offered to Julia from the jug had been exchanged for the tainted stuff that Tiburs had sent to his competitor, but he had no idea of just what my companion was up to. Tiburs's unexplainable actions had sent Julia into a rage. The Priest's attempt at murder was punished with the loss of his chief patroness.

Julia had already been seeking the blessings of Nephthys, even before her fallout with Isis's mortal representative. I suspected that more time and gold would be *spent* with the Oracle.

Leaving home, I set off on the short distance toward the city gate. Just outside of Pompeii, on the land that had not so long ago been dominated by the tombs of the dead, I entered the domain of those unfortunates who'd lost their homes and fled to open ground.

Even during the daylight of the late afternoon, I felt a growing trepidation as I passed. A few children played near vigilant mothers, who watched me slink by. I made eye contact and gave nervous smiles to the men who tended over open fires or stood huddled together. I was growing increasingly fearful of these people, as were many who still resided within the city walls.

The politicians promised food, medicines, and shelter for these people; if the talk didn't amount to something soon, desperation would drown out the empty words.

I reached my destination, rather quickly and unscathed. The grove that sat beside a trickling creek that sprang from the Oracle of Nephthys's adjoining cave was vacant, save for a familiar idol and a flock of small, dark birds.

In one fluid movement, the starlings took off and flew first to the left, and then swirled to the right. A good omen, I thought.

Hesiod, the slave who guarded the Oracle's cave, peered out from his realm. We made eye contact, and his head slipped back into the shadow. He had no use for me. In fact, I assumed he resented my presence. We both knew he was far more capable of protecting his mistress than I.

A moment later, I heard the wagon approach. Hesiod popped back out of the cave and walked past me to greet Cornelia.

The woman slipped off of the wagon with the help of Samson. Her open cloak billowed in the breeze, and the sunlight glistened off of her walnut hair. For an instant, in true character of a nineteen-year-old, I thought of nothing but how beautiful she was.

Completely aware of my weakness, and her power over me, we exchanged questionable smiles. Neither of us was really sure of the other's true feelings. We had only opened up enough to share confusing emotions. I had babbled youthful platitudes, and she contradictory insults and innuendo.

Hesiod led the donkeys and the wagon off to some secret location beyond the cliff face behind us while Samson and Cornelia entered the cave to don their mystical costumes.

I paced back and forth in front of the deteriorating idol of Nephthys. The original stone statue that had sat in the grove had been destroyed by Tiburs, his first act of violence against Cornelia. The new, temporary device was a random bust anchored to a wooden platform covered with weathered stolas. The makeshift form had two planks arranged like arms to hold a tray that still bore the offerings from the morning rituals.

One by one, or group by group, the devotees of Nephthys arrived. Coins, small loaves of bread, and random items of indeterminate value were placed on the idol's tray.

Despite being new to the group, I recognized each face. The loyal followers spoke amongst themselves for a moment. I was greeted, but nothing was asked of me. The devotees were under the impression that I sought Nephthys's aid in giving me speech.

In time, anticipation of the star attraction brought devout silence after the pleasantries were exchanged.

From the mouth of the cave, the Oracle and *her* veiled translator emerged. The Oracle was resplendent, as always. A tall, golden crown sat atop an elaborate black wig. The flowing, yellow gown somehow concealed that the demigoddess was, in fact, a muscular Nubian man. The Oracle's acolyte was clad in her simple attire, a sheer white veil, and a long white gown; she was otherwise unadorned.

I knew the ceremony, I had attended each of the rituals since Cornelia mistakenly assumed that the destruction of her statue was my fault. As with each rite, the Oracle chanted a few verses in Egyptian, which were translated. The acolyte spoke in a strange, high-pitched voice to mask her own low, sultry tone. Once several verses had been translated, Nephthys's mortal vessel began to touch us about the shoulders with her golden crook and beaded flail. We were all blessed by the divine Goddess, sister of Isis, mother of Anubis, and wife to Seth.

The early evening ritual concluded all too quickly, and had been a complete blur to me. The reason for this was because of the identity of the last devotee to arrive. As the others had fallen silent and gathered by the idol, Julia Felix joined the group.

My show of devotion to Cornelia was jeopardized by Julia's presence. The last occasion Julia had participated in the evening rites, she had shared her covered litter with me. A seemingly innocent gesture, allowing her neighbor's valet a safe ride home was hard to say no to, especially for a *mute*. Julia not only proved a disruption to my duties to Cornelia, but also a distraction.

Once Samson and Cornelia turned back toward the cave, the collection of devotees broke apart. A small handmaid tugged at my arm. My chest tightened, I was panic-stricken and somehow delighted at the same time. Cornelia had stolen my heart, but it had only been a few days since Julia had stolen a kiss from me.

I was, of course, worried that Cornelia would be displeased with me for leaving with Julia, but I was young and relished the opportunity to sit side by side, concealed with the woman who had discreetly shown me more attention in mere minutes than Cornelia, who'd had days worth of opportunity, ever had.

I was guided over to the litter, and Julia was already reclined within. With a soft sigh, she said, "I don't understand how Regulus lets you wander through *those* people unattended. It's not safe…here, get in."

Rather eagerly, I climbed into the litter, before I was settled beside the lady, she snapped her fingers, and the four hulking men who carried her hoisted us up. The last time, the only other time, I had traveled with her, the day had been cold, and she was fast to have the curtains closed around us. As the sun crawled toward the horizon, the air was still unseasonably warm, and to my disappointment, the curtains remained open.

We left the grove, and the men carried us over the winding road. After a few minutes of silence, Julia spoke, "I don't suppose you know what came over Tiburs the other day?" Due to the tone of voice and the arch of her brow, I was relieved that I was unable to voice a response. "He's always been a difficult man, but that outburst…" her smile made me think of a cat, batting at a mouse rather than killing it. "I think there's much more to his behavior than the insult of sharing wine from the Oracle."

She was correct, but all I could do was shrug. She smiled at me oddly, amused I suspected.

Julia gave another light sigh. "Regardless, I think I'm glad to be done with him." She peered outside of the litter; we were approaching the refugees. "Close the curtains," she told me. "I don't want them leering at me." I was as pleased to be closed away from the poor souls as I was to be concealed with Julia. I thought that perhaps she would kiss me once more.

The litter gently lowered to the sidewalk, and the handmaid pulled back the curtain next to Julia as she emerged. With far less grace, I scrambled out.

Before darting across the street, Julia told me, "It's silly for you to walk all the way out to the Oracle, I'll send for you before I leave tomorrow." I bowed my head and fled back home.

One of the Greeks opened the door for me. I darted into the atrium, unsure of what to do. Doubling back to the cave and escorting Cornelia, only to be chastised, seemed less than pleasant. Before I could make up my mind, I heard two voices moving closer to the atrium. I froze, unsure how to escape; and then the two were upon me.

"Well, he's back much sooner than I thought he would be," Tay told his guest. I could not help but notice that my companion's grin was rather devious. "Demetrius, this is Aemilius Celer." He was referring to the man who'd spoken to Valens in the courtyard earlier in the day. "He's impressed with that outrageous mural you are painting in the courtyard." I nodded and smiled. "He has a delicate work that needs to be touched up before his patron returns to the city, with so many of the known painters already busy, he thought, perhaps, I could be persuaded to have you do the work."

"A bust, of my late patroness, only slightly damaged, but I'd like to have it corrected before her son comes home." Celer smiled kindly at me. At that moment, I realized that he was a freedman, and understood what it was like to be another man's slave; loaned out, unappreciated, used. I was eager to paint for the man, pleased by his notice of my talent.

"Tomorrow then, I'll send him around the fourth hour." Tay told Celer, as they slowly walked towards the vestibule.

"Fine, good, I doubt the work will take him long." Celer's steps slowed, his eyes squinted, and he fingered a small bag on his belt. After fumbling for words, he asked awkwardly, "While I am here…I was wondering…is Sosia…busy?"

I bowed my head and passed by the two men, who were obviously done with me. I made my way to the back of the house to see what stew had brewed for dinner.

Geb, our mutt, met me in the cramped kitchen. Somehow, the dog always knew when I was about to eat. I ladled myself a bowl and found some bread.

Passing through the courtyard, I was happy to see Staphylus sitting on a bench near the side gate leading out to the alley. He was nearly recovered from being poisoned by tainted wine meant for Cornelia.

It was the time of day that a small group of men were departing before the next batch arrived to *visit* the girls that Tay rented out.

Due to the quake, the baths were closed. This presented the men of Pompeii, who were used to spending their late afternoons in the communal environment, with time on their hands.

Our five girls were adorned and primped for the well-off, middle-class men, whom Tay was happy to play host to. Secluded in their little chambers, the women earned our income, which, for good manners, was handed off to Staphylus at the gate. These men would depart, homeward bound, giving the women time to cleanse and take a bite to eat.

Once the sun began to set, the laborers and skilled craftsmen who toiled to rebuild Pompeii would arrive. Some might stop by the taverns or eateries along the way, while the more amorous fellows made no such diversions.

Despite the curfews and the brawn assigned to keep people off the streets after dark, members of the naval force commanded by Volvulus Proculus would be the last to arrive once discharged from their repairs to the local harbor.

I decided to take my meal upstairs to our peaceful room. A single oil lamp did little to illuminate the worn chamber, decorated with an aged fresco depicting a jungle scene. I went from lamp to lamp, lighting each one until surrounded by a warm glow.

I tore off a crust of bread and opened the little doors to my small shrine. While Geb drooled and stared at me, I said my prayers to the gods. I made the feeble offering of the crust, sure that Tay would toss it out to the birds later, and then I ate my stew.

My solitary moment was quickly interrupted. The door opened, and Tay peered inside and said, "Ah, there you are." He stepped in, and looked over my small meal before quoting Aesop, "*A crust eaten in peace is better than a banquet partaken in anxiety*" His grin appeared, and he asked, "How did you get home so soon? Cornelia still hasn't returned."

My whisper was rather loud, "Julia insisted I return with her…"

"And you couldn't argue," he retorted, with a rather devious tone.

"How could I?" My protest sounded rather weak.

"How could you, indeed." He laughed. "Doesn't matter, you need not follow Cornelia any more, she knows who's out to harm her now, and it's her own affair. I'll be glad to rent her the rooms above the shop, but she's no longer our concern."

I took in a deep breath. I had very mixed feelings on the matter. My youthful mind was coping with my emotions, and my desires. Cornelia had all but told me that perhaps she had growing feelings for me and, at the same time, alluded that she had no intention of letting these feelings get the better of her.

I knew that we would not unite at the end of the farce and live happily together. We were both living a shadowy life filled with deception and lies. If my truth was discovered, it would cost me my head, and if Cornelia's hoax was discovered, she would be off to the next town as some new seer, oracle, or soothsayer. I don't know that I can accurately describe my feelings, other than to say, I suspected that my lust was not going to be quenched by the woman who so enthralled me. But that isn't to say that I was ready to give up.

Following Cornelia also afforded me the chance opportunity to be alone with Julia, ever so briefly, yet it was ever so satisfying. She may not have been the object of my affection, but how flattering it was to receive her, alas brief, affections.

"I don't mind going, just to watch over the ceremony," I mumbled.

Tay laughed, "I'm sure you don't." Then he sighed, a signal that the subject was about to be changed. "I've sent Ajax off to get some paint and brushes for you. Celer is expecting his patroness' son."

"He's a freedman isn't he?" I wanted to confirm my suspicion.

"Yes, but strangely not to his patroness, he's a freedman of Valens's. Yet, he runs the house of a woman named Actia, who was killed in the quake. You know who her son is, Actuis Anicetus – *yes* I thought you'd know that name."

The look on my face no doubt registered a hint of concern. Actuis Anicetus, possibly as well-known an actor as Paris, was the nephew to the man who helped Nero kill his mother four years before. He proved himself even more loyal to Nero a few years later by claiming to have had an adulterous affair with Nero's wife, Octavia. He did this at the young Emperor's request in order to banish her. Of course, the poor Octavia was just too popular, calls for the end of her exile resulted in her death.

"I'm not repainting anything for that family," I snapped, feeling a bit of Spartacus's zeal run through me. "It's bad enough we've had Proculus under our roof for the past three nights." Volusius Proculus was a friend, and junior officer to Anicetus. He had assisted in the murder of Nero's mother, Agrippina.

Proculus, a bear of a man, had taken a liking to Servia, a rather harsh, prostitute whom Tay owned. Up close, the rough fellow lived up to the image that I had created of him. Of course, there was a touch of irony in the fact that I secretly was growing fond of the man. I still held him in contempt for his involvement in Agrippina's death. And yet, I had to remind myself, what fool would refuse Nero's orders?

"No, I think you shall do what he's asked." Tay spoke with a familiar condescending edge. "Valens will see it as a favor, and it's not a bad idea to do a favor for Anicetus as well; he knows Nero. Perhaps *the delegation* might ask Anicetus to join them when they solicit help from the Emperor."

The delegation he referred to were the political elite of Pompeii. Tay's private joke was that no actual delegation could be decided upon. Each leading man thought that it should be he and his lackeys who traveled to Rome. No progress had been made, aside from Tay catching a glimpse of just who was loyal to whom.

A leading member of the assemblage was Valens, who Tay had made fast friends with. Valens lived just down the street from us in a house barely standing after the quake. He had taken a liking to my companion, who was quick to join in on searching the neighborhood for survivors in the disaster's aftermath.

Tay went on, "Making the acquaintance of Actius Anicetus upon his return will be helpful. I need to build on the illusion of knowing as many people connected to the *Golden One* as I can."

I let out a disgruntled sigh. There was no choice but to play my part, I was going to paint the bust.

There was a gentle knock on the door, and Tay called out, "Come."

Free of her disguises, Cornelia slipped past the threshold. Her tone was sarcastic when she stated, "I thought I would find you in here, reporting on this evening's events." The comment was directed at me.

She crossed the room and gracefully sank into one of the little chairs nearby. Her eyes fixed upon mine, and she asked, "Did Julia comment on Tiburs's incident?"

I answered quickly, hoping to please the woman, who most likely suspected me of wrongdoing. "She did. She suggested that there was more to his outburst than the sharing of wine given to us by the Oracle."

"Did you scribe anything down on your little, wax tablet?" Cornelia inquired.

"No, she had the curtains of the litter drawn. It was very dim." I regretted the words even as they flew out of my dull-witted mouth. Quickly, I added, "She did go on to say that she was happy to be rid of Tiburs. She was tired of his behavior."

Cornelia allowed herself a slight smile. Although the pleased expression faded quickly, and she said, "Well, with the matter of Tiburs solved, for the time being, it isn't necessary for you escort me to the cave anymore." She turned toward my companion to avoid witnessing my reaction and began, "*Regulus*." There was an inflection on the name to remind us that she knew our secrets, "I'll pay you for the use of your donkeys and wagon, Samson can collect them. Let Ajax and Corax sleep, at some point someone will put together that we are connected if I'm always involved with your *slaves*."

Her tone of voice was not unfriendly, nor completely sincere. I speculated that perhaps my departure with Julia had hurt her feelings, or might I have only marred her pride?

I was unable to interject anything more than a plaintive look. A hint of guilt silenced me. I had relished the brief time alone with Julia too much to even lie to myself.

"I agree, however, I think Marcellus enjoys seeing the *show*," Tay put in his own jab, "I'll let him decide if he continues to seek the Oracle's divine blessings." A wave of his hands, a change of tone, and Tay went on, "The shop is cleaned up, and the apartment that is above seems fine. I'll have the essential furniture found, and then you should be able to move in. As long as Ursa will continue to cook for us, our kitchen is your kitchen."

"Fine, I'm sure we'll have more details to work out, but for now, I think the arrangements will suit us both," Cornelia replied, all business. She looked over to me. I was given an indifferent smile before I was told, "If you come to the morning or evening blessings, I prefer coins, it's the Roman gods who like the smell of burned pine cones, not the Egyptians." Her brow arched in the same manner as Tay's. After scolding me, she politely excused herself and left the room.

"And I thought *she* was going to break *your* heart," Tay quipped. I rolled my eyes in response. He was about leave me when he added, "Don't forget, you have an appointment tomorrow with Celer."

At the end of the evening, I found myself in bed, alone with my thoughts, while in the rooms below me, sailors, craftsmen, and the sly, little advocate named Varro were all having their needs tended to by the women of the house. Desire was stirring within me, almost consuming my thoughts, I was fearful about closing my eyes, unsure of whose face I would see, Cornelia or Julia's.

Chapter Two
The House of Actia

Corax knocked on my door. I looked groggily at the young man as he had to repeat himself, "Julia Felix's handmaid is here to collect you."

Thank the gods that I was simply too perplexed by his words to respond. Instead, I merely shook my head, *no*, and let my head drop back to the pillows.

I wanted nothing more than to fall back to sleep. Instead I thought of Julia, and the brief intimacy we had shared. I began to regret the refusal of joining her until I started to drift back to sleep. Visions of Cornelia took Julia's place, keeping me from achieving actual slumber. Between the two states, I tossed and turned, attaining neither.

Geb started to scratch at the door, he had quickly grown used to an early breakfast. I forced myself out of bed and joined the dog. He was easier to appease than anyone else plaguing my thoughts, and far more grateful.

Ursa, the stout, little cook, ignored me as I foraged for food. I'm sure she noticed that her mistress and Samson were gone, and I had remained.

I found some bread and covered it with honey. Geb and I went out to the freshly painted household shrine. The unnamed peacock, residing in the courtyard, concentrated on ignoring us.

With my prayers said, we ate our food near the brazier that was still burning from the night before. The air was cool but pleasant. The sun was just high enough that light crept over the high wall of the courtyard.

From the shadowed portico, I heard a door open, and Servia's voice echoed softly, "Stay away from those dock whores. Tell Regulus you want me to deliver some lunch to you at mid-day…"

"Lunch, I'll tell him I want…"

I blushed at what Proculus had to say. Rather affectionately, the hulking man said his goodbyes and assured Servia he would return in the evening. He noticed Geb before he saw me sitting next to the lifeless fountain. "Morning, Demetrius," the Admiral called happily in his booming voice.

The dog ran to him for a pat on the head. Indeed, it was difficult to dislike the man. After all, he was one of the few people who had bothered to learn *my* name. I waved, and gave him the expected smile of a good slave. Proculus then crossed the peristyle, headed toward Tay's study.

I waited a moment more, licking the honey off my fingertips. Another door opened, and this time, the little dark-haired advocate named Albius Varro poked his head out, seeing that no one but me was in sight. He smiled as if he had just tripped over something in a room full of people and only I noticed, then he walked quickly towards the side entrance of the house, leading out to the alley, and disappeared.

I bothered Ursa once more to find some clean water to dip my sticky hands in. Geb remained in the kitchen, hopeful for more scraps, while I proceeded to find Tay.

Proculus was just departing; one of the Greeks was holding the door for him, while the other was announcing a visitor.

Several disheveled and dirty men sat on newly acquired benches on either side of the impluvium.

One fellow was captivated by a life-sized, bronze sculpture of Venus, which had recently been added to the atrium. He glanced from Venus to me and quickly ducked his head as though he had been caught behaving in an unseemly fashion. The rest of the men stared at the mosaic floor, as if studying the interlocking patterns.

I knew that over the past few days, Tay had been busy acquiring clients, as a man of his alleged station customarily would have. This was my first chance to see his version of the morning salutations. The sight was somewhat pitiful. I wasn't sure if I was embarrassed for the assemblage, or for their host.

Quietly, I slipped into the study and took my place standing along the wall, like a good slave ready to be beckoned. A quick frown passed over Tay's face, otherwise, I was ignored. Tay was in the middle of giving instructions to one of his new dependants, "…after you've left Jucundus's go to Paquius's home and deliver this." He tapped at one of three scrolls on his writing table. "If he can't put you to work at one of his bakeries, come back here, and I'll have other work for you."

I could tell Tay was rushing through his performance, his style cramped by my presence.

A few coins were dropped next to the designated scroll. The young man thanked him as he carefully scooped up the items and departed.

Once alone, Tay asked, "You didn't go off to see the Oracle?" There wasn't even a hint of surprise in his voice.

I moved closer to his desk and whispered, "No, I'm here watching the *farce* that you are performing instead." The grin on Tay's face told me he hadn't been offended.

Feeling sorry for myself, I added, "Besides, she doesn't want me there."

Tay sighed, not for dramatic effect, and frowned, "You rarely give up so easily. I thought you were consumed with passion for her."

I mulled over my mixed emotions for a moment before responding, "I thought so, too." Rather theatrically, I pivoted on one heel and set off toward the door.

With my back to him, Tay quietly quoted Ovid, "*When I was from Cupid's passions free, my Muse was mute and wrote no elegy.*"

At the designated hour, Ajax led me to Celer's house, or rather, his late patroness's house. Tay had deduced that Ajax knew his way to the residence. The servant had delivered messages there on several occasions on behalf of his former master, Jucundus.

The dwelling was not all that far from ours, just over a few insulas to the West, and down a few insulas to the South.

We passed by the familiar sights of destruction and construction. Gangs of slaves, chained together, cleared rubble as more skilled laborers reworked crumbled masonry.

Upon freshly plastered, exterior walls, new graffiti was already decrying the faults of the incumbent politicians, or advertising the names of the men who had rebuilt the structure with questionable speed.

It was uncommon to travel far without seeing some sort of scuffle, or at least a hired thug moving someone along. Clad in a clean tunic, with a wooden box of clay pots, the needy assaulted me with pleas for money or food.

I was resigned to ignoring the countless beggars I passed. Tay had slipped Ajax a few coins in case we needed them, rather than me. Ajax, who was able to speak, apologized or argued as needed, and we made it to Celer's home safely.

The residence appeared to be midsize. The entrance was set within a modest slab threshold; the outer walls were typical of the city, a cream color washed with a repeating pattern of red rectangles that indicated the narrow span of the house from its neighbor's borders.

Ajax set down the basket of my painting supplies and gave the door a sound knock with his sandaled foot. We waited a few moments before a wizened elderly man struggled to open the heavy wooden doors.

After squinting at the squeaky hinges, the doorman peered at Ajax and reacted with a nearly toothless smile, "Ah, Jucundus's boy."

"Good fortune this morning, Xeus," Ajax said kindly. "I have brought someone here to paint, at Celer's request." The young Greek gestured toward me before adding, "He's mute, but good at painting."

I smiled dumbly, as I did so well.

The frail old man looked me up and down. "Jucundus sent him?"

Ajax was a smart lad, he saw that there was no reason to correct the old doorman's assumption. "Yes, we should let Celer know he's here so he can get to work."

The old man nodded his withered head, "Yes, Celer likes putting people to work." He pointed a bony finger at the bench near the raised impluvium. "Sit, sit. I have to go and announce you." He mumbled something unintelligible as he slowly walked across the atrium.

The house was larger than I had first suspected. On either side of the atrium sat six little sitting rooms. A drawing room occupied the traditional place, opposite the entrance, before the courtyard.

The atrium was painted in a pale green hue that reminded me of a foamy, shallow sea. Though sparse, the furniture in sight was ornate, and of a quality that Tay would have coveted.

Several minutes passed before a stern-faced man, walking several strides ahead of Xeus, came to see us. The strands of grey in the man's hair hinted that he was older than I suspected. A few faint lines showed upon his forehead, he was at the age when a healthy man appeared neither young nor old. He wasn't handsome in the classical sense, but he was attractive in a rugged, natural way.

"Jucundus sent you? I thought someone named Regulus sent you." The stranger didn't speak with the same Greek accent that so many of the locals had, his commanding voice was that of Rome.

Ajax shrugged. "Regulus sent us. I didn't want to confuse Xeus."

The old man was just reaching us, his breathing labored. He heard his name, but I think that was all.

"He's easily confused these days," replied the mild-mannered man. "Celer knows you are here." He turned to Xeus. "Show them to the courtyard, Actia's bust was moved out there for better light."

We slowly followed Xeus until the other fellow disappeared down the portico. Ajax placed a hand on Xeus's shoulder and told him, "We'll find our way."

With a sigh of relief, the doorman responded, "You're a good boy. Venus bless you."

Ajax led me through a narrow hall that ran alongside the drawing room rather than cutting through the decorated chamber reserved for the home's finer guests. The short passage emerged into a wide portico bordering the courtyard, before leading to a spacious dining room.

A low table sat in the middle of the garden, and atop of this was a large bust of a young woman. The work was vibrantly painted with great detail. The sculpture had black, wavy hair that was elegantly braided and coiled. The hue of her skin was dark olive. The bust had large, dark eyes and extremely plump, purple lips. One never knows how lifelike a piece of art is, it could have been created to flatter a woman's vanity as easily as to capture her likeness. Regardless, the depiction was of a very beautiful woman.

Grey stone showed along the ripples of her hair and the tip of her nose; a layer of soot concealed multiple blemishes that may have predated the more obvious damage.

While Ajax took the earthen jars of paint out of the wooden box we brought along, I inspected the bust curiously, wondering why the need to repaint so little damage.

Celer stepped through a wide doorway near the back wall of the courtyard. He seemed to be a perpetually happy man. Even the day before while sharing some information that troubled him with Valens, he had been pleasant to me. He smiled warmly and said, "I see you've found it." Celer pointed at the bust. "My patroness, *Isis protect* her, Actia Anicetia." He ran his hand down her cheek, as though the bust might come to life. After an awkward silence, he gestured about the courtyard. "As you can see, there was no structural damage to the house from the quake, but the bust tipped over and fell from its podium." Celer shook his head and added, "This is the only likeness of Actia, and I am sure her son will cherish it – that's why I wanted it repaired before he returns."

Several thoughts went through my head. I supposed that perhaps the bust was just as important to Celer as it might be to Actius Anicetus. Also, Celer was now without his patroness, he was sure to want to impress the actor on his arrival to his mother's home.

I nodded at the work, and, unable to ask him questions, I took the wax tablet from my neck and carved out a few words.

He read them and responded, "Yes, clean the soot, touch up any faded paint, I think you are right, the white around the eyes will need to be completely repainted…also make her lips more red, that shade of purple was never a color that she wore."

Celer pointed toward the dining room and jerked his thumb, indicating a small hallway to the right. He told me, "I shall be in my office, just past the kitchen, if you need anything." He was about to leave me when I noticed the smile melt away from his face. I followed his eyes and saw that the fellow who'd asked Xeus to show us to the courtyard was lurking nearby. Celer gave me a friendly pat on the back and said, "It's a good, sunny day, perfect for your work." And with that, he left me.

The other man, yet to be introduced, walked up to me and asked rather bluntly, "Do you know what you are doing?"

I supposed Ajax had sized up the man for being a fellow slave; unabashed, he replied for me, "He can't speak, but he is good at painting."

A rather skeptical grunt was the only reply.

Ajax ignored him and told me, "I'll collect you before the eighth hour ends."

"Which way does your new master live?"

"Near Valens–" Ajax began to answer the unnamed individual.

I noticed the man's dark eyes narrow before he inquired, "The younger or elder?"

"The elder," Ajax responded.

"Good, you can escort our cook to Faustus's garden." Ajax was led away, and I was left alone with the bust.

Taking a damp rag to the sculpture, I removed a layer of soot. The skin tone became a much lighter shade of olive in an instant. The rag was filthy before I even touched the lips, which, once cleaned, were a dark red, not purple after all. The face, that of a young woman's, became even younger, there were no lines around the mouth, and the forehead was smooth. She was not as beautiful as Cornelia, or as striking as Julia, but I was still left curious about the subject who had once modeled for the piece of artwork.

Gazing into image of the dead woman's face, I thought of her brother, Admiral Anicetus. I could only assume that the man, comfortably exiled to Sardinia, had received word of his sister's death.

The former commander of the fleet was little more than a tainted name to me, like Catalina or Sejanus. At Nero's bidding, he had commissioned a ship that was designed to collapse once at sea. The intended victim, Nero's mother, survived the incident and swam to shore. After his failure, he and Proculus were forced to finish what was started, with steel.

I was left to wonder what the freedman's sister could have been like; a plotter and schemer like her brother, or a nobler creature?

Her son, an actor of whom I had heard of but had never seen, was less than ten years my senior. I speculated that Actia must have been in her late forties, if not older, making the bust as old as her son, or a magnificent piece of flattery.

Actius carried the male version of his mother's name, which indicated that she was without a husband at the time of his birth. I was curious as to where her resources came from. Perhaps her brother, or perhaps a lover, I pondered. I was also intrigued as to where Celer fit into the equation. He referred to her to as his patroness, yet Tay had mentioned that he was the freedman of Valens. Might our friendly politician have *kept* the woman?

Once the bust was cleaned, I decided to let Celer inspect the object. I thought, perhaps, he might change his recommendations after seeing the work closer to its original state.

Lamplight flickered from an open doorway past the kitchen. I found the small office nestled toward the end of the short corridor near a set of stairs. Shelves lined the back wall, full of neatly rolled scrolls. Celer sat reading over something at a table that was far too large for the room.

I rapped at the open doorway to get his attention. I gave a little wave and pointed to the courtyard, my way of asking him to take a look at the bust.

The middle-aged man looked up from the document he was writing. A puzzled look crossed his face; of course, I had spent little time on the project, He must have wondered why I had disturbed him. His mouth opened, he was about to ask me something and then, instead, smiled, realizing it would just be easier to see what I wanted since I couldn't reply to his questions.

Celer followed me to the bust and gave a low whistle when he saw how different the object appeared. "By Venus, look at that." He put a hand to his chest, cocked his head, and gazed at the sculpture. "She was more beautiful in life, but by the goddess, how the artist captured her."

He had loved her, that much was clear to me. Had she loved him? Had she even known of his feelings for her? A jaded question crossed my mind; had she toyed with him? My unresolved feelings for Cornelia clouded my ability to be rational. It was all too easy to imagine Celer playing my part, longing for a woman just outside of his reach, and the rare times she did shorten the distance, all that happened was a fleeting touch, which made the desire worse than before.

Celer was as lost in thought as I. After a deep breath, he told me, "Well, the lips are fine, and you know the whites of her eyes seem fine, too; no need to risk upsetting the original pupils. You have done a good job." He stepped back and looked me over. "I knew you were the man for this task, as sure as if Fortuna had called me over to see your talented work...as if endorsing you." He pointed at my mouth, nearly touching my cheeks. "What's the matter with your tongue? Sosia said you can't speak a word?" I shrugged and made my silly half smile. Afterward, he pointed just below my waist, "Trouble there, too? Sosia said she threw herself at you and you wouldn't have her." I blushed and shrugged again.

Celer let out a high-pitched whistle and said, "To think, a whole house of girls; I'd be a very busy man...yes, very busy." His eyes fell back to the bust, and his smile changed slightly, it became somehow *forced.* He remained silent for a moment before giving me a pat on the back. "I'll let you get back to work." He returned to his little office.

I set out the paints and pondered what to mix to match the skin tone. The blemish on the nose was going to be the hardest area to fix. I had an eye for color, but wet paint seldom dries to the same hue.

I heard, faintly, a sound from within the house -- a strong knock on the door. It was several seconds before I could hear the squeak of the hinges. The sounds of sandals hitting the mosaic floor echoed through the portico. I stopped mixing my paints, but kept from glancing over my shoulder. It was several minutes before I heard the sound of voices inside Celer's little office; my perception was that the conversation had escalated into an argument. The exchange was brief, and after a few seconds of silence, the footfalls commenced under the portico behind me once more. I could not resist the urge to look, but I was only able to catch a brief glimpse of blonde headed man slip through the portico. An instant later, the front door squeaked open.

Returning my attention to the project, I painted the nose and paused for it to dry. While I waited, my eyes were drawn to an interesting fresco on the back wall of the courtyard. The depiction was of the local arena and the neighboring palestra. What made the image fascinating were the combatants outside of the arena. Rather crudely painted men fought savagely all about the fresco. I realized that this wasn't the captured image of a typical gladiatorial exhibit, this was a painting of the riot that had broken out four years before. I questioned what had compelled Actia to have commissioned such a work in her own home.

After studying the violent painting, I went back the bust to see if the paint had dried. Once more, I heard the front door squeak open. A moment passed before I heard someone walk in the direction toward Celer's office. Not a single sound from their conversation carried to the courtyard. Some time passed before the faintest echoes of movement startled me. I was engrossed in my painting, and swung my head back only to see the last of a shadowed figure fade into the hall. A moment later, the door made its familiar cry.

Once the bust's nose had completely dried, I was disgusted to find that the color didn't match the rest of the face. I started remixing my paint. As I did so, I heard the front door drawn open, yet again. Only a few seconds passed before I heard a nervous voice from the atrium. "I'll find him, Xeus, no need to trouble yourself." Before I could even look over my shoulder, the guest was halfway through the portico.

With my paint remixed, slightly darker, I went back to work. After my second brush stroke, the light footfalls of the last guest rapidly retraced their steps. The man's voice called to the doorman, "Xeus, don't mind me…stay on your bench." As the door squealed open, I could barely hear him say, "It was as if I were never here." And the door closed.

After the nose was once more repainted, I stood staring at the violent fresco for quite a while. It occurred to me that the incident depicted had an overwhelming effect on Pompeii, and had even shifted the course of my life. After the riot, gladiatorial contests had been banned as punishment for the violence against the visiting citizens of

Nuceria, a neighboring town. Popidius, whose house we had laid claim to, had profited from many fixed fights in the arena. With the reduction of income, he had been all too happy to borrow money from Tay, leaving him in our debt, and Tay as his sole benefactor.

Another series of knocks at the door echoed to the courtyard. That, followed by the squeak of the angry hinges, brought me out of my haze. I marveled at how many guests Celer had calling on him.

Moving toward the portico, a commanding voice told the doorman, "No need, I'll find him." This new caller walked briskly under the shadowed way, without as much as a glance in my direction.

I was inspecting the second attempt at the nose, when Xeus called out, "Porpurio, where is Fannius?"

I turned around to see a towering young man, with bright red hair, watching me from the portico. In a slow, childlike voice, he reported to the doorman, "Fannius left." I surmised that Fannius was the fellow who'd asked Ajax to escort the kitchen slave on his way home.

Xeus had wandered toward the young man and was squinting in my direction as he spoke, "He was just here? Did he go to collect Martha? She's been gone too long to be alone."

I could tell by both his voice and demeanor that Porpurio was simple minded. "I don't know."

Before Xeus responded, the guest, who had only just arrived, strode toward the two. Rather absent-mindedly, he said, "The blessings of the Muses to you both." He made an odd misstep and slipped past them. Looking down at his sandal and then glancing behind him, he added, "Xeus, I'll see my way out."

After we all listened to the door close, Xeus told Porpurio, "Go to the Faustus's garden and fetch back Martha."

The redheaded fellow sauntered off as Xeus told me, "If you get hungry, help yourself to some of the sweet cakes Martha made." He pointed down the portico, in way of direction to the kitchen.

Finally, the activities in the house ceased and quiet reigned. To my dismay, the nose still wasn't the same shade of olive as the rest of the head. I was resolved to paint the entire face, sure that I couldn't match the color.

A significant amount of time passed before the face was dry enough to judge my handiwork. I had done well, managing not to get any of the flesh tone on the lips, at least one feature I wouldn't have to redo. Next, I painted a thin line of black around the eyes. I had just finished and taken a step back to inspect my work when, again, I heard the door.

"No, Xeus, I'll find Celer, just need a moment of his time," came a voice from the vestibule.

I watched a middle-aged man cross the peristyle, he glanced at me, and for an instant, I think he frowned, but he was gone before I was sure.

Back to my work; the lining around the eyes was fine, and next, I painted a light coat of eye shadow. Before I was finished with this, the most difficult part, the visitor crossed back through the peristyle.

"Xeus, where did you say Fannius was..." the voice trailed off.

I stood and stared at the eyelids, not sure if I had matched the color or not; fretting a bit, I decided to fetch Celer to inspect my work.

Stepping into the shadows of the portico, I was momentarily blinded. My eyes were accustomed to the sunlight. I slowed my step, as the connecting corridor was extremely dim.

I peered into the little office. The oil lamp had been extinguished, and Celer was nowhere to be seen. I retraced my steps and entered the kitchen. I found the sweet cakes, and I ate two of them greedily, like the slaves my father had warned me about.

The stairs to the second floor were nearby, and I considered going up to look for Celer but thought better of it. I had decided, instead, to return to my work, when I noticed greasy footprints on the tiled floor of the corridor. Curious, I slid my left leg forward with little friction, and I realized that it was I who had left the track.

I returned to Celer's little office. My eyes had adjusted to the dimness, and I saw a pool of oil on the floor. I bent down to pick up the clay lamp, emptied and broken into two pieces. Bent on one knee, I noticed something slumped on the floor behind the desk. I sucked in a deep breath and dropped the ruined lamp. Celer was crumpled over on the tiled floor, completely lifeless.

I took another deep breath and sighed. Fumbling for my wax tablet, I was contemplating just what to write, but nothing appropriate came to my scattered mind. Perhaps it would have been best to just lead old Xeus back to the office without warning?

Stumbling back to the courtyard, I looked at the bust of Celer's late patroness. It struck me that perhaps I should return to my work. Let Xeus or the next visitor find him; surely someone else would come calling soon.

Somewhat in a state of shock, I studied the bust. Celer would not have the chance to critique the work, but I hoped that if his shade still lingered about the house that he might be pleased. I doubted that any other member of the household would even notice that the skin color might be a little light, or the hair was a bit too glossy. No, they would be consumed with the aftermath of Celer's death.

My work was done, but I needed to busy myself until the body was found. I remixed the black paint for the hair and tried to paint as slowly as possible. To my relief, I heard the door open once more.

"In his office....no, no, I'll find him...did Martha make any of those sweet cakes?" this was all said by the familiar voice belonging to Valens.

Xeus's reply echoed through the peristyle after the visitor. "Oh yes, next to the hearth."

I didn't turn around to see the man walk through the portico, instead, I stared at the bust and practiced at looking surprised. I inhaled sharply, dropped my jaw, and opened my eyes wide; too dramatic. I tried covering my mouth with my hand and repeated the wide eyes bit; better. Next, I cupped my mouth with both hands and, curled my forehead and squinted, but why would a mute cover his mouth? So, I wrapped my arms around my chest, frowned, furled my brow, and flared my nostrils. Yes, that was perfect. I repeated the steps a few times and stopped abruptly as I heard footsteps crossing behind me. I looked over my shoulder, anticipating that Valens would appear horrified, rushing to find Xeus. Instead, he walked under the portico nibbling at sweet cake.

Once he reached the atrium, he spoke to Xeus. I strained to hear his words, "He wasn't in there, are you sure he's here?"

I could not hear the old doorman's reply. Valens spoke again, but I couldn't make out the content. Whatever he said was followed by the sounds of the hinges grinding open and then closed.

Had Valens done as I had, glanced inside the office to see no one sitting behind the desk and gone in search of sweet cakes? He hadn't spent much time to look for Celer. Why hadn't he asked me if I knew where the freedman was, why hadn't he searched a bit more? I wished I could have heard what he told Xeus at the door, with his mouth full of cake.

It occurred to me that the guest before Valens hadn't seen Celer either. He had only spent a moment in the corridor and asked Xeus of Fannius's location. I looked back to the portico, and sprinted to where the fourth caller, who had been distracted upon his departure, had taken a misstep. On the mosaic floor, spot after spot of oil could be seen, leading from the corridor to the place he had slid. I decided that he too had stepped into the darkened room and observed the same sight as I – or he had killed Celer.

Returning to the center of the garden, I began elaborately pretending to paint the bust, now with a dry brush. Silently, I prayed to Jove that Xeus might go in search and find poor Celer. After another knock echoed from the front door, I felt a sense of relief, surely, this time someone would find the body. Quickly, I practised my surprised face and waited for footsteps to pass behind me.

"Demetrius, are you finished?" Ajax asked, walking towards me with a pleasant smile on his face. The smile wavered as he noticed the expression on my own face. "Something the matter?" he inquired.

I shook my head, no. I began to bite my lip, as always the sequence of events was not falling into place the way I wished. Ajax looked over the bust and nodded. "Looks good, fine job. Has Celer seen it yet?"

I shook my head *no*, a little wildly I think.

"Where is he?" asked the Greek.

I shrugged.

"I'll find him," Ajax told me, heading back to query old Xeus in the vestibule.

I could taste blood on my tongue as I bit my lip too deeply. I wished to be anywhere else while I anticipated what was about to happen.

Ajax reappeared under the portico and called to me, "He should be in his office." The young Greek pointed in the direction of the dark room. He seemed puzzled when I stood fixed beside the bust, as inert as the likeness of Actia. Ajax walked on without me.

I sighed, I wouldn't need to act surprised after all, Ajax would barely notice my performance. A moment passed before he skidded across the mosaic floor under the portico and shouted to me. "Celer's dead!" He took off running again before I reconsidered clutching my chest, furrowing my brow and flaring my nostrils.

Xeus, as quickly as he could manage, followed the flustered Greek. Ajax was forced to stop several times, begging the old man to hurry.

I waited a few seconds and joined them in the little room. Xeus was too old to stoop or get on his knees, so Ajax dropped to the floor to inspect the body.

"Leave him be, son, Fannius will know what to do," Xeus said, and I noticed a tear running down the old man's wrinkled face.

Ajax looked at me suspiciously, before asking, "Who could have done this?"

***

Fannius returned with the towering Porpurio and a diminutive young slave named Martha. Xeus was at the door, looking frightfully pale as he beckoned the steward to quicken his step.

"Fannius, oh, Fannius, something terrible has happened! Celer is dead."

Fannius furrowed his brow. Martha cupped her mouth with both of her hands, and Porpurio opened his eyes widely. They all appeared convincingly surprised.

Ajax and I were dismissed after the young Greek described how he found the body.

I am embarrassed to admit this, but my chief concern was Tay's reaction. Despite being intrigued by Celer's demise, he would be furious with me for unwittingly becoming involved in another murder. Yes, it was his fault for offering my services to Celer, but, of course, he wouldn't see things that way.

"Dear Moses," Tay mumbled, after Ajax excitedly recounted the events of the afternoon. Both the Greek and my companion had a cup of undiluted wine once the story was told. I was then quickly led upstairs to the privacy of my bedroom after Tay instructed Ajax to share the information with no one else. Ajax was an honest and loyal young man, yet I was sure the information would be shared with Corax the moment the two were alone.

"By Hades, how could this have happened – who did it?" Tay was having difficulty keeping his voiced pitched to a whisper.

In answer, I shrugged.

"You have no idea? Who was in and out of the house, you didn't hear anything?" He was disgusted with me, just as I had anticipated.

Whispering, I told him, "Six men called on Celer during the course of the day, the last one was Valens. He didn't see the body, he questioned Xeus and left."

"Xeus?"

"The doorman."

"Is he a suspect?"

I gave a little laugh, "He's old enough to have put bets on Antonius and Octavian."

Tay rolled his eyes at the pitiful cliché repeated from one of the histories that I had written. "Were there other servants in the house?" he inquired.

"Martha...no, she left when I arrived. Porpurio, but..." I began, but trailed off.

"Porpurio?"

"A big, simple-minded slave, he left the house to fetch Martha. Another man was there, Fannius. I couldn't quite make out his role, but he wasn't there for long either." I paused, collecting the order of the comings and goings about the house. "I think he left before I spoke to Celer last..." with that, I fell silent. I could not bring myself to tell Tay that I had found Celer's body and left the incident unreported.

Tay asked, "When did you last see Celer?"

"Just before the first visitor arrived," I replied sheepishly. I felt my face blushing and worried that my companion would realize that I knew more.

Tay seemed to mutter the next comment, more to himself than to me. "There must be a curse on you."

Perhaps Tay was correct and there was a curse on me. I had upset a few of my lovers' husbands. Countless men had parted my company with empty purses after the dice had been thrown. I was blamed for the death of my father, and actually responsible, inadvertently, for the death of several men. Might a relative, or even a victim of mine, have placed a curse on me? More important, what could be done to lift the curse?

Chapter Three
The Curse

After Tay asked me for descriptions of the men who called on Celer, I was released. I made my escape and paid a visit to the little shop attached to our house. Filled with lotions and tonics, my nose was assaulted by scents both pleasantly fragrant and pungent. I stepped inside the open workroom and smiled nervously at the antagonistic woman who owned the business. Gavia sat on a stool, with her raven perched on her shoulder. She ignored me as she mixed several powders together in a dry bowl, until the raven screeched at me.

"He knows trouble when he sees it," Gavia said in an ominous tone.

The shutters of the front windows were wide open to the street. The workmen in front of Julia Felix's property were watching. Their attention had been drawn by the bird's loud noise. I pointed to the doorway leading to the back room.

Gavia gave out a little grunt, but obliged me, and led the way. A single oil lamp attempted to illuminate the back room, which contained a steep staircase running against the left wall, another table, and several shelves full of unguents, creams, and ointments.

"What do you want, pretty boy?" she asked, her voice strangely sensual. "A moment alone with me, away from the eyes of others?"

I looked at the dirty leather cord holding a piece of stained material over her right eye. I glanced at her hair, which reminded me of two feral creatures that might have killed each other and died draped over the woman's head. Her face was blemished with soot, and something orange. At a glance, she was repulsive. But as I studied her, I had the vague impression that underneath the superficial ugliness, something unique radiated just outside the reach of my understanding. She seemed to sense that I was looking through her. The ugliness strengthened, and her voice turn gravelly, "Spit it out, boy."

She was one of the few people in Pompeii who knew that I could speak, still, I whispered, "I think there is a curse on me, do you have something that will remove it?"

Her eye narrowed, and for a moment, her expression softened. "A curse?"

"Yes, I have been plagued by one unfortunate event after another," I told her, still whispering.

"When did this begin?" she asked, her tone lacking the sarcasm or scorn that I was accustomed to.

I frowned. Her question was rather eye-opening. When did the misfortune begin? Not with the murder of Celer. Far before the local quake that occurred. Helen's death hadn't been the beginning of my misfortune. My father's death had merely been the conclusion to nineteen ill-omened years. Perhaps the day my mother disappeared was when it all began? Or had I just inherited a curse from my ancestors? My grandfather had been exiled and killed, his mother had lived a life of fear after being set aside by her first husband, Octavian. And my great-great grandparents, one killed along the road laid by his ancestors, the other a victim of political intrigue, her name synonymous with power-hungry women. Still farther back, my name sake, Gaius Sempronius Gracchus, like his brother, was destroyed due to his political beliefs.

As I was contemplating how Gaius's brother-in-law had destroyed Carthage, Gavia poked at me. My eyes focused on the raven bobbing its head while it perched on the little woman's shoulder. "A few hundred years ago...I think the Carthaginian's put a curse on my family," I said rather dumbly, not realizing how much like an idiot I must have sounded.

Gavia hadn't expected that answer. She licked her lips and narrowed her eye. "That would be a powerful curse, to plague your family for generations."

"A member of my family did something terrible to them."

She smiled strangely before asking, "How does a *slave* even know his family's past?"

"I know."

The solemnity of my voice vanquished her sinister smile. Gavia looked over to the shelves and then back to me. "This will take me a while to prepare. Come back in an hour or so," she told me. I thanked her profusely and departed.

Tay had left the house to speak with Valens. As the man's home was in still in shambles, the politician was staying with a client just one block over. Our dwelling was quiet while the master was away. Staphylus sat on a stool near the gate leading to the alley beside the residence. In exchange for food, lodging, and a bit of spending money, he was charged with greeting and dealing with the men who visited the women we had inherited. This suited Tay, who was happy to pay someone a cut and distance himself a bit from the actual business of the prostitution. Tay hadn't so much climbed Pompeii's social ladder, he more or less simply asserted himself.

Owning the women was acceptable among his peers, but renting them out himself was beneath their standards.

Servia, who dominated the pack of girls, went about the house instructing Mucia on where furniture needed to be placed. The two ignored me as I passed them.

I heard the mumbled voice of the gimpy Gallus Lutatius, from within Sosia's chamber, as I walked by. Only the prior day, Celer had occupied the little room for an hour or so. With a strange sense of mirth, Ovid's words came to me, *All love is vanquished by a succeeding love.* Well, love had little to do with the actives within Sosia's grasp.

As I crossed the atrium, Ajax was following Corax as he lit the oil lamps. Their whispered conversation stopped, and they both smiled at me. Guilt showed on Ajax's face, while suspicion shadowed Corax's.

I entered Tay's office and perused the growing collection of books he was amassing for me. I found one that he told me had been purchased from the man who owned a villa outside of the Herculaneum Gate that once belonged to Marcus Cicero. The implication was, the book, too, had belonged to Cicero. The work was a Greek piece by an author I had never heard of.

Just as I sat down to read, Mucia entered the study. Without preamble, she said, "Julia Felix is waiting for you."

"Demetrius," Julia said in greeting as I awkwardly climbed into the litter waiting outside of her house. Choosing not to display my rather dumb smile, I gave her what I thought was my coy grin.

She snapped her fingers, and we were hoisted up. She pointed to the inner, sheer curtain beside me, and I drew it closed as she closed the curtain near her. In the closed air,

I inhaled the woman's perfume. I was reminded of the smell of oranges. Had it not been *Demetrius* in the litter, but *Marcellus*, I would have told her that it was my ancestor, Scipio Africanus, who had introduced the orange tree to Rome. I had always taken great pride in sharing my family history. But that was another life, seemingly as remote as the lives of those long-dead notables. Instead, I remained silent, wishing to be someone else completely.

Julia was obviously perturbed. She complained the entire trip. I tried to listen to her as a distraction to my own woes. She had purchased the building next to her home and was negotiating buying the land that served as an alley that ran between the two properties from the town council. I had trouble following her, because she spoke as if I already knew her plans. It sounded as if she intended to build a set of apartments and shops, once she owned the entire block. I was intrigued by her wealth and independence but bored with her dissertation on how she planned to alter the point of entry of her home from the side street. It was no wonder Tay tired of explaining the town council's plans for the city to me. Such logistics seemed tedious.

At last, the litter came to a stop, and we were lowered. I let the grand lady stride ahead of me, as if I were her slave. After Julia had placed a gold coin on the offering table held by the crude statue of Nephthys, I dropped a single copper beside the other offerings.

From the mouth of the cave, the Oracle and her translator appeared. Samson was disguised in a beaded yellow gown, covered by a billowing white fabric as translucent as a spider's web. Placed over a coiled black wig sat a remarkable gold crown bearing the head of a cobra and a falcon. As always, somehow, the tall, black-skinned man appeared to be a divine female figure.

Behind the Oracle, the translator followed. Cornelia, always clad in a simple, white gown comprised of layer upon layer of sheer white material and a veil of the same material, bowed her head to the devotees. We all bowed to the Oracle, and the ceremony began.

I didn't hear the words chanted, instead, my mind wandered, as it usually does. Standing just beside me was a woman who toyed with me, while concealed from the world behind heavy curtains. Before me, disguised (not unlike myself), stood a woman whom I would have committed any sin for.

Had Cornelia, peering out at the loyal people who brought her coins and gifts from the cave, watched me arrive with Julia? If she had, would it have mattered to her? Might jealousy inspire her to invite me to her room? I tired over such thoughts, feeling as dramatic as a stock heroine pining for her lost love, in a Greek tragedy.

My thoughts drifted to poor Celer, dead now for mere hours. In my head, I had conjured the story that he had loved a mistress outside of his reach, and under my own roof, he had taken his pleasure from a woman who mattered not to him. What might Fortuna have been trying to tell me?

I was brought back to the group of devotees when the Oracle tapped my shoulders with her ceremonial crook and flail. The sun had dropped to the horizon while I had been lost in my own mind.

The assemblage began to disperse. I took my wax tablet and quickly wrote a message. I assumed that Julia could read, as wealthy women were usually educated.

Thank you for bringing me here today, I wish not to detain you, but would like to remain here to pray to the Goddess alone as Ra descends to fight chaos. I hope in no way to offend you. My thoughts are with a friend who joined the majority today. I bid you a pleasant evening, and may the blessings of Nephthys be with you.

Curious, Julia took the tablet that I handed her. Her lips pressed together as she read. "How eloquently you write, Demetrius." She looked into my eyes, as if she had discovered a living person within a statue.

I smiled and bowed my head, feeling a bit less than humble.

"Stay as long as you like, and for your safety, I will send the litter back for you." I bowed my head again. Julia's eyes lingered on me for a moment.

Alone, I stood beside the idol of Nephthys. My mind was a jumble of thoughts, all shouting at me...one louder than the next. The sky had transformed into three colors; a layer of orange bled into a foreboding shade of crimson, and above that was the hue of purple that was reserved for the Emperor. Below, Pompeii was consumed under the growing shadow of the omnipresent Vesuvius.

I heard the sounds of donkeys and the wagon rattling nearby. Within a moment, Hesiod would appear from the clearing on the other side of the nearby hill. I decided to wander towards the city rather than wait for Samson and Cornelia to come back to collect their booty. I didn't care to play audience to the closing scene of their lucrative performance.

I felt rather ridiculous being carried by Julia's men. Our house was a short distance from the city gate. Had my mind been clear, I would have waved the servants back to their mistress. Instead, I had complied with Julia's wishes even in her absence.

Gavia watched me as I climbed out of the sedan. As my weight shifted from the litter to the raised sidewalk, the men lifted the empty object back up and crossed the road.

"A *slave* with ancestors, carried about like a pampered woman, how very cursed you are," Gavia declared from her open shop.

I walked past the irritating woman, and without invitation, I went to the back room. She followed, laughing.

Once concealed, I started to explain, "Julia insisted–"

"I'm sure she did," The little witch cut in as she poked a stained finger at my chest. "*We desire nothing so much as that which what we ought not to have.*" I was puzzled as to if Publius Syrus's quote was directed toward myself, or Julia. I should have been more puzzled by the fact that someone like Gavia knew the expression.

"I don't know what you mean," I protested with little enthusiasm.

"Never you mind, never you mind." Gavia reached for a small pot on the table beside us. She handed the potion to me. "At sunrise tomorrow, go to the shore. Stand in the sea, at least up to your waist. Drink this down, all at once. Throw the empty pot into the water. While your eyes are closed, repeat, *Eshum heal me* until you hear the cry of a seagull. Afterward, make a promise to the goddess Tanit that you will bring your firstborn to the same waters, immerse the child, and swear that you will raise him to believe that the sacking of Carthage was unjust."

I frowned and bit my lip, the formula of the spell seemed sound, but, of course, there was one problem. I may or may not have already sired my firstborn child. Further complications involved my presence in Pompeii and his location in Rome. Immersing Appius off the shore of Pompeii would be quite a challenge.

"Is there something else I can do – instead of the part with the firstborn – I...I'm not sure, but I may have a son."

The wretched little woman began to chuckle. Her raven appeared from the nearby shelves and squawked out its own imitation of her ugly laughter. "Cursed indeed! May or may not have a son?" She caught her breath, "You *are* the folly of the gods, aren't you?"

I nodded my head in complete agreement with the wretched woman. "Surely there is another spell..."

She pointed at the pot in my hand, "Drink that all the same, tonight before you sleep, it will do you some good." Another laugh escaped her little mouth. "Come back tomorrow, I'll look into a different spell." She pointed at some tattered scrolls heaped on the top shelf above her potions.

Before Tay had left to see Valens, I'd asked him for money to give to the Oracle. Begrudgingly, he'd handed me two pieces of copper. I had dropped one on the Oracle's tray, the other I made to hand to Gavia. She frowned when she saw the coin. "Don't insult me. I'll give you my magic before I accept such a meager sum." Her laughter had stopped, and she shooed me toward the doorway. "Go, go before your curse taints me."

***

"There you are." Tay beckoned me to join him in his study. "I spoke to Valens and expressed my concern about you being in Celer's house when the murder occurred. After inspecting the body, Celer appears to have been strangled." He lowered his voice, "Apparently Celer had quite a few enemies."

I found this hard to believe. He had seemed to be a friendly, good-natured man. Tay went on, "Valens held his tongue, but assured me the man had been involved in more than one scandal. There is no question in anyone's mind that you hadn't anything to do with his death..."

"Me!" I did not whisper. "Why would anyone think such a thing?"

Tay rolled his eyes. "Everyone in that house is suspect, even you." He pointed a manicured finger in my face. "Valens will see to it that you are not questioned, I already told him everything you knew..."

"I don't know anything..."

"Yes, for once, we are in agreement," Tay remarked happily. I found his devious grin almost too much to bear.

Ursa had finished cooking the nightly stew, which I was enjoying when Cornelia and Samson returned home. Samson joined me in the kitchen, foraging for food and gossiping with the stout cook.

Said as if a mere afterthought, Samson inquired, "Demetrius, will you help me move my mistress's things? Regulus said that the apartment is ready."

I nodded dumbly. The second storefront attached to our new home was empty, as were the set of rooms above the shop. Cornelia would be no farther from me, the apartment could be entered from our courtyard as easily as the street, yet Samson's words were somehow unsettling. I thought that perhaps the gods had grown tired of my immature crush on the woman, and, in various stages, she was being separated from me. More than location was changing. Cornelia's aloofness and Julia's interest were both showing me a different path.

Cornelia stood in the foreign room, empty other than a small bed. The walls were rough, bare plaster, the floor was worn wood. A single lamp, hanging from the low ceiling, cast flickering light on the dismal space. The ceiling was darkened by the stain of soot and showed various watermarks and repairs.

"I'm not sure which is worse, this gloomy cell or Popidius's decadent chamber." She pointed to the corner and said absently, "Anywhere."

We set the largest and heaviest of her crates down, which dominated a sizable portion of the floor.

The cold tone in Cornelia's voice eased. "Perhaps you can paint this room for me, so long as no one is killed in the process."

Samson must not have been present when Tay relayed the story to his tenant. "Killed?"

The one advantage to the new location was that I didn't need to whisper as I said, "Celer was killed at some point in the day while I painted the bust of his patroness." The ebony man cupped his mouth with both hands, and his eyes opened wide.

"Actia Anicetia," Cornelia said, in a faraway voice.

"Did you know her?" I asked, and my words seemed to draw the woman back to us.

"She was a client, not just to the Oracle, but she came to the Sybil, too. A tortured woman, paranoid."

Samson frowned. "She's dead?"

"Killed in the quake, she was attending the sacrifice and was trampled by the crowd..." again, Cornelia's voice was far away. "She had a premonition that an awful fate would befall her. She asked us and the Sybil what the future held for her. She went to an astrologist too, he mustn't have been of any more good to her than we were."

"Why was she so fearful?" I asked.

"She played witness to something terrible, but she never explained. In her youth, she was a hairdresser to Lollia Paulina. That's how she became *friendly* with Agrippina."

Cornelia sounded more knowledgeable about the imperial family than I would have expected.

"Lollia was only married to Emperor Caligula for six months, I suppose that was more than long enough to witness many monstrous acts." I pondered a few questions and asked, "When did Actia come to Pompeii?

"After the death of Nero's mother, she had been a member of Agrippina's household at Misenum. When Actia first moved here, I believe she lived in the imperial villa outside of the city."

The fourth anniversary of Agrippina's death was less than a month away. The date would be celebrated, as Nero had seen to her vilification. The Senate treated her memory as if she were a despised criminal. Oddly, her greatest crime had been her gift of a son to the people of Rome. Certainly, she had paid for that sin.

"What kind of questions did she ask of you?" I inquired with great curiosity.

Cornelia took a deep breath and sat on the little bed. Our swinging scales had balanced, and once again, we were both at ease with each other, despite the drab room or the gloomy topic. "She wanted to know how she would die, and whom she could trust. She was also curious as to how to protect herself from the dead – not just in this life, but when she crossed the River of Styx as well. She was afraid of somebody, and afraid they'd harm her in Hades, if not here."

A chill ran down my back. Only someone who was witness to those whispered deeds that took place on the Palatine Hill could have lived under the same fear as Actia must have lived. "How awful," I muttered.

Samson and I left to retrieve more of their belongings, and when we returned, I noticed that another lamp had appeared, and a small statue of Apollo was placed in a deep niche within the wall.

Cornelia kindly thanked me for my help; this was a polite dismissal. I didn't mind, her manner had softened, and perhaps her feelings for me were as questionable as mine were for her. Maybe somehow, sometime, we would meet in the middle.

The morning following Celer's death, I awoke early, and prayed to the gods whose images I kept in my shrine. I told them each that I thought myself cursed and begged for their help and guidance. Afterward, Geb and I went downstairs for our morning repast. With little deliberation, I had decided to stay home. My interactions with Cornelia the evening before had been pleasant enough. There was no need to embark on a journey to the Oracle's cave and risk upsetting the balance that I had felt.

I tore a crust of bread into three equal pieces. The first, I placed on the shrine in the courtyard. I murmured a quick prayer to the household guardians. Geb took his share, and I sat on the cold, marble lip of the lifeless fountain and ate slowly as I contemplated what Tay had told me the day before.

My companion had made too general of a statement when he pronounced that everyone who'd been to Actia's house was a suspect. First, Xeus was too old and frail. I had no motive. The kitchen slave left before I last saw Celer alive. This left Fannius and the men who visited the house up to the point that I discovered the dead man. My instincts told me that it was one of the first three men who came calling, who had committed the crime. The man who had tracked the oil from the broken lamp had entered the dwelling with a confident air, and departed in a distracted manner. Had he killed Celer, I doubt he would have acted so perplexed. Instead, he would have steadied himself, regained his composure, and left the house without drawing attention to himself.

While my thoughts drifted, Geb snatched away my last bite of bread. He padded off toward the interior of the house, and the peacock followed, hopeful for crumbs.

From Servia's room, bordering the portico, I could hear what sounded like a bear snoring. If the little dark-eyed advocate, Varro, had spent the night in Sosia's neighboring room, he must have found it hard to sleep with all the noise.

The shuttered doors to Tay's study were closed to the courtyard; within, I could hear him speaking softly. I wasn't sure when the man slept. As far as I could tell, he had never joined me in our room during the course of the night. Although, I suspected with Cornelia's move to the sad little apartment, he would soon occupy Popidius's luxurious chamber.

I stepped closer to the door, trying to hear the conversation. I nearly jumped when I heard a single rap at the front door. Neither Mucia nor the Greeks responded. I had become quite the good slave in a very short period of time, so, without hesitation, I went to open the door.

Julia's familiar handmaid appeared surprised to see me rather than one of the Greek boys. She stuttered for a moment before telling me, "My mistress waits for you."

Indeed, she did, Julia sat in the litter, clutching an open curtain, staring directly at me from across the narrow street. The woman was too dignified to call out to me, but she need not, her eyes were expressive enough.

I capitulated to the change of plans and climbed into the litter beside Julia, who studied me as I situated myself. She snapped her fingers once I was settled, and we were raised upward. The curtains had already been closed to ward of the cool morning air, light seeped through the edges, but the environment was quite dim. We road in silence for what seemed a long time until Julia finally spoke. "I'm trying to remember every word that I have said in your presence." I detected no true concern in the woman's voice. I raised an eyebrow and cocked my head to one side as she continued, "You may not speak, but you are not altogether silent, are you?" My normal dumb grin was replaced with a rather sly smile.

"Do you write Regulus's letters?" she asked. I shrugged, not really answering. Julia remarked, "What an asset you must be." She fell silent once more, not for lack of words but because she put her lips to another purpose.

My first inclination was to stand as far from Julia as possible, after we joined the rest of Nephthys's devotees. Of course, that would have been as obvious as Julia's lip-stain smeared on my neck, which she managed to wipe off before we emerged from her sedan. Instead, I took my place not so far away from my neighbor, and attempted to concentrate on the ritual.

Chapter four
The Pantomime

To My Dear Appian:

May this letter find you well, as am I. Yes, it would seem that, once more, I was involved in a murder. While I claim Fortuna as my Divine Benefactress, I have often wondered if Charon has been the deity I should make my prayers to.

I had only just met Celer, yet I had taken a liking to the man. It is hard to believe that while I painted the bust of Actia, a quiet, forceful rage had seized the unknown person and sent Celer to the underworld.

Well, I must apologize for any confusion I create as I recall these days and my feelings for Cornelia. It may seem that I can't remember from one day to the next if I had been in love with her or not. Alas, I do recall, and it depended on the hour of the day. Remember, I was nineteen. I know I say that as if it's an excuse, but rather, it was the reason.

And what do I say of Julia? I was attracted to her, that I cannot deny. She was 'tangible' while Cornelia was elusive. I, of course, coveted that which was out of my grasp. Still, I very much appreciated finding myself in Julia's clutches.

I know that, thus far, I have made very little mention of Porcia and the infants. I shall remedy this in the following passages of my story. I often marvel as to the gods' designs. Those two children redirected the course of my life as surely as crossing the Rubicon changed Caesar's. Had not Porcia been with child, and we in need of a wet-nurse for our little orphaned girl, we would have never met Popidius, or inherited his dubious estate. Leaving me to ask, do I thank Fortuna or Charon?

Julia had little to say to me on the return trip form the Oracle's domain. That isn't to say she ignored me. Pleasantly distracted, the journey seemed rather brief.

As I fumbled out of the litter, a whistle from across the street caught my attention.

Gavia ushered me to the back room of her shop. The raven, perched on her shoulder, swayed as she walked, but never lost his balance. "Here, this time, I think you can manage the demands of this spell to repel your curse." Gavia pointed at a little chunk of salt on the table. Beside it was another pot of liquid and a piece of parchment folded into a square.

"I heard about the dead man. Does Charon split his spoils with you?" Gavia cackled at her own joke, "Go *home*, where Celer perished, sprinkle the potion in the jar around the floor of the room where he died, put the chunk of salt in your mouth, to suffer what the land of Carthage suffered, and read the words on the paper aloud to the dead man's shade so that he can take a message to Hades…"

"Come with me. I can never explain what I have to do, not by trying to write it all out on this." I rapped at the little wooded tablet hanging from my neck. "Besides, the old doorman won't refuse you, in fear that you'll curse him."

Gavia put a stained hand over my mouth. "I like you better when you are pretending that you can't speak."

I had begun to think that Gavia did not wear clothes, but a costume. The dark tunic that strangled her at the neck and draped down to her men's leather boots hid the fact that she was a shapely little woman. The rat's nest of hair must have been a wig, no human, however foul, could grow such a horrible, wiry mane. And the purple, orange, and green smears of herbs and dyes always seemed as deliberate as the eye shadow and lip stain that Samson wore to disguise himself as a woman.

When we left her shop, I was somewhat delighted to see the rest of the costume. Gavia covered herself with a patchwork cloak, made of what might have been decent rags ruined by cleaning the public latrines. Tied to the cloak and dangling from leather cords were a dozen odd brass charms, the dried head of a dead snake, and what looked like a wolf's tail.

I should have been embarrassed walking beside the woman, but I was far too amused. If someone stared at her, she cursed them, if a youngster heckled her, she spat at them. However, just as often, a mother, dirty from the streets, would drag a child over to us and beg for a blessing. Or a destitute man would ask her to speak good words to Fortuna, Venus, or Hercules for him. As quickly as she cursed, she blessed. From a deep pocket, some sort of odd token was dug out and handed to the person in need.

Entertained by the woman's eccentric behavior, I followed Gavia blindly; I didn't think to ask her how or why she knew the location of Celer's home. What a fool I was.

Standing at the front door, Gavia gave a heavy kick to announce us. As expected, we were left to wait a bit before the squeaky door opened. Xeus looked at me for a moment, and gave me a toothless smile of recognition, then he tilted his head toward Gavia. After a moment, his face froze into an awkward grimace. With a plaintive gasp, he whispered, "Gavia!"

There was venom her voice, "Xeus." After a long pause, in which time I began to wish I had come alone and carved my request out in wax, she explained, "Demetrius needs to cleanse himself from Celer's death. May he be allowed inside to make an offering to the dead man's shade?"

Poor old Xeus's eyes darted to mine, "Did she put you up to this, boy?" His voice was unsteady.

Before I could determine how to pantomime an answer, Gavia lied, "That Egyptian Oracle told him to come here, I just walked him here so the fool wouldn't get molested on the streets...it is a harsh world out here, old man..." her voice said more than her words.

Xeus seemed to shrink and squirm. After clearing his throat, he told us, "He can come in, but – but not you."

"I don't care to enter this place," she informed the old doorman. With a bit less scorn, she told me, "I'll wait down the street."

"Just go, girl. I'll have him escorted home when he's done," Xeus said, almost in a panic.

I thought Gavia might spit at the man, instead, she curled her lip and gave an odd snarl. Xeus took my arm and, rather quickly, closed the door before Gavia could utter a curse at him.

"By Pluto, what are you doing with her?" he shook his head at me as though he just caught me relieving myself in the impluvium. "Wretched girl, wretched girl…"

There was a flurry of activity in the atrium. A familiar man with thin, greasy hair was dabbing perfume onto the remains of Celer. The undertaker was the same who had dealt with our original host, Popidius, after he was killed in the quake. The short man went about his work without taking notice of his slaves around him, who were poking at pillows under the body, or adjusting the long tunic on the dead man.

"Now, what is it the Oracle told you to do…is this that Oracle of Nephthys, didn't she predict the quake?" I nodded. She had not predicted the quake, but was receiving the credit all the same. I pointed toward the back of the house, toward Celer's office. "Yes, go on. Do what you need to do. I'll get Porpurio to walk you home…oh, that wretched girl, how upsetting to see her…"

I walked slowly by Celer's body. The man was reclined on a simple litter. He wore a white tunic and few pieces of gold. His face betrayed no pain, or surprise having been in his final moments, just a peaceful expression. I had heard people mumble, "Ah, it looks as if he's sleeping" while viewing a body, only to judge for myself, *No, he looks dead.* But Celer did look as if he were asleep. I was hoping to wake him, at least for a moment, to hear my plea and take my message across the River Styx.

I crossed the portico, glancing into the courtyard. The bust I had repainted was no longer there, only the small table it had sat upon remained.

I entered the dimly lit office, and, as instructed, I sprinkled the liquid on the floor around the perimeter of the room. I put the chunk of salt in my mouth. It made me salivate and gag. Once it began to dissolve, I swallowed it. Next, I unfolded the paper and quietly began to read the words aloud so that Celer's shade might hear me.

"Ghosts of Carthage, bitter souls from the past, hear my words of repentance. I am a fool, I am dumber than a pumpkin, my head is full of rocks..." I frowned and skimmed ahead, silently. *I am an idiot who believes that words and a bottle filled with witch's piss can undo the harm caused two hundred years ago by fools braver, but no smarter, than I. My head is filled with mush, and I grope about blaming shadows for my idiocy. I pray, oh, dead souls of Carthage, that somehow all my misfortunes are your fault, not just my own poor judgments...fool, are you still reading this. Tell old Xeus you poured my piss on the floor, it's been many years since he's had to clean up after me.*

My face felt flushed, my heart began to beat rapidly, and my palms were sweating. I folded the piece of paper back up and tucked it into my belt. With some hesitation, I picked up the empty little jug and held it carefully to avoid the lip.

I was crossing the courtyard when I heard the door squeaking open. Entering the atrium, I watched the undertaker and his staff back away from Celer's remains.

A medium size man, perhaps twenty-five years old, slowly walked toward the body. The individual had a commanding presence. Without even looking behind him, he shrugged off his heavy cloak, knowing that the old doorman would catch the dusty garment. He was clad in riding attire, and the faint scent of horse wafted from him.

He was a handsome man, bearing classical features. With a cleft chin, strong cheekbones, and a straight, narrow nose, he appeared to be a statue that had come to life. His eyes were his most notable feature. They were small and dark, with something piercing about them. In an instant, I imagined first the sight of him laughing heartily at a good joke, then looking kindly on a beggar, and last, sneering while he kicked the porridge out of someone. While his expressions altered, his penetrating glare did not change in any way during the different moods.

I knew without being told who he was: Actius Anicetus, famous for his skills as a pantomime actor and known throughout the empire.

I would like to say that my father brought me up with traditional Roman values. Yet, this would be a lie. To my relief, he actually had little to do with my rearing. But he did impart on me the old prejudices against actors and sword fighters. Even if an emperor or two lavished attention on these lower class individuals, they were our social inferiors.

Observing Actius, there was nothing inferior about the man. Had I been the type who was indiscriminate toward the genders of my lovers, perhaps I might have desired him as I did Cornelia. Instead, I was instantly jealous of and intimidated by him.

Fannius entered the atrium from the drawing room and slowly approached Actius. He frowned for a moment when he caught sight of me, but my presence didn't keep his attention for very long. The two men made eye contact, and after a moment, Actius asked, "What has happened?"

Fannius looked about the room. Besides me, the undertaker and his staff, in addition to old Xeus were present. "It might be better to speak in private."

"Who are you?" Actius inquired, his tone changing from commanding to curious.

"My name is Fannius. I served Publius Memmius Regulus, as your mother once did."

Ever the performer, Actius tilted his chin upward, as his brow rippled with displeasure. He obviously didn't care to be reminded that his mother had been a slave.

In silence, Actius glanced once again toward Celer's body, and proceeded to the drawing room. As this happened, Fannius shot Xeus a stern look and swung his head back to me.

The old servant fumbled for words, "That Egyptian oracle told him to come here and cleanse himself, brought some kind of potion." The old man pointed at the pot that I clutched.

Before Xeus could say more, Fannius gave a wave of the hand to silence him and followed after Actius.

Xeus had the big, redheaded young man waiting for me at the door. Ushering me out as quickly as possible, he instructed my chaperone to see me home.

As the hinges ground open, a familiar face stepped toward the door. It was none other than the man who had tracked the lamp oil along the mosaic floor.

Porpurio liked to talk, and it didn't bother him that I only nodded, shook my head, smiled, or frowned. Porpurio talked so much about the most random topics that I have no recollection of what was said.

I was about to escape through the threshold of our front door when he followed me in. Perplexed, I frowned as he kept talking and looked about the atrium.

Ajax, greeted him, "Porpurio, look how tall you are."

Childlike, he replied, "I know."

"Did you walk Demetrius home?"

"Yeah, he's too little to be alone in the streets; and he can't talk. These benches are new, that statue of Venus wasn't here before..." Porpurio continued to list the changes Tay had made to the atrium.

He was now the Greeks' problem. I was just about to flee when the young man said, "I got some money...how much for a girl?" Well, not *totally* childlike.

Geb crossed the courtyard and met me in the kitchen. I plucked a few items, and then we sat at the lifeless fountain to share a midday snack. The dog's tail wagged gently, while I sat still and let the sun shine on me. I could hear several voices within the drawing room. My curiosity was drained. I didn't care who Tay was talking to, or what they were talking about, until I heard the name of my friend mentioned, Petronius.

I moved closer and sat on a marble bench just in front of the sitting room. The shuttered doors were partially open to allow light into the room from the courtyard. I recognized Valens's voice first. "Julius Phillipus dispatched his freedman yesterday with another plea, he heard from—"

"He needs to be working with us, not against us—" another man's voice interrupted.

"Then, by the gods, we need to decide who is going—"

Valens's voice once more, "Not until we decide what exactly we are petitioning for—"

"The aqueduct—"

"The harbor—"

"The harbor? Proculus is already fixing the harbor—"

"Not fast enough, the seas open in two months, do you want the trade going to Puteoli—"

"Maius, the harbor will be completed in a matter of weeks, Proculus knows what he's doing and the importance of–" once more Valens interrupted, only to be interrupted.

"We need cash, cash on hand. The Emperor needs to help us feed these people and get them settled. It's getting dangerous out there. My own son was attacked, beaten for his cloak–"

"He shouldn't have been out after curfew–"

"Damn it, Terius–"

And then I heard Tay's voice. "My friends, we can agree that our community's needs are many. I think we should write up a list, and then prioritize our most urgent necessities based on what will bring the most benefit to the most people. We need, above all, civil accord. Without peace, the harbor, the bridges, the basilicas, even the temples, are nothing to us. Sickness and hunger are far more dangerous than crumbled buildings and ruined sidewalks–"

"The aqueduct must be our first concern…"

I grew bored and left the politicians and their new friend to argue. I had my own matter to settle.

"How long did you read out loud?" Gavia chortled as she spoke.

"Not long," I lied. "I don't understand; you gave me a real speech to recite while standing in the sea, but you made a fool of me at Celer's home…"

A lean, white finger nearly poked my eye out. "That house doesn't belong to Celer, or his mistress." Her tone was sharp, and her single eye glared at me. "What I told you to do in the sea was no different, just rubbish. But maybe if you believed in something as stupid as curses then it might ease your feeble brain to think the curse had been lifted."

"Then why the change of heart, why make me do something so foolish…"

The finger was back in my face, as she snapped at me, "Painting a bust of that bitch, what are the chances that you would end up…*there*." She sighed, fatigued by her frustration.

"I don't understand, what is your connection to Actia?"

"Look around you, boy, we all live with our own curses." For an instant, her façade faltered, and I saw a small young woman who was not crude or spiteful, but frail and hurt.

"Get out, leave me." She snapped her fingers and her raven flew from the worktable to her hand. The creature let out a low croak at me, irritated that I had annoyed its master.

I walked out of the shop and absentmindedly collided with a person walking down the sidewalk. I was about to excuse myself when I caught my tongue. I stepped back and recognized the man I had run into. I could tell by his slight grin and piercing brown eyes that he recognized me as well.

"You're Demetrius." Actius's remark sounded less a question and more like an accusation. I nodded. "I want to speak to you…"

"He can't talk," one of the Greeks said, as he swept dirt out of the entrance of the house, onto the sidewalk. Corax eyed the handsome fellow who had me cornered with a hint of concern and curiosity.

Actius made an exaggerated frown. "So I've heard." He pointed toward the open door, indicating I should enter. I was used to being ordered around, but I doubted anyone ever argued much with Actius. He followed me inside the house, despite Corax's disapproving glare.

Actius glanced around the elegant atrium and started to lead me toward the drawing room. Pointing at the wax tablet I wore dangling from my neck, he said, "I have some questions for you..."

"Most guests are invited in, and speak with the master of the house before interrogating slaves." Tay's voice was as commanding as Actius's.

The actor spun on his heel to face my companion, who was striding toward us from his study.

"I'm sorry for my intrusion. I have been laid low with some bad news, and I feel my manners might be lacking," Actius said with meager sincerity.

"Yes, I understand." Tay paused, attempting to soften his tone despite the obvious discomfort he felt. "I am sorry for your loss. Celer was a pleasant man. And, of course, your mother, I had not met her, but my sympathies are with you."

Actius bowed his head, his eyes closed for a moment, and his shoulders dropped. The actions expressed sorrow, understanding, and appreciation for the comments. He was a renowned pantomime after all, the skill could not be set aside. After a pause, and in a polite tone of voice, he said, "You seem to know who I am, but I don't believe we have met. I am Actius Anicetus."

"Octavius Regulus..." he paused, noticing a puzzled expression on Actius's face. "It was rather easy to deduce who you are. Few people have reason to speak to my servant."

Slowly, Actius replied, "Yes." As if debating whether to ask, he frowned, smiled, and shuffled a bit before saying, "Regulus? Any relation to Livineius Regulus?" As Actius spoke, he patted a hand at the back of his head and winced.

"No," Tay responded with a slight edge in his tone. This question had been put to him so many times over the past few weeks that I'm sure he had regretted choosing the name *Regulus* from thin air. The entire town blamed a man named Livineius Regulus for the riot that had occurred in the town's amphitheater nearly four years before, the same riot depicted in Actia's courtyard.

"I thought not, but...well, never mind. I do apologize about the intrusion." He smiled weakly and stepped toward me.

Tay shot me a nasty look and said as pleasantly as possible. "Demetrius is unable to speak, however, he can write. I have already asked all of the pertinent questions regarding his presence in your mother's home when Celer was murdered. If you would come this way, I'll share with you what we know." He led us to his study.

Tay sat behind his writing table and motioned toward a small, backless chair for Actius. I was about to sit until Tay's raised brow and pinched lips reminded me that I was *still* a slave. I stood at attention near the desk.

Ajax appeared with a tray of wine, water, and two delicate glasses. Tay poured for his guest, who took his wine with little water, and then he poured his own glass.

"I'm not sure what you have been told already, but Celer asked me to send Demetrius to touch up some damage on a bust of your mother. The paint was chipped, I believe. Celer was anticipating your arrival and wanted the portrait fixed." Actius nodded as Tay spoke. "Demetrius was painting in the courtyard, his back to the portico, for the most part. There were a number of visitors...six?" I nodded. "And there was a man named Fannius, who came and went, the old doorman, and the half-witted young man. Demetrius interacted with Celer shortly before the callers arrived. I know that one of our local leaders, Valens, was the last to stop by. He merely glanced into Celer's office and didn't see him. "

Actius looked over at me with an odd grin, which caused me to squirm. "That confirms what Xeus told me, three men came calling after Fannius departed." He looked back to me. "You didn't hear anything odd?" I shook my head, *no.* The man grinned again. "Thank you for your time. I am sorry for my rudeness before."

I could tell he didn't mean what he said. He was suspicious of us, and hadn't taken to Tay's manners.

"No trouble at all. I am truly sorry for you, coming home to mourn for your mother, only to find out that another member of your household had been killed." Tay rose from behind his desk as he spoke.

Actius also stood from the little chair. "Yes, a shock, indeed."

"Forgive my curiosity, but would any of the men who called on Celer have reason to kill him?"

"I intend on finding out." After a brief bow of the head to Tay, Actius glanced at me once more. He seemed to be purposely unable to suppress his grin.

Corax was called upon to walk the guest to the vestibule after Tay and Actius exchanged forced pleasantries. Once Actius had departed, Tay remarked, "He's going to be trouble." I believe my companion had said the same thing regarding Cornelia just a few weeks before.

I lingered in the study as Tay stepped toward the door. I had not told him that I suspected Celer had been killed before the last three visitors arrived. I had hoped to keep this my secret. However, I had an inkling that the gods possessed different plans.

"What's wrong?" Tay asked, noticing the pained expression on my face.

"I left something out...Celer was dead before Valens arrived. I went looking for him." Tay's brows arched as I confessed. "I didn't see him in his office. I went into the kitchen and then back." Tay sighed, while I fumbled for the right words. "I noticed that I'd tracked lamp oil on my sandal. I stepped back into the dark office, found the broken lamp on the floor...and there was Celer, dead."

Tay groaned. "Why didn't you alert the doorman?"

I told him the simple truth. "I just wanted someone else to find him."

Ajax was dispatched with a note asking Valens to meet with Tay at his first chance. The note only mentioned that *Regulus* had discovered a bit more information regarding the guests of Celer. The man's curiosity had been piqued; he arrived within an hour.

Ushered into the study and quickly offered some refreshments, Valens asked, "Now what's the *new* information?" He glanced at me with a nervous smile.

Tay clasped his hands and looked toward me, the innocent but foolish slave. "I'm embarrassed to tell you this, but my valet withheld an important detail about yesterday."

Valens's forced smile slipped from his face.

"Out of fear, he kept this to himself; not all that long before you arrived, Demetrius discovered Celer's body." Tay went on to share the rest of my story, "He also suspects that Celer was dead before the two men who arrived before you paid their visits. One of them seems to have tracked oil from a broken lamp through the portico. Demetrius says the man seemed rather startled."

Valens's mouth dropped open, his hands clenched. "Eros?" he let out a long sigh, "Ianvarius told me he didn't see Celer...well, this is..." he took a deep breath and raised his finger to his mouth. "This must stay between us." He looked at me nervously, then back to Tay. "I will deal with this information. Regulus, you must promise me that you'll share this with no one."

I could tell that Tay did not care for the man's reaction, but he promised anyway. "I'll be content to remain out of the matter, so long as justice will be done."

Valens' eyes darted to me "Good that you came forward with the truth..." His mind was reeling. I disappeared before his eyes as he wrestled with the information.

Tay's voice dropped to almost a whisper when he added, "Actius Anicetus came by today, asking what Demetrius knew, this piece of information wasn't shared with him..."

Valens nearly leapt from his chair, "Anicetus...he was here...no, tell him nothing. The man is trouble...just like his mother was." Valens was obviously flustered.

Tay asked, "His mother was killed in the quake, and it's taken him over two weeks to get here? Where was he?"

Valens just shook his head, still upset by the information. "I must go. I will speak with you soon..." He departed without another word.

"He seemed rather upset," I whispered.

"A bit *too* upset." Tay remarked. He was weighing Valens's words, and I could tell that he didn't care for what was adding up.

Mucia came looking for me in the courtyard. I was watching the dog chase the peacock about the fountain.

The bird was a brave creature, he would peck at Geb and then run. Their antics were a pleasant distraction.

"Julia Felix has sent for you," Mucia said dismissively.

I had lost track of the day and was surprised to note that the sun was, in fact, slipping toward the horizon. Blessedly, Julia hadn't crossed my mind since the morning. Interestingly, neither had Cornelia.

I joined our neighbor in her litter. She inspected me silently for a moment, her eyes moving across my face and down my chest slowly, deliberately. "Blue suits you," she commented. I looked down to make sure I was wearing a blue tunic. I hadn't really paid attention to what Tay had laid out for me to wear.

We had been in motion for several minutes before Julia spoke again. "Does Regulus ask what I say to you when we are alone?"

I opened my little wax tablet and wrote a reply. *He has not. I assume he thinks we ride in silence. He's distracted now with members of the town council. I believe they are sending a delegation to the Emperor to ask for assistance.*

"Yes, I've noticed the company he's been keeping. I imagine his friendship with an ex-consul will get him appointed to whatever post he chooses... if the knuckle-bones fall correctly. His *generosity* has been helpful, too." She meant the bribes Tay had made in acquiring Popidius's property after the man's death. "Your master is an interesting..."

The litter came to an abrupt halt. Julia was reaching for the curtain when we both heard her handmaid scream. An instant later, the litter jilted backwards and fell to one side.

I was lying on top of Julia; she struggled to get up. Without thinking, I whispered, "Stay still, don't move."

In darkness, with the strewn pillows and wads of curtains, I was unable to see the reaction on the woman's face.

I heard a grunt, a howl of pain, and the maid's voice calling for help at some distance behind us. I leapt up blindly through the heavy fabric as I heard a man yell, "Get the rich woman!"

The advancing gang looked surprised to see me emerging from the toppled litter. Yet my appearance did nothing to halt their actions. Each man bore a club over their shoulder, ready to take a swing. One of Julia's slaves had been struck down and lay motionless beside the dropped sedan. The other three were attempting to repel the attackers. Unarmed, they were at a disadvantage to the men who had ambushed us.

The scene was chaotic, we were just outside of the makeshift refuge with eight men encircling us. The cry for help from the maid was whipping up another group of figures from the tents and shelters clustered about the tombs. These people were coming to join the fight, but on whose side?

I am not a brave man, but I am decisive. The three litter carriers who were still standing seemed to be putting up a decent fight. I pulled Julia from the wreckage of her litter, threw her over my right shoulder, and took off running through a gap in the calamity.

To my relief, the new band of recruits who were rushing towards the altercation meant to offer us help. Several women flanked my side while I carried Julia to presumed safety, as the men went on to rescue Julia's slaves.

These less fortunate women were fawning over my ward as I let her down from my shoulder. The look on Julia's face when we made eye contact was indescribable. Obviously, my rescue of her had not offset misleading her.

The numerous female refugees fussed over Julia as if she were a member of their sad community. The woman did her best to be polite and thank them for their efforts despite her obvious disdain for them. She waved her maid away to check on the injured slave who had been carried nearby.

The attackers had dispersed into the crowd that formed around us. While we'd been saved from them, no one seemed too willing to point out just who had set about capturing Julia. Neither did she push the issue, instead she thanked those who helped her and gave them the coins meant for the Oracle.

Once the commotion had passed, and Julia had been deemed healthy and unharmed, the men and I righted the litter and settled the injured slaves inside the damaged conveyance.

Inside Julia's home, a veritable construction site, the woman gave orders for the injured slaves to be tended to. She then snapped her fingers at me and pointed toward a wide portico.

I was led through the large home, which was a maze of projects. Fresh plaster, new masonry, and incomplete mosaic floors spoke of the place's damage. Once as far away as possible from anyone else, we entered a small, unfurnished room. Julia slammed the door behind me.

"What a deep and commanding voice you have, Demetrius. Would you care to explain why you don't use it?"

I understood her anger, no one enjoys being fooled. "I would rather not lie to you, and I'm certainly not going to tell you the truth."

Her face softened, just a bit. "A necessary deception?"

"Yes." I offered her no more.

"You may have saved my life…"

"I didn't, your men would have protected you, and the others were on their way to help."

"You fascinate me, young man." Her curious gaze had returned, and her anger was either abated or, perhaps, driving her. I knew that I could easily silence the questions, if only for a short time. With unnecessary force, I put my lips to hers. I felt her anger; it was the most emotion a woman had bestowed on me in some time. More powerful than lust, Julia's wrath directed my own passion. Until that day, I had been an inexperienced youth, fumbling about with random women between the bedclothes. With Julia, I became a seasoned lover.

"He's here!" Corax shouted toward the atrium as I sauntered through the front door. I smiled at him, and he looked at me oddly as I passed.

Cornelia and Samson rushed toward me, Tay following with greater dignity. "Look at you, oh, you are a mess," Samson exclaimed with worry.

Cornelia reached out to touch my lip. "You're bleeding." I pulled my head back and caught her hand with mine. I held her wrist somewhat tightly, and for a moment too long. She pulled away, and I released her at once, but not before we exchanged quizzical glances.

Tay joined us and sighed, "That beautiful blue tunic is ruined."

Once inside Popidius's empty bedroom, I was asked by Cornelia, "How is Julia?"

"Shaken up, but otherwise, fine." I noticed Tay stood behind Samson and Cornelia, his devilish grin told me that he knew why my hair was matted flat to the sides of my head with sweat. I'm sure he surmised just how the neck of my tunic had been ripped.

"What happened?" Cornelia asked, wanting all the information at once.

I licked my lower lip. Julia had bitten it as she dug her nails into my back. I had been in far greater danger in her arms than when encompassed by the men who attacked us. "We were just past the encampment when the litter stopped. The handmaid screamed and, in an instant, we toppled over. One of the litter carriers was struck at the back of the head; knocked out. The other three pushed the attackers back. I picked up Julia and ran with her towards some of the onlookers that her maid had managed to rouse."

"Random or deliberate?" Tay asked me, his grin had faded.

"Deliberate, I heard one man shout, 'Get the rich woman.' They were out for her, or at least for her jewelry and the offering meant for the Oracle." I was looking into Cornelia's eyes as I spoke. I knew what Tay was going to say next.

"It's just not safe right now; your flock shouldn't be traipsing beyond the city walls twice a day, and neither should you." That I expected, the next statement, I had not. "Move your rituals into the vineyard. I'll see to it that some of the ground is cleared…"

"The vineyard?" I had never thought to ask who owned the property next to us. I hadn't given much thought to where our donkeys were kept, or where the wagon had come from. At this point, I wanted to know. "What do you have to do with the vineyard?"

"I bought it." Tay made an expansive gesture. "This was once all one property…"

"You bought it, and you didn't tell me?"

Samson looked worried, Cornelia looked irritated, and Tay shook his finger at me. "Not right now, we can have this talk later." Of course, I doubted that we ever would.

"There's nothing *mystical* about your dried up vineyard..." Cornelia's tone was unnecessarily hostile. I think at that moment she was starting to regret her relationship with Tay. Somehow, he had managed to gain influence over her. Like almost any woman who wasn't married to an Emperor, she was naturally dominated by men. Without a husband or male relative, Cornelia's dubious career could lead her into some trouble. In reality, Tay was her best candidate for a patron. She knew as many of his secrets as he knew hers. They were both actors, well-versed in their parts, and perhaps too much alike.

"No less *mystical* than Octavius Quartio's courtyard, which is where Tiburs is holding the ritual's dedicated to Isis," Tay countered.

The Temple of Isis had been badly damaged by the quake. Tiburs, the High Priest of Isis, was a rather sore subject with Cornelia, since the man had tried to poison her only days after the disaster.

Cornelia's nostrils flared and her eyes narrowed, but she remained silent.

Tay sighed, "Do what you will..." He hesitated, as if to say more and then left the room.

Tay's strategy worked. Once the door was closed, Samson clasped his accomplice's hands and made an exaggerated shudder. "Mistress, he's right, it's not safe outside the city gates...let the devotees come to us here."

Cornelia's eyes were unfocused, she was somewhere far away.

Chapter Five
The Actor's Stage

🔲🔲🔲🔲🔲🔲🔲

Under Cornelia's critical supervision, Hesiod and I had struggled with the sarcophagus that the *Oracle* appeared from at the beginning of her private appointments. The prop, rather less authentic than I had first thought, weighed more than anticipated. Cornelia's sour slave and I managed to get the casket out of the cave and onto the wagon with only three stops along the way. I had wanted to set it down a few more times to get my strength back. Hesiod still believed me to be a mute, which limited my ability to ask for a moment's rest.

Afterward, Samson and Cornelia packed their costumes while Hesiod and I carried the blessedly light throne out to the wagon. We covered the gilded props with blankets, and despite the pleasant temperature, we covered ourselves in hooded cloaks.

Cornelia silently rode in the back of the wagon as we departed from her arena. All that remained of the Oracle's presence was the sad, makeshift idol standing in the clearing, its weathered gown billowing in the morning breeze.

A friendly old man had hobbled out of the ramshackle structure near the vineyard's gate. He called the donkeys by name as he unhitched them from the wagon. I assumed he came with the property, *another asset belonging to Octavius Regulus.*

Cornelia still seemed distracted. She hadn't even mentioned any concern that yet another person was being introduced to her duel identities.

Always good for his word, Tay had seen to it that a section of the scarred land had been cleared. Near our house, to the west, a fresh piece of open space awaited Cornelia.

The vegetation within the lifeless vineyard had been burned. Knurled and charred growth stood in strange symmetry atop the blackened soil. The place was cold and eerie, conjuring images of the banks of the River Styx. The hair on the back of my neck stood when I heard the cry of a nearby raven. I felt foolish when I realized that it was Gavia's little monster, residing just on the other side of the vineyard's wall.

After helping Hesiod with the mummy case, I left them to their task, feeling somewhat ignored, or perhaps merely forgotten.

Upon striding through our open front doors, I could see that the house was alive with activities. Mucia was pulling back the sheer curtains to open the drawing room to both the atrium and the courtyard. Ajax and Corax were arranging chairs and little tables about the open rooms. Freshly arranged garlands were being hung by Sosia and Delia. The household was all in good cheer, excited to celebrate the naming day of Porcia's newborn son.

In search of my companion, I entered his study. Dressed, not as a prostitute, but as the matron of the household, Servia's narrow face swung in my direction. As always, when she caught sight of me, Servia frowned. The woman was seductively posed, leaning across Tay's writing table. Her master sat behind the desk speaking to her in a hushed voice until he noticed her frown and spotted me. "Ah,

Demetrius." He beckoned me forward with a lazy wave of the hand.

Servia, snakelike, slithered off the desk and coiled onto a low, backless chair.

"I trust everything went well?" Tay's raised brow told me that a simple nod would do for the time being. With that motion, he understood that the Oracle of Nephthys, through her translator's voice, had explained after the morning ritual that the devotees were invited to commune with the Goddess within the secure walls of the neighboring vineyard until the Goddess determined the grotto to be safe once more. The small collection of followers responded well to the change of locations, the grounds weren't as hallowed as one might think.

"Good, well, go get yourself cleaned up, it won't be long until our company starts to arrive." Tay's smile seemed less devious than usual. He was genuinely looking forward to actual guests, rather than the typical visitors looking to buy a bit of soft flesh or the city slaves picking up taxes and bribes.

I found a clean tunic laid out for me on my bed. I defined the bed as mine at this point because Tay had taken the room Cornelia had occupied over the past eleven days. I had not had a room to myself in nearly four years. Sometimes, I snuck a woman into my bed at a friend's house where I was a guest and Tay was left to find another place to sleep. Other times, I found myself in an inn or a woman's home, and my companion would be waiting for me in the exact location I anticipated he would be. But day in and day out, we cohabitated more often than not, and I had grown accustomed to his perpetual presence. With his departure to another room, I felt another change occurring that set me at ill ease. Our new life seemed to be stable, and yet still growing, adapting, as if the play's author occasionally corrected something amiss along the second draft.

The celebration forced Ursa to prepare something other than stew for our meal. I was curious to taste her offerings. A rather grand meal, considering there were shortages of food throughout the crippled city, was spread out on a long table in the drawing room. Pickled eggs, roasted ducks, and an assortment of questionable cheeses caught my eye before I noticed two silver trays of elaborate pastries.

By day, when the sailors and craftsmen worked, our home was so very different than the evening. Staphylus was throwing a stick across the courtyard, and Tay's mutt eagerly chased after it. Dressed in cheerful yet homely stolas, Delia and Sosia quietly argued under the peristyle as they tied ribbons about the evergreen garlands. Mucia rested beside the lifeless fountain, gazing at the peacock while he preened himself.

How normal the setting appeared; I was almost lulled into thinking that the gods had stopped setting me up for follies to amuse themselves. That somehow, I had stumbled into a regular life to live, not mine, but a strangely adequate situation all the same.

My wandering thoughts were disturbed when the gate to the alley swung open and our neighbor, Curtius, arrived, followed by his slave Carus. The servant was a fair-sized, good-natured young man. Curtius was as kind as he could be, despite his intimidating stature.

Servia appeared and took charge. She welcomed the men, thanked them for the wine they brought, and directed them to set the gifts next to some clay cups.

Only a moment later, I heard voices from the atrium. Ajax and Corax excitedly welcomed their former master, Jucundus. The older fellow was carried in a chair by four sturdy slaves. As they moved en mass toward the courtyard, Jucundus exchanged pleasantries with the two young men whom he had given to Tay as a gift for saving his life after the quake.

Fetched by Servia, Tay emerged from his study to welcome the man. "My dear Jucundus, I'm so happy you could make it."

"Yes, yes, so am I. Kind of you to invite me, good to be out of that house," the kindly man replied.

Tay directed the brawn to the portico, where the injured man was gently placed. They pulled the carry poles from the chair, and then Tay snapped his fingers and looked at me.

My eyes opened wide, and I bit my lip, unsure what I was supposed to do. After an awkward moment of being stared at, Tay suggested, "Show Jucundus's servants where to wait." I stared back dumbly until Tay nodded toward the kitchen.

I gave a grunt to the men and led them to the little room. Humiliated, my face was burning red. They didn't seem to notice. Instead, they glanced about at the food still in the kitchen, eager for me to leave them.

I was just rejoining the group as Curtius and Jucundus tried to make conversation with each other. I gathered they were acquainted, but they didn't seem to know each other well.

"I remember when Porcia was first…" Curtius stumbled for a phrase that didn't contain the word *bought*, "came here…and now look at her, a freedwoman, and a mother."

"Mother to a son no less, yes, the gods have seen fit to bless her…" said Jucundus, kindly. He then lowered his voice a bit, "She's the auburn-haired one, yes?" after Curtius confirmed the older man's assumption, Jucundus smiled. "Such a nice girl."

Tay sat down after Curtius took a seat. Carus, aware of his station, remained standing until Tay pointed to another chair. Afterward, he invited Staphylus to join them under the portico and then asked Jucundus, "So tell us, how's commerce?"

Jucundus sat back in his chair. "Active. I've witnessed a dozen land transactions in half as many days. Cornelius Tages just bought four homes grouped together, plans to make himself one big place out of the lot of them. In fact, your neighbor across the way, Julia, she's bought the entire block…even arranged through Primus to buy the alley and close it off from wheeled traffic."

"I hear she plans to build shops, apartments, even a small bathhouse," Curtius interjected.

"There's nothing more intolerable than a wealthy woman." Tay quoted the old saying and all of the men laughed.

I noticed Servia sneer in her master's direction. Landowners, money men, and the gentry never realized just what their servants and women heard. I had to question what random comment was spoken before an otherwise mild-mannered slave turned into Spartacus, or a good-natured wife added hemlock to her husband's sweet cakes.

Jucundus continued the conversation, "There are as many people out to sell as to buy, oh, yes, there's fear that the old nobility is going to abandon the city. Well, that happened years ago." The old fellow shrugged. "I'm the son of a freedman, so I can say this, Pompeii's been run by *new men*, upstarts and wealthy ex-slaves, since Sulla left the city. Marcus Licinius Crassus Frugi may be our noblest inhabitant, but Julius Phillipus, a descendant of an imperial freedman, has just as much clout around here. The Empress's family may have a home overlooking the river, but how often do they visit it? Claudia Antonia, who once frequented the city, hasn't been here in …perhaps four years." The old man had winded himself. He gave a wave of the hand, and brought his thoughts to a close. "Let them have their mansions in Baiae."

Curtius put his hand to his chin and shrugged. "Let the nobility leave, I sell more cheap wine than the good stuff anyway."

Jucundus gave the tavern owner a polite chuckle and went on, "Speaking of business, someone who visited me this morning asked me about you." This statement was directed toward Tay.

"Really?" he responded, only mildly curious.

"Actius Anicetus, the pantomime, he had some business to see to, his mother's actually. He told me about the *unfortunate* death of Celer." Jucundus's eyes drifted toward me, lingering under the portico.

Tay picked up his cup of wine and took a deep drink before asking, "And what did Anicetus want to know?"

Jucundus shrugged, "Yes, well, I couldn't quite figure that out. Wanted to know how long you'd been here, how you came to own Popidius's home…asked about him…" the fellow pointed at me. "Wanted to know how long he'd been mute? Well, he wasn't direct about it, yes, but he wasn't as subtle as he thought he was. He's a pantomime mind you, when they start talking, they never really know what to say."

I couldn't help but think of our recent trip to Jucundus's house, when Tay had delicately probed him for information about an old slave named Darvus. Had the shrewd man seen through Tay's array of questions as quickly as he had Actius's?

"Well, I understand his curiosity; Demetrius was in the house when Celer was killed," Tay replied evenly.

"Yes, yes, he was." Jucundus still had a bit more gossip to share despite his host's seeming disinterest. "I gather I wasn't the first person he'd asked about you. He mentioned that Eros had told him that you were from Nicopolis, he even knew that your father's second wife had laid claim to the family business."

Tay's brow arched rather high as he took a long swallow of his wine. "And I wonder how it is that Eros knows this?" he remarked with forced humor.

I recognized the name, Eros. It was he who tracked the oil from Celer's office, and then arrived as I was last departing from Celer's house after the trick played upon me by Gavia. Had I yet know whose freedman he was, I would have been even more concerned.

Jucundus replied, "Eros is a nosy creature, perhaps he found out from Ptolemy, the linen trader?"

Tay's brow could raise no further, but keeping his tone in check, he remarked, "I don't believe that I am acquainted with Ptolemy."

Curtius earnestly jumped into the conversation, "Ptolemy, *the eunuch*. Besides linen, he can get you anything you want from Egypt—for a price."

In response, Tay only nodded.

Jucundus concluded his story, "Actius knew as much about you as I, he changed the subject, and we came to business. I told him who owed his mother's debts and that was really that, well, and he asked about…"

Jucundus was silenced by the appearance of the guest of honor. The entire household converged on Porcia and her son. Mucia trailed behind with little Regula in her arms.

The group, considerate of Jucundus's inability to move, gathered around the peristyle and passed Little Popidius around as if he were on fire. Which, with his bright red hair and crimson skin, he did, indeed, seemed alight.

The noise of the commotion carried through the courtyard, and only a few minutes passed before Gavia, without her raven, appeared. She was as disheveled as ever.

I noticed an odd exchange of cold glances and sublte nods between Jucundus and Gavia, before the little witch snatched the child from Carus and told him, "The food is over there, don't get confused and gobble this little thing down like a pickled egg."

From the doorway that connected the abandoned basket shop to the courtyard, Cornelia and Samson emerged. I was rather taken aback by this. Each had been seen by every member of the household, but just who they were was still shrouded in mystery.

Tay had obviously invited the two, as he showed no sign of surprise. However, the rest of the assemblage was attempting to casually study them, in the most obvious manner. Even Ursa, who belonged to Cornelia, eyed them suspiciously, keeping up her appearance as a new member of *our* household.

Tay looked to Servia, who had learned to read his facial expressions almost as well as I. He raised a brow and turned his eyes to the table filled with food. Servia gave a crisp clap with her hands and said, just loud enough to be heard, "Guests, please help yourselves."

This was an informal occasion with a very odd mixture of attendants. Couches would not be used for reclining and as most of the guests were slaves, hands and feet would not be washed nor would little plates be passed about.

As the ensemble helped themselves, Tay prepared a little plate for Jucundus, ironic because when he was my slave, he seldom did the like for me.

I held Little Popidius for a few minutes, he was like a wild animal, and he could sense my fear of him. He cried and thrashed until Gavia plucked him away from me. The child, the center of attention, was the least happy guest. While his mother, Porcia, was delighted by the attention of her friends.

Cornelia was introduced to both Jucundus and Curtius as *Regulus's* new tenant. She had been displaced by the quake and was renting both the shop and the rooms connected to our house. It was Jucundus who asked, "How long have you lived in Pompeii?"

"Close to a year, I moved here after my father died." The woman lied, or at least, I assumed the story was a lie.

Trying to be pleasant, Curtius asked, "What brought you to these parts?"

Cornelia's smile never wavered. "I had a distant relative who lived here; he died in the quake."

I had learned that mentioning a death in the quake was a quick way to get people to change the subject. The topic was a dark cloud over the city. On the day of the disaster, the inhabitants had been about to celebrate to the city forefathers. It was whispered that those who died had been singled out by the shades of those long dead men for transgressions unknown.

Jucundus asked, "How shall you use the shop? Yes, the last tenant wove baskets. Spent all his profit on Curtius's wine and Popidius's women."

Somewhat rehearsed, Cornelia replied, "Samson," she pointed toward her ebony servant, who smiled gleefully, "is an excellent barber. I think I shall put his services to work."

Curtius couldn't help but laugh. "A quick drink, a haircut, and then a girl, makes for a nice afternoon."

Playing her part, Cornelia bowed her head, while the men chuckled. Convinced by her false display of modesty, Curtius apologized. "Sorry about that, I was just joking."

Cornelia smiled demurely and lowered her head again. I didn't care for the performance. I missed her normal scorn and haughty attitude. This woman, who lived above the old basket shop, seemed shy and broken. I thought of that faraway look in her eyes earlier in the day; perhaps she was broken.

Gavia fussed over both of the infants, keeping her distance from Jucundus, and completely ignoring her host. From time to time, she noticed me glance in her direction and made mocking faces at me.

As the naming day celebration drew to an end, the baby boy was taken to the freshly repainted shrine. We all knew that the infant had been given the name of the former owner of the home. Still, Tay held him before the assembled group, and officially presented him as Popidius Metellicus, and then he asked us to watch over the child and think of him as our own. He recited a few prayers, or made them up, I'm not sure which, but they sounded convincing.

Jucundus, as the eldest man present, was asked to say a blessing over the bulla. He strung together a few pious phrases, and the gold amulet was pressed to Little Popidius's swaddled chest.

We drank what was left of the wine, and then it was time to prepare for the evening.

Jucundus departed after making his gracious farewells. He was carried off by his slaves, who had devoured nearly every morsel of food left in our little kitchen.

Curtius and Carus returned to the tavern, while Gavia pestered Tay about the crack in her floor. She left, pleased with herself once her landlord was uncharacteristically flustered.

The girls went to their rooms to don their more sensual attire, while Ajax and Corax removed the fragrant garlands and returned the furniture to the proper places.

Cornelia and Samson slipped out of sight. The Oracle would practice her first evening ritual in the vineyard before the sun set.

Tay had retreated to his study, while the others readied for the evening performances. The expression on his face told me to withhold the comment that I was about to whisper. I rephrased the jab into a mild question, "Octavius Regulus isn't a name plucked from thin air after all?"

Tay exhaled a long sigh before he made his reply. "A ghost from the past."

"Is this Egyptian trader going to be a problem?" This wasn't the query that I wanted to ask, but it was the more pressing concern.

"One mystery at a time, *Demetrius.*" I could see through his attempt at sarcasm; he was apprehensive. "The man you believe to have first stumbled upon Celer seems rather interested in you and me."

I just nodded, while lowering into the chair across from my friend. His arched brow told me that he was waiting for a reaction. "Eros?" I whispered, unsure of what statement was expected of me.

"I'm surprised…you don't know who Eros is?" After I shrugged, he informed me, "Quintus Poppaeus's freedman."

Poppaeus was the uncle of Nero's wife. Displeased by the new correlation, I choked out the following statement, "Poppaea's uncle, he left Pompeii after the quake."

"Yes, but now his freedman who is assigned to run the local house. This is a man whom we do not wish to investigate our story."

The sun would touch the horizon in another hour. For late Februarius, it was warm, but I could feel a chill coming. I threw a cloak on and slipped through the alley gate, only to walk around to the front of our house towards the vineyard.

Gavia was inserting heavy wooden shutters into open windows. Her bird flapped its wings and shrieked from his perch atop her little head. The scene would have been comical if I weren't afraid of the creature and suspicious of its master.

"Headed out, are you?" Gavia asked without looking at me. I only nodded, I wouldn't be tricked into speaking again by her. "Which of your lovers are you off to see?" I missed a step, but tried not to react.

The vineyard was a large piece of property, extending nearly to the city walls. Devoid of growth, the land sat strangely without purpose.

I recalled Jucundus mentioning that the deceased and nearly bankrupt Popidius had originally owned the vineyard. Perhaps there had been some sort of insect infestation that only fire could cure. That would explain where part of the man's wealth had gone.

Hesiod, concealed by a heavy cloak with the hood pulled over his bowed head, pointed a devotee ahead of me to our left; I followed.

Along the wall of the property, that was, in fact, the exterior wall of our house, stood the golden sarcophagus. Beside the dazzling casket was a tall, three-legged table that I recognized from our sitting room. Atop the pilfered item, a silver tray with burning incense collected the gifts to Nephthys. The area was somewhat secluded, a row of tall hedges that were only burned to the trunk fenced in one side of the clearing on our right, while we faced Popidius's home, and to our left was the back of a stable. Though the domain was not mystic, it was still otherworldly and strange. Charred ground and the skeletons of long dead grapevines dangling from blackened posts made me uneasy, as if I were somewhere I shouldn't be.

The familiar faces were gathered, with the exception of Julia Felix. We waited in silence for the Oracle and her translator to appear. I heard movement from somewhere behind the scarred, wretched, wooded bones to our left. From the macabre scene came the performers.

The Oracle was dressed in a resplendent gold gown, a traditional crown sat atop a beautiful beaded black wig that touched the demigoddess's shoulders. A yellow veil rested between the crown and wig and fell to the mystical figure's waist. She carried her flail and crook, crossed over her breasts like the image of the dead pharaohs. I nearly forgot that behind this majestic façade was Samson. Almost unnoticed, the veiled translator followed in her simple, all white attire.

With bowed heads, we listened to the foreign words, which the Oracle almost sang. The translator welcomed us, blessed the new environment, and then the evening ritual began.

Before departing the Oracle's new domain, I noticed a patch of bricks in the wall that didn't match. I had a good guess as to where in the house the former doorway had led before Popidius sold the vineyard.

Resisting the urge to inspect the newer brickwork, I followed the other devotees. With Ra on the horizon, long shadows fell from the stone wall concealing Cornelia and Samson as they waited to collect the offerings.

Standing on the cobbled sidewalk leading the short distance home, I felt little purpose and rather melancholy. Gavia's shop was closed. She wouldn't be lingering to torment me. Across the street, Julia's house evaded shadow, yet still stood lifeless.

I had a few coins stashed inside my wax tablet. Curtius's tavern beckoned to me. Not that there wasn't wine at the house, but there was a strange privacy to be found in a populated tavern, that couldn't always be obtained at home.

I passed by Gavia's shop, boarded up and dark. And then the closed door of our own dwelling, freshly painted dark red with a costly bronze lion's head affixed to it. At the corner of the inherited property was the sealed door to the abandoned basket shop; Cornelia's new refuge.

I crossed the alley and then ducked into the open tavern. Smoke hung in the air from burning lamps, dangling from the ceiling. My eyes stung for a moment, and my nostrils curled at the scent of soured wine and sweat. A group of rough-looking men eyed me as they leaned against the counter.

"Evening, Demetrius," Curtius called. He pointed to an amphora of his better wine and I nodded. "Just you?" he asked. I smiled big and raised my eyebrows up and down. He handed me a crude clay cup, and poured the dark liquid into it. I didn't signal for him to stop, but he still left plenty of room to add water. I was digging for a coin when the friendly chunk of a man told me, "First one's on me." He leaned in closer and lowered his voice before adding, "Successus, over there by Isis, he likes to gamble...she's been squirming about for a while, I figure she's got to get back to her mistress soon." I glanced toward the young couple. The girl looked like ants were climbing up her legs, while the young man appeared to be at that perfect state of intoxication when everything seemed pleasant and tranquil; this was also the point leading up to jolly laughter or blubbering self-pity.

I reached, and quite a reach it was, over the counter and patted Curtius's sturdy shoulder. There was an open table near the door, within sight of my potential adversary. I sat down and drank slowly. Curtius's good wine wasn't really that good, only by comparison to his lesser wines was it worth the two coppers that he charged. Of course, my first helping was free, so I had no right to complain.

I watched the girl named Isis, a young, nervous thing, as she peered at the door and then back to her companion several times. He talked constantly, but, thank the gods, his slurred voice blended in with the rest of the crowd.

The two old whores, who seemed to be ever-present at the tavern, were without victims and drinking heavily. One would start singing a song only to be interrupted by the other and corrected with a different word or pitch.

A number of bland men sat in small groups, most covered in dust, as a sign of their earlier labors. Many of them had most likely come from Julia Felix's construction site. Wasn't it Crassus who said: *No man is truly rich unless he can afford his own army*? If not, it sounds like something he would have said. Well, Julia had an army, and they had set siege to her property.

Few faces were familiar to me. I doubted any of Proculus's sailors were part of the crowd, they knew Tay would supply them with the drink, if they had already meandered across Pompeii. Over the past few days, a number of taverns had reopened about the city that were much closer to the demolished harbor. No doubt the many displaced prostitutes of the city were lurking in the establishments, quick to draw away from our customers.

I set my wax tablet down and flipped it opened. I pulled my little bronze dice from the wool bag that dangled from my belt. I dropped them a few times onto my tablet. The action went unnoticed.

After finishing my first cup of wine, I went back for another. Once I returned to my table, I watched Isis pull her wrist out of Successus's hand. They argued a bit before she stood, and he called her a foul name that momentarily caught the attention of the crooning whores until they realized the familiar comment wasn't directed at them.

Isis returned the insult with a crude hand gesture and stormed out of the tavern with more self-confidence than I would have anticipated.

A few eyes were on Successus, and he loudly informed us all as to what we could do to ourselves. The two wretched women looked over once more before determining the explicit suggestion wasn't a solicitation for their services.

Curtius called out to Successus from behind the counter, "Calm yourself, friend, I don't want to kick you out…"

"Yeah, not until you have all my money," Successus replied back, in surprisingly good humor. There was a round of chuckles from anyone paying attention.

Successus met my gaze and then looked to my dice. The young man, tanned-skinned and fair-haired, gathered his cup, his jug, and a small satchel and came over to my table. Without preamble, he told me, "Damn girl's owned by Adelpha. She's at her inn, spreading her legs for everybody but me," he took a long drink from his cup as he dropped into the bench across from me and continued, "and I love her…dumb girl." He dropped his satchel on the table and nearly spilled his wine as he slammed it down. "One day I'll buy her, then she'll love me." He sighed and closed his eyes for a moment. "Got money?"

As I was nodding, one of the old whores called over to Successus, "That one don't talk."

I picked up my bronze stylus and wrote an "I" and an "II" on either side of the wax-covered leaflets of my tablet. Successus looked over the etchings and then back to me.

"I don't know, bad luck to gamble with a cripple."

The same woman who'd called out before shouted, "*No Tongue* will win, he's blessed by Fortuna." This was just the necessary challenge, and then the game commenced.

The young man, a stone mason by trade I had learned, was not without luck himself. We both exchanged the same coins a number of times until, finally, my pile of bronze and copper started to grow larger than his. While he had stopped drinking, I had continued, thus we met in the middle and were well-suited for each other. I almost shouted (both from joy and frustration) a number of times, but managed to contain myself.

Successus was just dropping his dice from his cup when I heard Curtius mention *my* name, "...Demetrius is fine..."

I turned to see one of the Greeks, Corax or Ajax, poking his head into the tavern. He gave me a quick smile and disappeared. Always the junior partner, I was being checked up on by my companion. I surmised that the need to see where I was indicated that Cornelia and Samson had already returned to the house. There were few locations I could be, making it easy for Tay to keep an eye on me.

Successus rebounded for a few throws, but never won back half of what he had lost. His tongue grew dry, and he was becoming irritable. He shouted to the counter for Curtius to bring him another jug. When I looked to see how the friendly man was going to respond, I saw a new customer leaning with his back to the counter watching us.

It was Actius Anicetus, and when our eyes met, he gave me a little nod of the head and an odd smile, as if we shared a secret. He watched us, or perhaps me, for some time. I felt my skin flush, and my palms grew sweaty.

Finally, Successus won back just enough of his money to quit.

"I knew it was bad luck to gamble with a cripple!" my opponent said while scooping up his coins. "I've had enough."

Actius, still grinning, stared me down, while I thrust my winnings into my little bag and hung my wax tablet back around my neck. He slid to one side of the counter to make room for me, and I tried to avoid eye contact with him while I slapped a few coins down between us, but it was impossible.

Like a scared rabbit, I darted for the door, hoping that the fox wouldn't follow me.

Chapter Six
A New Performer

I was halfway across the narrow alley when I heard just the words that I had expected, "Hey, I want to talk to you!" I didn't look back, instead I picked up my pace, and then a firm hand was on my shoulder. Actius swiveled me around to face him. He gave me rather benign smile, and jovially said, "I just want to talk, alright?"

Horrified, I smiled and nodded. He took me by the elbow and directed me back toward the corner, onto the uneven sidewalk and then we walked along the front of our house. He led me farther away, and after passing Gavia's shop, we slowed our pace.

The sun was gone, the sky was illuminated only by stars. None of the night watchmen seemed to be near, I contemplated shouting for help but thought better of it. We finally stopped in front of the gate to the vineyard.

"This will do, we are far enough away from the stray ear," Actius mumbled, his face barely visible to me. "I want to know what happened the day Celer died."

I was reaching for the tablet around my neck, unsure that either of us would be able to see what I wrote in the darkness, when the man firmly put his palm against the tablet and pressed it onto my chest. "It would be a lot easier if you just tell me, I know that you can speak." I looked at him dumbly before he told me, "I'm the most famous pantomime performer in the empire. I can speak more with my little finger than most men can with all their words. Now you, all you can manage is that dumb look," he tapped rather firmly on my chin. "That's because you can talk."

My secret wasn't much of a secret, it seemed. I sighed and shrugged. Once more, he asked, "Now, tell me what you know." He was no longer menacing to me, his expressive eyes told me not to be scared but to trust him.

"I was painting…" I started speaking, and his smile transformed into a bit of sneer. I had proven him correct. "…the bust of your mother's…" I blinked my eyes three times and spit to the right, it was never good to talk about the dead in the dark of night under the naked sky. "Celer kept to himself in his study most of the time, as…" I almost said *Tay,* but caught myself, "as Regulus told you, six men came calling, and, at some point, Fannius left…"

"I don't trust that man," Actius mumbled. "I know that he is hiding something from me."

I was about to go on when I saw some strange figure appear behind Actius. My mouth gaping open, I pointed behind him. I had momentarily lost my mind, thinking that perhaps his mother had heard us and had been conjured from the cold air. The man started to turn to see what I was looking at when a club swung and caught him on his right shoulder. He attempted to lurch at the silhouette and took a misstep. Actius fell off the high curb of the sidewalk and cursed Minerva rather boldly.

The frightening specter, was, indeed, an ominous creature, she was about to take a swing at the downed man when I hissed, "Gavia, stop!"

Tay clasped me by the elbow, as if I might take flight. Condescension and scorn merged into a tone of voice fit to give execution orders as he asked, "Again, how did this happen?"

Actius was lying on a couch in the closed study, the only private room on the ground floor that wasn't occupied by a lustful client. Ajax and Corax had carried him there after I summoned them for help.

The Greeks had been quickly dispatched after depositing the injured man before their master. Only Tay, myself, Gavia, and the injured man were present. Nonetheless, I whispered as I explained, "Actius led me away from the tavern, just down the street to speak with me." Tay's brow nearly leaped off his forehead. "Gavia heard something, got a club out, and came to defend me."

"Stupid bitch…" Actius mumbled, even though she was crouched beside him inspecting the wound on his forehead. He'd split the flesh when he fell and hit the stone curb. Besides the healthy blow that little Gavia had landed on his shoulder, he'd also twisted his ankle in the process of falling.

"She didn't know it was *him*…" I attempted to defend her.

"It would have been a lethal blow if I knew it was *him,*" she quipped. This didn't surprise me, as she certainly had some sort of grievance with Actius's mother and her household.

"Who are you…what's wrong with you?" Actius swatted Gavia away.

"Gavia Servia," she told him, as if Actius should recognize her name.

I could tell by the confused look in Actius's eyes, the woman's name meant nothing. "I don't know you. What do you have to hold against me?"

The little witch snarled and spat in the man's face. He momentarily forgot about his injured leg and struggled to get up, but thank Jove, he was in too much pain to put his weight on the ankle. Tay and I gently sat him back on the couch, while Gavia enlightened us.

"Your mother took my family's home. I was thrown to the streets after my father killed himself." There was a deluge of curses and foul language followed by a stream of tears.

We remained in silence, watching the woman attempt to stifle her crying. When she recovered her voice, she choked out, "That old bastard, Xeus...I trusted him...my family trusted him..." she looked over to Tay, "Your friend Valens, you watch out for him."

I simply can't repeat verbatim what was told to us, her words were beyond foul. Simply put, her father, for reasons she did not explain, had been ruined and took his own life. The suicide occurred shortly after Gavia's husband, nameless to me at that point, had been killed. Members of the town leadership then seemed to have given the late Actia the family's home. Gavia was left with nothing other than disgrace. Well, that was the gist of what she uttered before storming off. I must admit, though, I have retold the account knowing the full story, in retrospect, much of what she said did not make clear sense to me at the time.

We three men, left alone, mulled over the woman's rage in silence before Tay finally relaxed and sat down behind his writing desk. "You really don't know who she is? Or why she hates your mother so?" His words weren't scornful, just inquisitive.

"I have no clue who that little creature is, or what she's talking about. My mother moved to that house maybe three, four years ago, once she settled here." He took a deep breath and winced. "I wasn't really that close with my mother. She never explained why she chose Pompeii as her home after Agrippina's death."

"Your mother was a freedwoman to Agrippina?" Tay asked, confused by the reference.

Before answering, Actius sniffed at a tonic that Gavia had mixed for him while he had been carried to our house. With a shudder, he drank the fluid in one swallow.

"Not exactly, she had belonged to, and was freed by, Lollia Paulina. When Lollia's property was confiscated by *Claudius,* Agrippina invited my mother to become part of her entourage. I don't know much more about the business, I was already learning my trade and traveling with a guild." Actius's tone hinted at some disdain for the story.

Lollia Paulina is said to have been one of the most beautiful women of her day. I was six years old when she was forced to commit suicide, so I must believe what I've been told. Her beauty had been her curse; coveted by the Emperor Caligula, she had been forced to divorce her husband in favor of a brief marriage with the young Emperor.

After being married to Caligula for less than a year, Lollia was divorced and forbidden to remarry. Yet the subject of remarriage may have caused her death. She was one of the women whom Emperor Claudius considered marrying before he decided to seal his fate with his niece, none other than Agrippina.

Agrippina was proficient in eliminating rivals; Lollia was charged with sorcery, exiled, and then forced to take her own life.

Pliny the Elder, never to be confused with one of my dearest friends, Pliny the Younger, bless his memory, recorded that Lollia was ostentatious. He stated that she wore half of her fortune in jewelry. Well, if a woman is deprived of a husband, by decree of an emperor, let her relish her possessions, I say. They were all she had to substitute for love and affection.

"Why did you ask me if I was related to Livineius Regulus?" Tay asked our wounded guest.

"The name was on the top of a list that I found in Celer's office," Actius explained.

"Regulus was involved in a riot that started at the amphitheater—" Tay started to say.

I interjected, "The riot that's depicted in your mother's courtyard fresco."

Actius's eyes darted back and forth from mine to Tay's before my companion asked, "Who were the other names on that list?"

Actius shook his head and winced at the same time. "I'm not sure. After I arrived, Fannius was about to tell me what had happened to Celer, and then a freedman belonging to Poppaea's family barged in. He bullied Fannius out of the room and then described the day of the quake, when my mother was killed. He went on and surmised that a man named Valens had arranged for Celer's death..." Actius sighed, indicating he didn't believe a word that he was repeating. "...apparently, Celer had belonged to Valens and he'd outlived his usefulness." Actius swung his head dramatically towards me. "Eros also told me that *he* was in the house at the time of the murder and that -" his head swung back to Tay, "-you and Valens were in each other's debt."

Tay's sarcastic wit returned to him. "Thank Jove that Eros has this all neatly solved for you."

Actius, grimacing from pain, continued, "When he finally left, I began wandering the house. I came to Celer's office and discovered a list of names on his desk." Actius paused for effect. "I had only started to read it - then I was on the floor seeing stars, the scroll was pulled out of my hand, and I heard footsteps running away. Old Xeus didn't see or hear anything, and Fannius was with the overgrown boy."

"Did you hear the front door open before you were struck?" I asked. Actius shrugged and I explained, "Then they were either in the house already, or came from the alley. The front door squeaks loud enough to wake Pluto."

I had been accompanied to the house by Gavia earlier in the day. I was left to ponder where she had gone after Xeus dismissed her.

"Who else was on the list?" Tay asked, completely intrigued.

"I didn't recognize most of the names. Celer and my mother's names were on the top of the list; then Regulus... Frugi... Poppaeus... Valens. There were initials too, C.A." Actius's voice drifted off.

"How many names where there?" I asked.

"Ten or so, I'm not sure." He tried to stifle a yawn and winced.

I could tell that whatever Gavia had given the man was making him drowsy.

There was a loud knock at the door, and, startled, I jumped. Tay called out, "Come in."

Servia's narrow little head appeared. "Master, Proculus has arrived." Tay had given strict instructions to be informed when the admiral was under our roof. He acknowledged her with a quick nod of his head.

Once the door was closed, Actius asked, "Volusius Proculus?" The name seemed to lift some of the fog clouding his mind.

"The same," Tay responded, perhaps not making the connection.

With more hostility in my voice than I meant, I added, "An associate of your *uncle's,* I believe."

The man's piercing eyes narrowed. "You know who my uncle is?"

"Of course, while you are *famous*, he is *infamous*." I noticed Tay roll his eyes, and realized that Actius's dramatic effect had rubbed off on me.

"You're an odd young man, a mute who can talk, a slave who seems fairly useless..." he raised his brow and glanced back and forth between Tay and me.

Tay offered, "I can explain all that - later. I have business to see to." I remained seated beside the desk until Tay cleared his throat. I jumped up and followed my companion, in full agreement that I couldn't be trusted with Actius alone.

The gods, always with a good sense of humor, had positioned the little hermaphrodite, Mucia, just in the atrium as we passed. "Take a tray of food in to our guest, speak to him as little as possible." She made for the kitchen, and he mumbled to me, "If he's amused by things that seem to be a contradiction, let him figure *her* out."

Actius was unable to walk, and we hadn't really finished our business with him. Tay invited him to spend the night. Staphylus would move to one of the unused rooms upstairs, and Actius would sleep in his room on the ground floor. To my surprise, the man was immediately agreeable.

My clothing was laid out for me when I awoke. Geb, at my feet, was eager to go downstairs and see what I might find us for breakfast. I had missed the morning blessing of Nephthys. No one had woken me, nor did I care. Perhaps my absence would intrigue Cornelia.

Ursa was mixing the stew that the entire household would feed off of over the course of the day, while I slipped past her to find some bread and honey. She seemed to purposely get in my way, reminding me that I was in her domain. But I knew a trick. I went to the marble-faced latrine and began to hike up my tunic. She departed as quickly as her short legs could carry her bulk.

Already halfway through the motions, I went ahead and took advantage of the solitude. But my true intent was to inspect the plaster. As I had surmised, a section of the kitchen wall seemed to be reworked. This was about the same place on the outside of the house that the pattern of bricks looked different.

Geb followed me to the household shrine and drooled while Venus, Hercules, and the unnamed household gods received my offerings. I tore off a chunk of bread for him and devoured the rest. Geb left me to chase his friend, the peacock, and I went back to the kitchen to put together a plate for our injured guest.

I knocked softly upon the wooden door, but there was no answer. I knocked again with a bit more force, and then I opened the door. Actius held his hand over his face and repeated some of the curses that Gavia had unleashed upon him the night before. Between the profanities, I was told to come back later, much later.

Next, I found Tay in his study; his eyes might have set me on fire, if his snapping fingers and incoherent hiss hadn't run me away so quickly. The man sitting in front of his writing table hadn't even so much as turned his head to look at me. I guessed the man was Primus, the town slave who saw to taxes, fees, and bribes. Tay had been particularly keen at keeping me out of the man's sight.

I went in search of distraction and found Porcia too busy with crying babies. Irritated, Servia shooed me from the room while she tended to little Regula.

I was bored, and a bit lonely. The girls would all be sleeping late; their work kept them up past most people's hours. Ajax and Corax were busy cleaning the house and preparing for another day.

I decided to step out and see if Gavia had recovered from her hysteria of the night before. I was surprised to find the shop still shuttered. I rapped at the door and heard her scream, "Be gone with you!"

Curiosity replaced boredom. What had the riot to do with Gavia's family and their downfall? The strange fresco depicting the incident became even more perplexing.

I knocked on the closed door of Actia's home. After waiting a few minutes, old Xeus answered. The squeaky hinges made my teeth tingle, and I cringed. When the old man peered at me, he seemed to wince just as I had.

I handed him a letter that I had written before departing from home. The note explained that Actius had fallen and twisted his ankle - not quite the whole truth - and that he was staying with Octavius Regulus. The letter went on lying and stated that I was there to pick up clothes for the man. "Dear Jove, is he alright?" Xeus asked, sincerely concerned.

I nodded as I was allowed inside the house. Xeus pointed to a bench and told me he would fetch some of Actius's things.

Celer's body remained on the litter in the corner of the atrium. Strong perfume wafted off of the corpse, concealing less pleasant smells.

I waited for old Xeus to round the corner and then made my way to the courtyard.

I studied the painting of the riot at the town's amphitheater. The arena was one of the largest I had seen in my travels, and something of an oddity in Italy. Few permanent structures dedicated to gladiatorial events were to be found at that time.

The painting was rather crude. The size of the people in comparison to the structures was incorrect. Fighting people poured out on the grounds, mostly in the direction of the Palaestra nearby. The arena itself was depicted as a strange misshapen thing, and there was something off about the number of archways beneath the main stairs leading to the top of the structure. I wasn't familiar enough with the actual place to know what was amiss, but I knew something was incorrect. I counted the painted archways - there were eleven.

Painted on the walls of the Palaestra, were banners which read, "Good Fortune to D. Lucretius." This was in Latin, while in Greek, another banner stated, "Good Fortune to Satrius Valens, Augustus Nero."

I was examining another crude painting to the right of the riot fresco when Fannius entered the courtyard.

"What happened to Actius?" he asked, his voice a bit more harsh than necessary.

I handed him the letter I had written, and then held my own right ankle and grimaced. Actius's words had stuck with me; I needed to work harder at playing the part of the mute.

Frowning, Fannius read the letter and handed it back to me. "I can arrange for a litter to bring him back here." He sounded genuinely concerned.

I opened my little wax tablet and quickly jotted out, "He's fine at my master's house, for now."

Fannius let out a sigh of displeasure as he read my tablet.

"Here are some of the master's things," Xeus called from the peristyle. It would have taken the old man too long to walk over to me, so I sprinted to him, snatched the satchel in his hands, and with a quick bow to Fannius, I departed.

A young man covered in dust was pacing in our atrium when I returned home. Ajax, staring at the dirt the fellow was tracking about the mosaic floor, informed me that the master was looking for me and could be found in his study.

Tay was writing a letter when I stepped inside, he only looked up for a moment as he acknowledged me, "Ah, there you are." His eyes were lowering back to his work before he asked, "What's in the satchel?"

I took three quick strides, and whispered, "I fetched some of Actius's things from his mother's house. I wanted back inside." Tay's eyes remained on the document before him, while his right brow arched. I sat down and explained, "There is a fresco that depicts the riot in the amphitheater that took place–"

"Yes, get to the point."

"There are banners with names painted on it, Valens's name…

"What of it?"

I shrugged, not really sure. "I noticed another odd fragment of the riot. There is a crudely sketched woman attempting to stop two gladiators from fighting."

"Stop snooping, this has nothing to do with us." His tone wasn't convincing. He pointed at a scroll and told me, "Read that." He went back to writing whatever it was that kept him preoccupied.

I recognized the handwriting in an instant, the letter was from my friend Petronius. Unlike his previous correspondence, it was written in Latin rather than hieroglyphics.

"My Dear Regulus, I trust you are blessed with good fortune and good health as I am.

I thought I might mention to you that the uncle of my dearest friend, Poppaea, owns a home in Pompeii, and that I spoke with her about you. Her uncle's name is Quintus Poppaeus, if you should meet him, please give him my regards.

I shared with Poppaea how we met, your dear late father and I happened to be in Caesarea at the same time, and we were introduced. I was left reflecting on what a pity it was that your stepmother inherited the bulk of your family's wealth after his death. That aside, I'm sure you and Quintus would make fast friends given the chance.

Poppaea hopes to see the damage for herself soon. The Golden One has already listened to the requests of a delegation from Herculaneum and awaits the visit from Pompeii's representatives.

From your last letter, it does sound as if the gods have seen fit to protect you, and I am ever so pleased by this. Pompeii, despite the recent tragedy, should make a good home for you and your dependents. Also, think nothing of my little gift, and if you need anything else, do let me know.

May the gods bless you, much love, Petronius"

"What is he talking about, your father, your stepmother?" Already whispering, it was a challenge for me to lower my voice even more to state, "This *ghost from the past* seems well-known."

Tay frowned and replied, "So it would seem." He cleared his throat and went back to writing.

I knew better than to ask any more about *Octavius Regulus's* namesake, he was clearly irritated, and I would gain nothing from prying.

Tay sprinkled sand on the piece of parchment, and without offering to let me read the return letter, rolled it up and sealed it with a smearing of hot wax off his signet ring.

"Take this to the courier; the faster it gets to Petronius, the sooner Eros will be distracted." My companion didn't sound all that convinced by his own words.

I was pointing out to Tay where the old doorway to the vineyard had been closed off from the kitchen, when Mucia poked her head in and blurted out, "The man in Staphylus's room is calling for you."

I found Actius sitting up in his bed, rubbing his ankle. "Zeus, I'm in pain."

Tay leaned in to me, "Get more of the tonic from Gavia."

"No, no. Now, not her, you heard what she said, she'll poison me." Actius remarked.

Tay sighed, "There are people with crushed bones, and amputated limbs right now who are keeping the few healers around here busy."

Actius rolled his eyes, "Tell her it's for one of your girls – " he smiled and pointed at me, " – or for him. I think she likes him."

Tay jabbed me in my ribs; that was all the instruction that was needed for me to go off on my mission.

Gavia sat at her worktable, mixing something slimy. Both she and her giant raven, perched on her right shoulder, stared at me as I nervously entered her untidy shop. "What do you want now, fool?"

No one was present; still, I whispered the first thing that came to my mind, "Thank you for coming to my rescue last night." I hadn't thought to thank her before due to the fact I hadn't needed rescuing in the first place.

She merely shrugged in reply.

Regardless of Actius's suggestion, I knew better than to lie to Gavia, so I said, "Actius is in pain from his fall. I was wondering if you could make up more tonic for him."

"Ha, he's in pain..." the bird sensed his mistress's aggravation, and he squawked and flapped his huge wings, beating little Gavia in the face. "Let him suffer," she mumbled.

"What did his mother do to you?" I sat at an empty stool, across the table from the odd little woman. She put aside her concoction, and reached for an empty clay pot.

"She took what belonged to my family," Gavia whispered, mocking me.

"So I gather, but how?"

"My husband was killed in the riot" – she watched the expression change on my face – "that's right, my husband. I wasn't always like this." She pointed at her stained tunic, and waved about the little shop. "He was an aedile, just starting his political career with my father's help." She sneered at me, as if I might not believe her, "Ask anyone, they'll tell you, my father was duumvir." I did believe her, she had no reason to lie to me. "Livineius Regulus was sponsoring the games." She spit on the floor after saying the man's name. "He, my father, and my adopted brother put on a big show, spared no expense on Lucretius's best fighters."

Her single eye glazed over, and she fell silent for a moment. "There was a brawl, in one of the stairways, someone pulled a knife. The two men that started fighting were both dead long before the bloodshed ended. My husband, Licineius, was killed, his body was barely recognizable. He went into the thick of the fighting trying to break the people up, instead they butchered him." Something caught the raven's eye, and it flew off of the woman and perched itself on a high shelf.

Gavia started to mix some liquids while she explained, "The town council sent off a delegation to plea for *forgiveness* from Nero; at the same time, the Nucerians dragged their wounded to show them what the citizens of Pompeii had done to his colonists." She paused to pick up a vial from the nearby shelf. "The town council exiled Livineius Regulus, just like his father had been exiled from Rome, my adopted brother – despicable bastard – was killed in the clash as well. He deserved it. My father was left to bear the shame, the town council wanted a name to place all the blame on." She smeared a bit of a dark green paste into her mixture. "He killed himself, opened a vein." Her voice grew somewhat eerie, "He never told me goodbye." She paused for a moment, seemingly lost in her memories. "My husband's family abandoned me, moved away, I don't know where they ended up – doesn't matter, they had no use for me."

She clutched a little wooden spoon and started mixing whatever was in the clay cup. "Old Sextus Pompeius Proculus was made *Special Prefect* to tidy up what had happened. Your *friend* Valens and that sly Poppaeus used him as their puppet. All of my family's property was seized, the proceeds went back into the town's coffers to pay some of what was lost due to the riot." She spat out an odd laugh. "And that wicked woman of Agrippina's got my house. Old Xeus was throwing my clothes out on the street while she was being moved in."

"Why was it given to her?"

She looked up at me and brushed a tear away before she replied, "I don't know, never found out – all part of the secret they are keeping."

"So you ended up here, making potions?"

"Say what you will about old Popidius, but he was the only one who helped me. He told me I could stay upstairs," she pointed to the room above her shop, "as long as I needed to. He used to sell wine out of this storefront, until the moths got to the vines."

"When did you start your business?" I asked, intrigued by the woman's past.

"When Popidius started buying whores. I didn't want to become one of them. So I would go off to the groves, the public gardens, even the vineyard, and pick what I needed to make lotions, tonics, what have you." She picked up the clay pot and pointed to it. "I went around collecting trash, found what I needed – broken pots, empty glass jars – a ground-up cricket soaked in honey can be whatever a wealthy woman wants it to be for six coppers." She laughed, a hint of self-pity in her tone. "But after a while, I learned to make real tonics and remedies. Even the shit I mix together for *love potions* is a least good to cure a headache." She laughed again with a bit more mirth. "There, now you know." She pointed a stained finger into my face, "And I know your secret, too."

I stared at her in silence, wondering if she was bluffing, mistaken, or actually aware of who I was and what I was hiding from. "Thank Jove then, that you are better at remaining silent than I."

Gavia flashed me a wicked grin that reminded me of Tay's evil smile. "Take this to your injured *friend*." She handed me the clay cup.

I studied the liquid mixture before asking, "You aren't taking this opportunity to avenge yourself, are you?"

She took the cup back and drank a sip from it, and as I sighed with relief, she cleared her throat and then spat into the cup. "It's poisoned, my own special ingredient for the son of a bitch." She winked her good eye and handed back the cup.

"By Hades, what took you so long?" Tay demanded, leading me to the back room housing Actius. I rolled my eyes, unable to speak under the portico.

With the door shut behind me, I retold Gavia's story. Tay at first scoffed as I spoke but fell silent at the mention of her young husband's heroic death. Actius listened in complete silence, grimacing as he drank the tainted elixir. I omitted Gavia's confession that some of her tonics weren't magical and ended the tale with Popidius offering her shelter when no one else would.

Tay looked to our guest. "Your mother moves to Pompeii after her patroness's death, and comes into possession of a house confiscated by the city leaders?" Tay's eyes lit up. "Celer was a freedman of Valens's. I am curious as to how he ended up running your mother's household?"

"Were they lovers?" I asked, somewhat boldly.

Actius sneered, "They could have been, I don't think my mother was all that stingy with her affections." He took a deep breath. "Celer was killed because he knew that she had been murdered. He was out to prove who killed her."

Tay and I looked to each other and then back to Actius. "I thought your mother died in the quake?" Tay's remark sounded forced, giving away that he had already heard the rumors.

"No." Actius drained the last of his medicine and cringed. "Could I get some wine?" he asked, with a pained look on his face.

Tay glanced to me, waiting for his servant to go and fetch the request.

"Call for Mucia or one of the boys, I want to hear this," I protested.

Actius's piercing eyes narrowed as he watched the exchange. Tay would not make a scene in front of the guest; he opened the door, called to Mucia, and we waited only a moment before she returned with a tray bearing her master's request.

The actor took a deep drink and then informed us, "Celer wrote me a letter, telling me that my mother was killed in a quake while attending a local festival. I was in Athens, performing. I made arrangements to travel here. The day before I left, a second letter from Celer came." Actius paused and took another sip of wine. "The second message was that she had been seen, alive, after the quake. He believed that someone killed her and took advantage of the disaster to hide the crime. He hinted that he knew the culprit, but did not state the name." He paused to let the information settle and then added, "When I walked into the house the other day and saw Celer dead, that just confirmed that she'd been murdered and Celer had to be silenced."

"Who is Fannius?" Tay asked, hinting toward his own suspicions.

"Now that is a good question. He is yet another mysterious freedman living under my mother's roof. I recognize, but can't place him."

"When did your mother acquire Fannius?" Tay asked.

"I don't know." Actius shrugged. "She may have mentioned him in a letter…" He had more to say, but I could tell he chose to hold his tongue. Actius's tone changed as he said, "I'm not sure. I didn't pay much attention to her household. Not all slaves are as interesting as you." The comment was directed at me, even though it actually applied to Tay.

"Do you know who visited the house the day of Celer's death?" Tay asked, ignoring the insinuating comment.

Actius closed his eyes for a moment, and then began to pull the names from his memory. "Xeus told me, as if I already knew the men. The first person to visit the house was Ianvarius, a freedman of Crassus Frugi. He came after Celer had sent a messenger out with several letters. Then your man here arrived." With a flourish of his hands, he pointed at me. "Next was Eutychis, then Siricus, I have no idea who either of them are. Then someone named Balbus stopped in very briefly. None other than my *helpful friend* Eros arrived next. Xeus said that Ianvarius came back again, but he didn't seem to be able to locate Celer. Leaving your friend Valens, who indicated that he didn't find Celer either, as the last one until the body was discovered." Actius took a deep breath and let it out very slowly.

"When Eros came to you yesterday, did he mention calling on Celer the day before?" I inquired.

Actius cocked his head and overdid a suspicious frown before replying, "He did not."

Tay had promised Valens that he would not repeat this to Actius; I had not, "I believe that Celer was dead before the last three callers walked unescorted to his study." I watched a blank expression appear on our handsome guest's face as I spoke. "I also suspect that Eros saw that Celer was dead, and said nothing."

"Why?" The word sounded as if a thought had emerged from his mouth, rather than an intended question being asked.

Somewhat perturbed with me, Tay quipped, "Because that is exactly what he did." My companion mimicked Actius's flourish and gestured at me.

Chapter Seven
Foreshadowing

Julia Felix made her first appearance after the attack at the evening rituals. The Oracle's disciples gushed over the woman, politely ignoring her previous disdain for them.

Listening to the questions and comments, it became clear that my rescue of her had been omitted. The gracious lady protested as she was called brave. She said, generously, that Nephthys had been watching over her, and saw to her safety. A reverent murmur of agreement rippled through the small group.

Julia took in the new surroundings before she allowed our eyes to meet. The faintest hint of a smile shadowed her face.

After waiting for the excited group to fall silent, the Oracle of Nephthys joined us. She was clad in a shimmering, golden gown. Her transparent veil was weighted with beads of blue glass that rested on her bosom. A golden diadem held the sheer veil in place to disguise the face underneath.

Easily forgotten, the translator followed her mistress. The acolyte's standard, all-white attire appeared particularly ominous in the shadowed, foreboding vineyard.

The nightly prayers were recited. We were each, in turn, blessed by the Oracle, as Ra fell to the horizon. The

Goddess Nephthys was once more charged with seeing to our safety until dawn's break.

The devotees left the vineyard once the ritual was complete. Julia hesitated for an instant, gazing briefly at me. There was no litter to conceal us, instead her brawn waited at the gate to escort her the short distance across the cobbled stone avenue. I gave her a knowing smile and then bowed my head.

Cornelia had been pleasantly surprised by the existence of a doorway from the house to the vineyard. Tay seemed mildly irritated that he hadn't detected the bricked-up entrance nor thought to investigate himself. Of course, he rewarded me for my discovery.

Hesiod and I chipped away at the bricks separating our kitchen from the vineyard. We worked by torch light, and as carefully as we might to make as little noise as possible.

Tay had started the waiting sailors in the house on a round of songs. Their crude tunes wouldn't do much to mask the sound of a wall being taken down, but their own reveling made for a good distraction.

One layer of bricks was removed before Tay came to inspect. Hesiod, a true laborer, wished to continue the work, however, Tay relinquished me from any more toil.

Inside the house, I was surprised to find Actius propped up on a couch exchanging stories with Proculus. I was curious as to how well the two men knew each other. They glanced at me as I walked by the drawing room, and kept talking.

Geb met me in the kitchen, and we found a bite to eat. While I filled a bowl with warm stew, I could faintly hear the clatter of Hesiod removing the bricks. It almost sounded as if he had doubled his efforts now that I was no longer there to receive partial credit.

Once in my room, I collapsed on the bed. I was so tired that when I closed my eyelids, I only saw darkness.

I had no desire to get out of bed after my introduction to manual labor the night before. My back and arms ached. My dreams had been plagued with dirty bricks and splinter-laden axe handles. Despite the sunlight seeping through the shutters of my window, I was on the verge of falling back to sleep when Tay opened my door and barked out an order, "Get up, dress yourself. I have been *summoned* by Valens."

Geb was at my heels as I darted into the kitchen and snatched a dry scrap of bread. The gods would be owed their due, as I tore the food into two and devoured my share as quickly as the dog ate his.

I encountered Tay's growing collection of clients, assembled in the atrium. Tay, dressed in a pristine white tunic bordered with a dark brown, Greek key pattern, was giving orders to Servia. Her harsh features softened as she realized she was being left in charge of the house.

Ajax, Corax, and I trailed behind Tay's group of eight dependants as we made our way to the house that Valens was temporarily residing within. As we walked, those who recognized *Regulus* greeted him warmly.

I was the last to realize that we were not en route to the nearby temporary lodgings that Valens had taken to while his home was under repair. Our destination was an impressive residence, north of the forum.

I heard one of Tay's clients let out a low whistle as we approached the fine house. Fronted by four shops, it was a monstrously large home, fit for any nobleman.

The Greeks lingered outside with the clients while Tay and I were ushered in and welcomed inside a beautiful atrium.

The doorman left us waiting for several minutes while I studied the brightly painted room. A bronze faun sat on the corner of the tiled impluvium. Beyond the atrium was a large drawing room, open to the peristyle, a familiar layout, yet done on a colossal scale.

The doorman returned, only to take us into a small anteroom to wait a bit longer. Valens was reminding Tay of his social stature. My companion was on the verge of biting his nails before we were finally collected and shown to the peristyle. After another short wait, Valens joined his guest.

I had remained standing under the portico, while Tay had taken a chair offered to him by the doorman. Valens's forced smile wavered for a moment as he looked me over.

"Morning, Regulus. Good of you to come so early, and on short notice." The meaning of our host's statement was rather obvious.

"May Fortune smile upon you today, Valens," Regulus said, mirroring the fake pleasantness.

The wealthy man sat down and gestured around the surroundings, "My son, Satrius's, home. After Decimus Lucretius Valens adopted me, he moved here with us, where we could take care of him. After his death, I moved to his residence, and my son remained here."

"Very impressive," Tay remarked, waiting for the awkward topic at hand.

"I understand you have a guest staying with you." Valens's tone became more familiar; he was a direct man, not used to acting coy.

"I surmised Actius's presence in my home was the reason for your request to meet with me." Tay's devious grin could not be concealed.

"You are correct. It's better to just get to the point." He forced a laugh. "Regulus, I'll tell you straight, keep your distance from Anicetus, you're new to town, but you are well liked. Anicetus will cause you nothing but trouble."

"Anicetus will? Or will it be others who actually cause me the trouble?" Tay asked. There was just a touch of humor in his voice, enough to take out some of the sting from his accusation.

Valens tried to smile. "Anicetus will be your problem. Regulus, I don't want to see you involved in this. I consider you a friend."

Tay took a deep breath before responding, "I'm not out to cause trouble. Anicetus was at Curtius's bar and twisted his ankle. Demetrius recognized him and brought him home."

"I understand, I just don't think you should let him stay any longer than necessary."

Tay nodded his head. "I will send him on his way once he's well enough to defend himself."

Valen's eyes narrowed. "You misunderstand, the man is in no danger."

"He was struck on the head, almost knocked out, on the very day he came home…"

"I know nothing of this, please believe me." Rattled, Valens went on, "He is a friend to the Emperor. We have no desire to upset, let alone harm the man. Where did the assault take place?"

"In his mother's home, more precisely, Celer's office while he was going through some letters."

"Who would do such a thing?" Valens appeared genuinely outraged.

"Rather hard to speculate, as you told me, Celer had his enemies." Tay's remark nearly sounded like an accusation.

After a long period of silence, Valens replied, "Well...perhaps he is better off in your home." The man's eyes seemed to lose focus as his mind raced. "But once he is well, you must send him on his way."

Tay's voice lightened as he replied, "I intend on doing so." He raised a hand to his chin, and said, as if an afterthought, "You should know something that Actius told me; Eros called on him after he arrived in Pompeii. Eros told him that with Actia dead, you had no purpose for Celer. He went on to suggest that you eliminated your freedman."

The color drained from Valens's face. He was left speechless.

Tay stood from his chair, all nonchalant, and finished the interview by telling his host, "I told Actius that Eros was mistaken. I made sure that he understood that I have the most complete trust in you."

Tay quickly became annoyed with his little entourage only a block away from the magnificent home we had just left. We came to a stop. Tay handed out coins to his collection of clients and issued instructions to disperse the group. Ajax and Corax were both sent back home, and we made our way to Jucundus's house.

Even at the early hour, we were quickly admitted to a small sitting room where Jucundus was reading over a stack of wax tablets.

"I apologize for coming so early without sending a messenger ahead, please forgive my manners."

"Think nothing of it. Yes, now what has you out so early, and so near my home? Let's see, Satrius Valens lives rather nearby." The older fellow raised a brow in imitation of Tay.

"Tell me, what is it that I don't know, that everybody else seems to be in on," Tay said with a sigh.

"I'm sorry to disappoint, but I don't know the secret."

"But there is a secret."

"Oh yes, it all has to do with the day the riot broke out. There was a lot of talk at the time, accusations where the words trail off before the sinister deed is actually named. I hadn't thought of it much until today. Yes, I've had a number of men stop by to ask me questions about you, about Anicetus, and even that little wretch that rents from you – poor Gavia."

"I can name the men, Proculus, Frugi, Poppaeus..."

The older man chuckled, "Close, yes. Very close. But rather, their freedmen." His smile disappeared, and his tone became slightly grave, "I understand Anicetus is your guest; a friendly piece of advice," he stressed the following words, "get rid of him."

"You are the second person today to tell me that."

"Don't wait for a third," Jucundus replied.

"How did Actia end up with Gavia's family home?"

Jucundus took a deep breath, "I don't know. Truly, I don't. But I will tell you this, Actia was a guest of the late emperor Claudius's daughter, they were staying at Zenobia's villa. On the morning of the riot, Claudia

Antonia left by ship to Baiae. Actia went to the amphitheater and had to have witnessed something. Valens and Poppaeus whisked her away to Rome. Within seven days of their return, she was moved into poor Gavianus's home."

"What happened when Antonia returned, did she—"

Jucundus shook a bony finger toward his guest, "She didn't come back. Yes, hasn't come back since." He paused as if debating whether to add the rest, "Not a single member of the imperial family had set foot in the house for years other than Claudia Antonia. You know that Zenobia runs the place as if it was her own, and it might as well be." Jucundus frowned and covered his mouth for a moment. "Now, listen to me...yes, I sound like a slave at the corner fountain, telling stories." Jucundus forced a laugh, "Regulus, whatever this business is, keep out of it."

"Jucundus, my friend, that's good advice," Tay responded. I knew the tone of voice, he agreed with the man's suggestion yet he had little intention of heeding the recommendation.

When we returned home, we found Actius sleeping soundly, so soundly that Tay put his head to the man's chest and sniffed the cup of Gavia's pain-relieving tonic. Satisfied the man was no worse off than when we left him, Tay slipped into his study after suggesting I check on Porcia and the children. This was his polite way of brushing me off.

Porcia greeted me excitedly, and whispered, "Is the actor Actius Anicetus really a guest in this house?" I nodded. "Servia told me so, you know the Admiral served under Anicetus's uncle." I nodded that I knew that too.

"She said that he is very handsome." And at that comment, I frowned.

"What do you know about his mother?" I asked in a whisper. Porcia was one of the very few among the household who knew that I could speak, or at least I hoped that the number was few.

"She died in the quake, Celer told Sosia that she was killed after she was separated from a worthless brute that had been undermining him."

"What else?" I was excited that I might solve the riddle so easily.

"Gavia hates her, she put a curse on her. I suppose the curse worked?"

"Don't say that, or the whole city will blame Gavia for the gods' wrath."

The normal innocence that filled Porcia's voice was absent when she responded, "Gavia wouldn't care."

I was tempted to ask Porcia more about the little witch, instead I stayed on task. "Tell me more about Actia."

Porcia took a deep breath and sighed slowly, "I don't really know much more."

I could tell that she was holding something back. "There is something more, what is it?"

Porcia hesitated before answering, "Her name was mentioned once to Popidius. He spat out a curse and said that she had brought about his downfall."

As I was formulating my next question, Porcia's son began to cry, waking little Regula as well. In an instant, we were both pacing the room with the irritated infants.

The nameless old man who occupied the vineyard's stable pointed me toward a macabre structure located along the vineyard's west wall. Directly in front of, in fact concealing, the hole in the wall of our kitchen was a newly fashioned pergola. Freshly painted wooden planks supported several beams wrapped in gold cloth. Heavy curtains hung from the beams and were tied back, just enough to let those who gathered see the golden sarcophagus and the dazzling throne lit by a flickering brazier. Another heavy curtain hid the newly discovered entry point into our house, acting as the backdrop to Cornelia's stage.

I dropped a coin on the ornate three-legged table, near a lively brazier. The other devotees did likewise as they approached the new sanctuary.

Keeping with her typical fashion, Julia was the last to arrive. The beautiful woman wore a plastered smile as she looked toward the other worshipers. Cheerful greetings were hurriedly said, but all notice was focused on the adorned pavilion. After the previous day's fanfare, I believe Julia was disappointed by the lack of attention she received. As the serene expression on the woman's face crumbled, I felt embarrassed for her.

The acolyte of the Oracle beckoned us to gather near the draped pergola. In her breathy, high-pitched voice, she welcomed us before the star attraction emerged from her new shrine.

Despite the change in location, the performance followed its same routine. Samson, in his elaborate disguise, *spoke* the words that would appease the Goddess Nephthys and Cornelia translated for us. We joined in as directed, chanting the invocations we had come to remember. Each devotee was blessed, and the rites were concluded. The Oracle and her translator returned to the seclusion of the curtained structure.

On leaving, a few well-wishes were given to Julia, who uncharacteristically lingered behind. I slowed my own step, certain to be the last person out of the vineyard. Julia shot a dismissive look to the hefty men waiting for her. They reacted to her silent command and dispersed. The lovely woman reached a hand toward me and asked, "Demetrius, perhaps you might escort me across the street to my home."

And I did just that.

"There you are!" Tay led me into his study the moment I returned from Julia's. He was obviously distracted, for he made no comment on my tussled hair or idiotic grin.

Once seated at his writing table, he suggested, "That pumpkin head of yours is filled with all the boring details regarding the imperial family, perhaps you can shed some light on the subject of Claudia Antonia?"

I took a deep breath, delighted to share what I knew. "Claudia Antonia is the Divine Claudius's eldest daughter. I think she's about twelve years older than I. Her mother was Aelia Paetina, who was the adoptive sister to Lucius Aelius Sejanus. Old Tiberius had Claudius married to her to connect Sejanus to his family. I don't think they were married long before Antonia was born, because after Sejanus fell from power and was killed, Claudius quickly divorced Aelia. Antonia was raised by Claudius's mother, until, when she was seven or eight, her grandmother died. Not too long afterward, Claudius married Messalina. Messalina was Caligula's second cousin and—"

"You are drifting off topic," Tay interjected.

"Messalina was wealthy and well-connected, that's important, and I'll come back to that." I smiled and continued to empty my cornucopia of knowledge,

"Claudius arranged for Antonia to marry Gnaeus Pompeius Magnus, both of his parents could trace their family bloodline back to *the* Pompeius Magnus. In fact, I was tutored alongside Gnaeus's little brother." There was much more to that story, but it had nothing to do with the current mystery. "Their brother is none other than Marcus Licinius Crassus Frugi, whose local freedman is Ianvarius, the man who called on Celer twice the day of his murder."

"Frugi is going to be one of the consuls next year. Valens and the rest of the town council are counting on his support to encourage Nero's generosity," Tay interjected, already pondering the implications.

"Frugi's great-grand aunt was none other than Scribonia, second wife of Augustus and mother to Julia the elder."

"Are there so few nobles that you all have to keep marrying back into your own bloodline? Let me guess, you're related to them, too," he sneered, knowing that I was.

"Scribonia was related to three branches of my family," I replied with great pride. *"But I'm getting off topic.* Antonia was only married to Frugi's brother for three or four years. He was murdered – a scandalous affair. I think he was stabbed to death by a male slave he had taken as a lover." I took a deep breath and realized that I was speaking rather rapidly. "Afterward, she married Faustus Cornelius Sulla Felix, the half-brother of Messalina."

Tay sighed. "You did warn me that we'd come back to her."

I smiled. "So, Antonia is married to her own step-uncle, Faustus. Maybe a year passes before Messalina's downfall and death. Faustus weathered that storm. However, shortly before I left for Alexandria, Faustus was involved in a few

140

court intrigues and then exiled. Nero had him killed, just last year."

"How do you remember all of this?" Tay asked. I just shrugged. It was easy to remember the history of Rome and her leading families, because I remembered little else. "So make the correlation for me, Antonia and Actia?"

I bit the inside of my lip and thought about the dates. "Well, let's see. Antonia's second husband was in exile at the time of the riot, accused of vying for Nero's throne." I pointed a finger at Tay. "Not a good time to be the daughter of the last emperor and married to a man who might be using his relationship to the imperial family to overthrow Nero. I imagine she was attempting to stay within sight of her adoptive brother, but a respectable distance from the capital." I took another deep breath. "I know little about Antonia's relationship with her stepmother, Agrippina, but it is possible that Antonia would have been familiar with Actia. Both had reason to be cautious, Actia's patron, killed just four months before, Antonia, never far from Nero's suspicious thoughts. They both find themselves at the imperial villa here outside of Pompeii. It wouldn't be surprising for them to keep company with each other."

"The daughter of an Emperor and a freedwoman?" Tay sounded skeptical.

"No stranger than the descendant of Publius Claudius Pulcher and an Alexandrian con-man," I retorted. Tay forced a guffaw. "Remember though, Actia wasn't a freedwoman to Agrippina ...she was the freedwoman to Lollia Paulina."

Tay's brow raised, unsure if this was important information or merely another dissertation on unfortunate aristocrats.

"Lollia, an ex-wife of Caligula, was a candidate for marriage with Claudius. Agrippina received the honor instead. And then she went on to destroy her rivals, including Lollia. Curious that Actia would first find herself as part of Agrippina's entourage until the woman's death."

"And upon Agrippina's death she ends up with Nero's eldest stepsister?" Tay sighed, unsure that any of this information mattered. "Next, after the riot at the arena, she is somehow rewarded with a large house and slaves. Why does she have a fresco of the event painted in her courtyard?" Tay was merely thinking out loud.

I said the very first thought that entered my mind, "To remind those involved of her part…and theirs." I snapped my fingers, "Valens told Celer there wasn't a conspiracy, *this time*, when they spoke of Actia's death in our courtyard."

Tay slumped and shook his head. "Meaning there had been a conspiracy before – and they were all part of it."

"The list of names that Actius found…" At that moment, I had an epiphany. I jumped up from my chair and said rather loudly, "Follow me!"

Caught up in the moment, Tay followed me through the atrium, out of the house, and down to the nearest street corner. I pointed at the amphitheater looming at the end of the road, the last of the sunlight reflected a deep orange off of the stonework.

"What?" he demanded, unsure of why we were gawking at the structure.

I looked about only to realize that, despite the setting sun, there were still workmen all around us. I covered my mouth as if I had sneezed and whispered, "Eleven arches."

He looked back to the massive staircases built into the exterior wall. Both of his brows rose as he mumbled, "Six?" Tay steered me back toward our house by my elbow. We were just passing Gavia's shop as she appeared with the shutters to close the place up.

"Actius out of his tonic yet? I just picked some fresh hellebore today." She cackled as she hung the shutters.

Tay snapped at me, "Help Gavia...we need to have a word with her."

Actius looked surprised to see Gavia follow us into his room. The two exchanged unfriendly glances before each crossed their arms and shifted their gazes away from the other. Actius's actions were a perfect imitation of Gavia's.

Without preamble, Tay began, "You mother was involved in a conspiracy, and it had to do with Claudia Antonia and the riot at the amphitheater."

"C.A." Actius remarked.

In a low but excited tone, I interjected, "One of *eleven* names on the list you found."

Actius asked rather loudly, "Why does he whisper...who doesn't know that he can speak?"

Tay's posture stiffened, and he replied, "Let us stick to the subject at hand. Your mother played a part in the event surrounding the riot, as well as Celer, Frugi, Poppaeus, Proculus and Valens..."

"Plus, Balbus and Siricus who called on Celer," I added. I counted the names on my fingers and mumbled, "Who are the other three?"

Tay ignored me, and Actius asked, "What other three?"

"The fresco depicting the riot shows the amphitheater with eleven, rather than six archways supporting the staircases. It's a reminder that eleven people know the truth."

Gavia's voice was completely changed, she sounded the part of an educated young woman, brought up in a fine home. "Siricus and Balbus took my father and adopted brother's seats as Duumvir. Proculus was appointed Special Prefect, in charge of the whole matter."

"What did the others gain?" Actius asked.

Gavia's harsh tone returned, "A house!"

"But what else? Was Celer already a freedman, or did Valens free him when he took over the running of the house?" Tay inquired to no one in particular.

I looked to Tay and hesitantly said a name, "Cornelia?"

My companion grimaced. "She might know."

I didn't wait for the order, instead I quickly went to the second floor apartment and rapped at the door.

Samson was delighted to see me, but I impolitely rushed passed him and blurted out, "Regulus needs you. We have some questions that you might be able to answer."

Cornelia, radiant as ever, glared at me from a little writing table stacked with coins. The hostile expression triggered my guilty conscience, but she made no mention of Julia. "Now I'm his servant to be summoned when he wants a piece of gossip?"

Samson rested a heavy hand on my shoulder and carefully suggested, "Does this have to do with Regulus's new houseguest?"

And with that, I noticed Cornelia's eyes light up. "Actius Anicetus, yes?"

I felt my face turn red, now it was I who was jealous. "Yes," I muttered.

She waved Samson to her, and told me, "I would be delighted to answer any question he might have. I'll be down once I am *presentable.*" She looked toward a mirror and started running her fingers through her hair. I waited for a moment to see if she would glance at me with a raised brow, or a devious smile, to make sure she had landed the desired blow. She did not; I was already forgotten.

Cornelia entered the little drab chamber, and at once, the oil lamps seemed to burn brighter. Her hair was coiled and pinned back, fresh make-up enhanced her perfect face. She wore a loose, pink tunic that draped off of her sleek frame.

Tay introduced his guest, "Actius Anicetus, may I introduce to you Cornelia Vibia."

I noticed Actius's Adam's apple bob, and his pupils grow larger. "It's a pleasure to meet you." He gave a wave of the hand to the unadorned room. "I'm sorry to have you called down to this little cell." He apologized, as if he were the host rather than guest. "I *fell* and twisted my ankle. I'm barely able to move."

"Has the injury been seen to?" Cornelia spoke not in the tone of voice that was used on Samson, Tay, or myself, but in that breathy, excited tone of voice that husbands remember, but seldom hear.

Actius's skills were not hampered by discomfort or pain medication. His smile twitched, he gave a little shudder, and then pointed dramatically to Gavia. "Well, according to her, I'll be fine."

Gavia only sneered. Cornelia turned to glance at the woman and thought better of making a quip that might enrage the little witch. "I can only hope that she is correct." A performer herself, her smile subsided, her face darkened, and she said, "I'm so sorry for the loss of your mother. She was a fine lady."

"You knew her?" He sounded surprised.

"We met, on several occasions." Her answer was specifically vague.

Tay was more than ready to speed things along, "Cornelia is intimately connected with a local soothsayer, she has met many locals and has gathered some useful knowledge from those meetings."

Cornelia could not help but frown, however, she shook it off and said, "*Marcellus,* told me that you had some questions I might be able to answer."

"Marcellus?" asked Actius.

With her point clearly made to Tay, she corrected herself, "I'm sorry, I meant to say *Demetrius.*"

Gavia gave a little chuckle, at which Actius mused, "There is more going on here than meets the eye."

"Indeed," quipped Tay in an effort to get us past the moment. "Cornelia, what can you tell us about the aftermath from the riot?"

Awkwardly, the beautiful woman looked back to Gavia and replied, "I would think she could tell you more, I was in Cumae when it happened."

"True," remarked Tay, "but we wish to discover what connection Poppaeus, Frugi, and Actia have regarding the riot?"

Cornelia let out a long sigh before choosing her words. "Actia visited the Sybil not long after the riot. She wanted to know how she would die and how she could protect herself in the afterlife from further harm. All I can say of Frugi is that he's rarely here. Ianvarius, his freedman, tends to his household and several businesses. I believe Ianvarius has a number of married ladies of good family who seem to be well *acquainted* with him. As to Poppaeus, he is fond of reminding people that he is the uncle of Nero's wife. He isn't as wealthy as he appears, nor is he particularly close to his niece. A man named Eros is as much his spy as his freedman." She touched her forefinger to her brow and nodded. "I can't think of any connection." After a moment, her face lit up and she said, "Zenobia would know."

In a mocking voice, Gavia repeated, "*Zenobia would know*." She laughed. "Zenobia!"

"Who is Zenobia? The name sounds familiar," Actius asked.

Cornelia explained, "She is in charge of the imperial villa, just outside of the city. Not the big estate at the foot of the mountain, but the house overlooking the sea. If the gossip can be believed, she's the child of Emperor Tiberius and one of his favorite slaves that he kept at Capri." She paused, gathering her thoughts. "There is much local lore about Zenobia. People fear her. It is said that she knows black magic and that she can read people's minds."

Tay scoffed, "I'm surprised that you would believe that."

"I didn't say that I did, only that I've heard it said," Cornelia replied dryly.

We all remained silent for a moment until Actius said, "Thank you very much for the information you have shared."

The two smiled at each other, causing my chest to ache, before Cornelia replied, "You are a magnificent performer. I saw you in Baiae two summers ago." Once more, she spoke in that seductive, breathy tone.

Actius, accustomed to flattery, shrugged and replied, "A gift – I'm blessed."

Tay thanked the woman as graciously as he was capable of and ushered her out of the room, but not before Actius could invite her to visit *any time* she liked.

Gavia donned a nasty smile intended to irritate me. She succeeded, and I shooed her out of the room as well. "Don't forget, I have fresh hellebore," she said with a cackle as I closed the door on her.

"Well, I thought she would have been more help," Tay said apologetically.

Actius eased back on his pillows and replied smugly, "She was of some help, she nudged my memory. Another name on the list was Zenobia's."

Chapter Eight
Zenobia

░░░░░░░░

To My Dear Appian:

I pray this letter finds you well, as I am. Cursed indeed, Gavia had played quite a trick on me. Of course, the gods had played a rather ugly trick on her. I knew all too well what is was like to believe a particular destiny awaited and to find out otherwise. Gavia had lost more than her intended future, she lost those whom she loved. And where I had the luxury of escaping a besmirched name, she was left to live in the shadows of what might have been.

Actius, the name brings back mixed feelings. He was a talented actor, and that is the best possible description of him. He could 'act' charmingly, thoughtfully, and even scandalously – but it was all an act. He had worked too long to perfect his art to let anyone see under the performer's mask.

You asked if Julia pressured me to explain myself, and my deception. In private, she toyed with me, but at heart, she knew I would admit to nothing. I rather think she enjoyed the mystery. Besides, little of our time together was devoted to conversation. I shall say no more.

Well, before I continue, I must make mention of youth, yet again. Not only was I a mere nineteen years old, so was Tay. My steadfast companion has always been far more clever than I. In some cases, he has been too clever for his own good. A certain recklessness accompanies cunning and youth, and this threatened to displace Tay's better judgment in the days following Actius's arrival. To continue the theme, Tay was caught up in his role. To his disadvantage, however, the men he was about to pit himself against were far better rehearsed.

I look back to when we were too young to know any better and marvel at the life we lived. Perhaps after I finish this letter, it seems fitting that I should make my way to the household shrine and give formal thanks to Fortuna.

Morning came all too soon. I had lain awake for much of the night, brooding over Cornelia's obvious attraction toward Actius. The nocturnal activities that had taken place in the rooms below hadn't helped my mood either. There was something unsatisfying about knowing that quite a bit of lust was being quenched while one nestles against a dog in need of a bath.

With sunlight seeping through the closed shutters of my little window, I almost dreaded to ponder what the day might bring.

Geb at my heels, wanting his breakfast, I paused while passing by Porcia's room. I felt obligated to enter, I could hear her son's wailing and knew she needed a hand. My bravery was rewarded with sweet thanks and a kiss on the cheek. The slight redemption was gratifying. At least Porcia still looked on me kindly.

Once downstairs, I found that Hesiod had completed his work. There was now a sturdy, wooden door in our kitchen, leading to the curtained pergola.

While I foraged for bread and honey, I imagined Cornelia just beyond the new door preparing for the Oracle's morning rituals. Rituals that I had decided not to attend. She didn't want me there, and I had no desire to draw attention to Julia's behavior toward me.

I was crossing the peristyle with Geb at my side when I heard Tay's raised voice echo from his study, "I can't believe this..." There was a pause, and his next statement was muffled.

Curious, I made several abbreviated prayers, gobbled my third of the crust, and headed for the atrium. Along the benches, a few of Tay's new dependants sat with heads held low. Standing at the doorway of his study, Tay was telling a frowning man on his way to the vestibule, "I'm very disappointed, I will remember this."

The man turned back with pleading eyes, but said nothing. Tay gave him a point toward the door, and the man shuffled on. Once Corax closed the door behind him, Tay asked the remaining clients, "So that you do not suffer the same fate as the last three men, will any of you be so good as to *volunteer* to deliver a message to Zenobia?"

Miraculously, the collection of clients seemed to shrink. The men's shoulders dropped, and their chins went to their chests. Tay let out a disgusted sigh. "I can't believe this," he repeated. Each man was handed a single coin by their agitated patron and dismissed with simple instructions on who to help, or call on.

One brute of a man, the last to depart, was directed to collect some owed fees. It was at that point I began to suspect that Tay had become a money lender in addition to a procurer.

I would have spurred an unwinnable argument on the subject of money lending, had Tay not forced a wax tablet into my hands and informed me that all of his clients were too afraid to go to Zenobia to request an audience for him.

I was not invited into the study where I could whisper my own protest; but, instead, told that Corax, who was too afraid to enter the property, would at least walk me so far as to the city gate leading to the residence. Tay gave us both a shove and we were out the door.

Gavia was wrestling the shutters off of her shop as we stepped outside. Her raven struggled to balance on her shoulder. "Aren't you missing the Egyptian charade?" she asked me mockingly, referring to Nephthys's morning salutation.

Less afraid of her than Zenobia, Corax answered for me. "The master wants him to deliver a message to…" his voice quivered when he said Zenobia's name.

She barked, "It takes two of you?"

"I won't step foot on the property…the dragon!" He shook his head. "I'm just leading Demetrius to the Herculaneum Gate."

Gavia shook her head. "You are a pretty little fool. Go back in and do whatever it is you do. I'll take this idiot to Zenobia."

Rather gleefully, I was abandoned by the Greek. Gavia reentered her shop to exchange the raven for her bizarre cloak. She forced a heavy wooden box into my arms and lifted a patchwork satchel over her shoulder.

I knew the imperial villa sat on the other side of town near the sea. However, Gavia led me in the opposite direction toward the nearby gate just down the thoroughfare. She explained it was easier to walk the outer road encircling the eastern and northern walls of Pompeii. I wasn't so sure, considering the numerous homeless who were encamped along the tombs of the dead. But there were already enough ears about the street to deter me from arguing.

Out of the city gate, we quickly encountered the same people who came to Julia's rescue, as well, I am sure, as the same people who attacked her. Gavia was instantly recognized by a group of women huddled under a makeshift hovel. They smiled and, as one, came to greet her.

To the elder of the group, Gavia extended her hand in greeting. I could tell by the smile that graced the homeless woman's dirty face that she had just been palmed a coin.

"Good blessings to you on this morning. Any sickness, discomfort?" asked my little companion in a motherly voice.

The women all began to speak at once until the elder silenced them and told Gavia who was ill, injured, or suffering from bad dreams. Gavia had something to prescribe for each symptom. Either from the box that I held or from the bag she carried, an item was produced. A few little pots with honey and medicine were distributed for injuries; a vial of something clear that should only be smelled was given out for illness. She handed off a few crude charms carved from porous stone that were to be placed under cushions to ward off bad dreams.

Others came to the woman for help, all of which was given to them without charge. Gavia's generosity wasn't surprising to me, knowing that she, too, had once been left desolate. I was witness to Virgil's words playing out before me, *Myself acquainted with misfortune, I learn to help the unfortunate.*

Before we headed on toward the narrow dirt path hugging the old city wall, the box I carried was half-emptied.

Down the pathway bordering the impressive outer wall surrounding Pompeii, I asked Gavia, "Why is Zenobia feared?"

She grunted, perhaps envious of the woman. "Zenobia's mother was *a gift* from Cleopatra's grandson to Emperor Tiberius. She was one of the old monster's favorites, lived with him on Capri. They say she was some kind of sorceress." She scoffed at the notion. "After the Emperor died, she found her way to Livia's villa. Rumor was, Zenobia was Tiberius's daughter. He didn't acknowledge her, but mother and daughter were freed in his will, with a handsome largess promised to them. Zenobia's mother died young, and if the tale is true, one of her own spells killed her. "

Gavia used the voice a parent might employ to frighten a child, "They say that Zenobia is a sorceress too. When a fishing boat floats back to the bay, her fishermen missing – Zenobia did it. A man turns into a wolf and kills his family – Zenobia wished it so."

Gavia stopped in her tracks, and pointed toward the thick line of trees beside us. "When two people disappear in the Northern woods – Zenobia took them!"

As the hair on the back of my neck stood, the rancid little women cackled.

We passed two more gates, each with refugees in need of Gavia's supplies, before we neared the gate leading to a row of impressive tombs.

Jetting from the fortification was a low wall bordering the road leading out of the city. We were about to pass through the wall's small gate when Gavia tugged at my elbow and pointed to a modest marble tomb built into the outer wall. I caught sight of the name, Titus Terentius Felix. A cold chill ran down my spine as I read the epitaph.

To the memory of Titus Terentius Felix, the Elder, son of Titus, of the Tribe Menenia, Aedile. This place of burial was given by the city, with two thousand sesterces. His wife, Fabia Sabina, daughter of Fabius Probus built this monument.

Gavia pointed a stained finger at the man's resting place and told me, "Be sure and remember this location so that you can bring the dead man's daughter here to pay respect."

Perhaps Gavia did know the entire story we were keeping from her. Somehow, this notion caused me little concern. She might attempt to tease me in her own way, but in my heart, I knew she wouldn't expose me.

While I stared silently at the freshly chiseled marble tomb, Gavia went to a nearby grave. She bent down, kissed her index finger, and then touched a small stone protruding from the ground. I knew that I was witnessing something she didn't care for me to see. I wandered away, drawn by the sounds of the sea.

The nearby gate opened to a wide, cobbled street. The road sloped downward, away from the city, lined by large monuments to the dead. Just behind many of the countless, ornate tombs, the land steadily dropped off and gave way to a steep coastline. Past the bay, just beyond the Isle of Capri, the swaying sea and the listless sky blurred into one.

Gavia came to my side, and we walked on down the sloping street. There were no refugees needing necessities. Order was maintained by several big men pacing the sidewalks past the tombs. Beyond the monuments to the dead were several large buildings of clustered shops and the entrances to several sizable homes built outside of the city walls.

Craftsmen worked at rebuilding archways and patching plaster, while those with ready coin did their shopping. This was a different world, devoid of the suffering occurring such a short distance away.

Past the last buildings that crowed the city gate, we followed a winding road until we came to a private lane emerging from a row of neatly trimmed hedges. A small man, about my age, dressed like a soldier, stood at attention; he was under a parasol held by the tallest woman I had ever seen. I almost laughed at the peculiar sight until he lifted his hefty sword.

Before Gavia could speak, the giant woman told the little guard, "They may pass."

Gavia plucked a small jar from the box I carried and handed it to the young man. "This will help you grow into that *gladius* of yours."

The guard blushed while his companion chuckled at Gavia's double entendre.

Past an orderly vineyard, we came to a large flower garden, and beyond sat a sizable home silhouetted by the ever-looming Vesuvius. The land surrounding the house sloped gently toward the sea, its landscaping climbing toward the second floor where the formal entrance was located, opening off of a wide, stone landing.

Fragrant incense wafted from the sprawling house as we approached. The scent reminded me of an exotic temple, foreign to Rome.

Ornate doors stood open behind a closed iron gate, a shadowed figure sat just within the vestibule. As we approached, the individual stood from a luxurious, ivory chair. I paused, waiting for the man to come to the gate.

Instead, a deep voice echoed about the vaulted vestibule. "Come in, my mistress is waiting for you."

I glanced sidelong at Gavia, who was unfazed by the doorman's statement. She pushed the gate open, and we entered the dimly lit space. "He's come with a message from his–"

"She knows who you are." The servant interrupted Gavia as he spoke, "This way." The man pointed us toward the atrium. Even in the murky light of the vestibule, it was obvious to me that he was an albino. His skin was even paler than the ivory chair he'd reclined on. Enhancing his unusual appearance, the man was engulfed in a blood red robe that trailed behind him along the mosaic floor.

The servant walked through the shadows, avoiding the natural light that crept in from the open courtyard. He paused in front of an open doorway. Gesturing toward a spacious sitting room, the servant said, "You may wait here, the mistress only wants to see *him*." The doorman was pointing a pale finger at me.

Gavia gave me a rueful smile and said teasingly, "He doesn't speak."

The servant shrugged; his robe reminded me of Gavia's raven adjusting his wings. "It is he," the white finger nearly jabbed me, "that she wishes to see."

Amused, Gavia bowed her head and whispered to me, "Remember what they say, *Zenobia is all-knowing.*"

The doorman ignored my escort and picked up a parasol. Cautiously, he glided under the protection of the peristyle.

"Careful," the man told me. I thought he was warning me about the sunlight above. Instead, he pointed toward a lush little garden in the center of the space, or rather, he was pointing at what lurked in the garden. My eyes fell onto a monstrous Komodo dragon. I quickened my step, so that I nearly tripped on the blood red robe ahead of me.

I was led through a spectacular drawing room with lavish furnishings and superb artwork. The smell of spices and incense was almost overwhelming. The fresh air from the courtyard behind us was unable to penetrate the dense fumes hovering about the dusky chamber.

Beyond this room stood what could only be called the inner sanctum. Two large doors stood open, framing a dimly lit interior. Smoke billowed from several braziers, and the spices that I had never smelled before, or have since, coated my nostrils.

My escort bowed to me and waved a pale hand toward the entrance. With great trepidation, I took a slow step inside. There were too many fanciful details to describe, and no one would believe me if I tried.

A large couch of gilt, covered with blood red bedding, dominated the smoky room. Unfamiliar scenes were painted on all of the walls. The shadowed images looked so lifelike, I wouldn't have been surprised if they moved.

Finally, my eyes fell on three female pigmies, wearing golden collars and little else. They sat about their mistress on the over-sized bed. Their dark skin made for an odd contrast to her unique hue.

The little women each held a dish and a stylus. They were painting the woman with henna. Zenobia, although reclined, was obviously a tall woman, her uncovered limbs lean and long. The woman's legs were crossed at the ankle, one pygmy painted Zenobia's exposed thigh. Another applied the henna to an outstretched arm, and the other was repeating the elaborate pattern on the woman's exposed breasts. Besides the orange-brown dye, she was completely bare. Zenobia's skin was a strange ash-like color. An African descent mingled with Roman blood had created a stunning and unique example of flesh.

After realizing the woman was completely nude, my steps faltered, and I averted my curious gaze to the tiled floor. Zenobia spoke in a low, sultry voice, "I'm not embarrassed, nor should you be." I forced myself to meet her gaze. I found a beautiful face studying me. "My name is Zenobia, of course, you know this. You are Gaius Sempronius Gracchus Marcellus. I'm honored to have someone of such illustrious ancestry in my home."

I can't say that her knowledge surprised me, after all, she was referred to as *all-knowing*. I made no attempt to insult the woman by protesting to the truth. "The honor is mine. You are revered by the community…"

Zenobia let out a strange hiss of laughter. "I'm *feared* by the community." She raised her one free hand and gave a flourish about the room, "It matters not, fear is as useful as wealth – and power can be derived by each."

I noticed that the henna was the same color of the woman's unusual copper hair, which was drawn tightly into a coil atop her head. The repeated pattern of stain began at her neck, like a painted lace collar. Ovals of varying size interlinked one another, creating an endless chain atop her light, grey-brown skin. The pigment trailed along Zenobia's shoulders, encircled her arms at various points, and bloomed at her wrists. The woman's hands were covered with the most detailed of the artwork. I can only describe the backs of her hands as the interior of lilies. Zenobia was transformed into a living, breathing piece of art.

"Do I even need to ask you my question?" I felt a strange boldness in the woman's presence.

"Actually, your *companion* has been asking the wrong people, the wrong questions," she told me with a bit of mirth. "You want to know about the conspiracy?"

Zenobia brushed away the pigmies who labored on her artwork, and leaned toward me. "It was nothing more than a group of small men reacting to the scheme of a deceitful woman; petty lies, from petty minds." She fell back to her cushions. "Actia's murder had nothing to do with the riot, you are irritating *the good men* of Pompeii for naught."

She was part of the conspiracy, with as much to hide as the rest, yet I had no doubt she was speaking the truth. "Then who killed Actia and Celer?"

Zenobia gave me a coy smile. "*Can you keep a secret?*" She was barely able to contain a little laugh, and then, adding to the irony off her words, she whispered, "I'm not all-knowing."

"Then how do you know their deaths had nothing to do with the conspiracy?" Something about the woman told me that no question might offend her.

"Your *companion's* inquiries were brushed off or half answered, mine were not." Zenobia smiled warmly and went on, "Let the matter be, or those who you pester might retaliate. And that would be a shame, you are a very attractive young man. I would hate to see misfortune upon you."

Still feeling bold, I asked, "A warning, or a threat?"

Zenobia waved for her servants to continue their work. "A fact!" she responded jovially, before adding, "Actia deserved her fate, and Celer merited worse."

"Should I tell her son that?" Perhaps I had felt too bold.

She scoffed, "You shall soon regret taking him into your home." The woman looked at her wrist and smiled at the glistening henna, I could tell that the audience was concluded.

"Thank you for seeing me," I said humbly.

"I will send for you once I know who killed Actia and Celer," Zenobia informed me, confident that she would correct the infraction and again become *all-knowing*.

I handed Tay the scroll that had been meant for Zenobia. He looked perplexed when he saw that the seal was unbroken, "She won't see me?"

I nodded toward the study and began to fiddle with my wax tablet, assuming that Ajax and Corax, watching us, still thought that I was mute.

With the door closed, I began to whisper, "She met with me..." Tay's brow arched dramatically, he was searching for an indignant response, but I went on, "She knows who I am, and she was expecting me."

Tay dropped to his chair and rubbed his brow. "Well, as they say..."

"She is all-knowing, yes. Well, she told me that Actia and Celer's death had nothing to do with the conspiracy. And that they each deserved their fate."

"Yes, so says a co-conspirator," Tay snapped.

"She warned that we should drop the matter and..." we had been told this before, "...that we would soon regret inviting Actius into our home."

Tay sighed. "She didn't happen to tell you who killed them or why?" There was only a hint of sarcasm in his voice.

I decided not to repeat her confession, Tay might scoff at the notion of her magic abilities, but her reputation of being all-knowing was safe with me. "She chose not to enlighten me at this time."

Gavia was pouring honey into a little pot as I entered her shop. Uninvited, I slipped into the back room where her raven picked at some millet on the worktable. She let me wait for a bit before she joined me.

"I thought you were waiting for me at the villa." I remarked with a perturbed tone.

"You made your way back, no reason for me to waste time there. I have business to see to."

"So you do," I responded absently. The wooden box I had carried for her sat on the table. It was filled with freshly picked herbs and a few of the spring flowers from Zenobia's garden. "Zenobia told me that Actia and Celer deserved their fate, and I should leave well enough alone. What do you think?"

"I think the last time you and Regulus pried into someone else's business you nearly got yourselves killed. Instead, Staphylus was poisoned and Lucius Terentius died."

"You handed his sister-in-law the poison," I retorted.

"He would have died all the same, I just wanted to let her have a taste of vengeance." Gavia's voice was strangely tranquil despite the nature of our conversation.

"Vengeance, what about vengeance for you?" Zenobia's words had repeated in my mind as walked back home alone. If what she told me was true, rather than misdirection, another suspect was required. I had a shadowy concern that perhaps Gavia killed Actia after the quake. She had been in shock for days following the disaster. But had it been from the gods' wrath, or an action she had committed?

"There will never be vengeance for me, for my husband, or for my father." Her tone was becoming less tranquil.

I didn't have the spine to voice my theory. Instead, I asked, "Should we continue to seek their killer?"

The woman snapped her fingers and pointed to her shoulder; in an instant, the idle raven flew to his perch. "Makes no matter to me, but I suggest you do so with care."

There were more questions that I wanted to ask her, but the moment was lost. Upon my return home, unescorted, I had stopped at the stone she had so tenderly touched. It was nothing more than a rock, pushed into the ground. All that defined it as a grave marker were the letters, crudely, carved into the stone that read: *My husband.*

My instincts told me that Gavia was more than capable of murder. If she had made the slightest hint to me, I would have attempted to persuade Tay to drop the matter, as everyone else had suggested.

Ursa had made a grand mid-day meal for Actius. She loaded a silver tray with pickled eggs, dried figs, green olives, garlic encrusted dormice and some sweet cakes. I pointed at the food and licked my lips. She pointed at a simmering pot of stew.

I reached for a bowl, and she departed the kitchen. With her back to me, I firmly placed the bowl back onto the table. Ducking my head out of the kitchen, I peered down the peristyle and watched Ursa enter Actius's room. I darted through the garden, Geb at my heels, and sat down beside the lifeless fountain.

Ursa laughed at whatever Actius told her and went on to assure him that the meal was nothing too special for him, before bowing her hefty little body out of the actor's presence.

The woman floated back to the kitchen, oblivious of me. I gave Geb a pat and we made our way to the little feast. I did not bother to knock on the door, but instead, entered in silence. With the door closed behind us, I asked, "How are you feeling?" Uninvited, I pulled a chair very close to the little table bearing the silver tray.

"My leg is throbbing. I understand there is a shortage of physicians, but I don't trust that rancid potion maker." Actius spoke with a strained tone and a grimace on his face.

"Do you want more tonic for the pain until Regulus can get you a healer?"

"She hasn't poisoned me yet...I guess so." He reached for a goblet of dark wine and took a long draft.

I pulled my wax tablet from my neck and carved out a few words. Actius grinned and asked, "Why the façade?"

I shrugged and replied, "Ask Regulus." Actius laughed. I opened the door and started clapping. From the end of the peristyle Ajax peered at me, and when I waved him over, he sprinted toward the room. I tapped at the tablet, and he frowned as he read my request.

"She likes you, I don't know if she will give me any," Ajax responded. He was fairly certain that he need not follow my directions.

Actius piped up, "Do as he says, I need a moment with him."

Ajax looked past me to the commanding man stretched out on the bed. He was no less immune to Actius's charms than the women of the household. The young Greek smiled, bowed his head, and apologized before sprinting back down the peristyle.

I closed the door and sat back down, waiting to be offered some of the food.

"Proculus thinks highly of Regulus," Actius remarked in an off-hand manner.

"Does he?' I replied dryly, gazing at the dormouse.

"Servia told him that you two just recently arrived in Pompeii, traveling from Rome." I nodded as he spoke. "The owner of this place and he were old friends, Popidius – was that his name?"

I nodded again and Actius went on, "She said, though, she'd never seen or heard of Regulus before." Actius picked up a dormouse and ate it.

Tay would have been proud of my quick lie, "Regulus met Popidius before he bought me, I had never heard of the man either until we arrived in town."

"Arrived in town with a baby, how did that happen?" He popped another dormouse into his mouth and stared at me.

I wasn't a good enough liar to retell Tay's version of what happened, "Ask Regulus."

Actius laughed again. "Servia says you are as useless as Porcia when she was eight months pregnant. She can't figure out why Regulus keeps you around." He picked up two dormice and tossed one to Geb before putting the other into his mouth.

"I make him feel smart," I responded with a shrug. "I entertain him."

Actius studied my face. My flesh wasn't red because I hadn't lied. "That might be true, but there's something more to it." He ate another dormouse. There was only one left on the plate. He looked from my eyes to the last garlic-encrusted delicacy. "These are delicious, have the last one."

I smiled, relieved to get at least a taste of something other than stew. I picked up the offered item of food and placed it in my mouth. Just as I was savoring the flavorful garlic, Actius let out a slow laugh. "No slave would take food from a guest's plate, especially the last dormouse." He reached for his wine, but before he took a drink, he winked at me and said, "I know, ask Regulus."

We both laughed, but the lightness of my mood was quickly cut short when Actius said, "Tell me about Cornelia."

I took a deep breath and let out a long sigh. I fumbled for words, and then Actius grinned before asking, "Her too? I thought you were busy with the woman across the street."

My face began to burn red. "Who told you that?"

"Now, I can't betray my sources." He rolled his eyes and covered his mouth with a flat palm before he winked at me, as if on stage.

"Julia is...complicated..."

"Because she thinks that you are a mute slave?"

"I don't know what she thinks. I don't much care either," I admitted.

Actius's face lost all expression, "But you do care what Cornelia thinks?"

I confessed, "That varies from day to day. She confounds me."

Actius shrugged, "Your young, that's only natural."

"I think I'm in love with her, but I don't want to be..."

Actius laughed again, "The moon hasn't completed a cycle since you met her. You aren't in love. You are smitten."

I asked, "How do I become un-smitten?"

"That's easy – have her."

"She's not that type of woman."

Actius lifted his cup of wine in a mock toast and said, "There is only one type of woman."

I thought perhaps for a famous performer who kept the company of Nero, this might be true. From Cornelia to Ursa, the women under our roof seemed instantly enchanted by the man. I envied him.

I had given up my birthright, I was deprived of my family's wealth, my future was uncertain. All that I still possessed were my good looks, which paled in comparison to the charming actor's. The irony wasn't lost on me – he was the son of a slave, living a charmed life; I was the stock of nobility, living no life at all.

Before I could muster a response, there was a knock at the door. Looking slightly rattled, Ajax came inside the little cell holding a clay cup close to his chest. Actius reached a hand toward the young Greek, but Ajax frowned and glanced at the item in his hand before saying, "She mixed up the tonic...and then she spit in it."

Actius gave a comic smile indicating delight, and wiggled the fingers on his outreached hand. "I don't care. I'm sure she has spit in every concoction she's made for me."

"A real healer should look at his ankle. He still can't put any weight on it," I whispered to Tay, who sat at his writing table pretending to ignore me.

"He just injured it two days ago. It will take time to heal. Gavia seems to know something about medicine."

It was rare for him to give any credit to the woman. I'm sure that the comment must have left a bad taste in his mouth.

I decided not to tell him that most of her concoctions were nothing but fool's magic. "All the same..."

"Fine, I'll find a physician. Do not pester me on the subject," Tay burst out.

"What's the matter?"

Tay pointed in the direction of our guest's room. "Our list of suspects are men who shouldn't be annoyed," he snapped.

"We don't owe him the answer to this mystery." I was surprised by my own words. I had thought of Gavia, and dreaded the idea of where the truth might lead us.

"If he heals and goes about digging for answers, one of two things will happen: he'll get killed, or he will find out the truth. It's just possible that neither outcome will serve the best interests of this town."

I dropped to a little backless chair by the table and made my confused pupil expression. Not that I didn't understood Tay's comment, what I didn't understand was where he stood on the matter.

Tay looked into my eyes, and his voice was free of sarcasm as he explained, "The trivial local politicians aside, we have Nero's stepsister, Nero's uncle-in-law, and next year's Consul somehow involved in this plot. On the other side, we have Nero's favorite actor, a man whom he's shared the stage with and is the nephew of one of his steadfast allies, the man who killed his mother and ruined an unwanted wife. One way or another, Nero's simply going to prefer this matter is dropped."

"Then tell him that, he's no fool."

"He isn't a coward either, his mother has been killed and someone attacked him; he wants the truth." Tay sighed, "I just want to find out the truth first."

"So you can manipulate it?"

"Handsome *and* smart." Tay flashed me his devious grin. "If I can find the answers, I might save face with both our local *acquaintances* and please the Emperor's friend. Think of the favors I will be owed, this will truly establish me in this community."

Suddenly feeling less smart, I remarked, "You don't want him to heal. You want him off his feet until you figure out who killed his mother and Celer."

"*And* devious too, you make me proud," Tay quipped with his usual zeal.

I had just stepped out of the study when I caught sight of Cornelia striding down the peristyle toward Actius's borrowed room. She knocked at the partially opened door and then entered. The door closed firmly behind her.

I stood frozen for some time until I noticed that Ajax was sitting on a stool nearby, trying hard to act as if he hadn't observed me.

Nearly stumbling, I forced myself onward. Geb waited by the kitchen door, the intelligent dog had sensed that before I saw Cornelia, I was headed there for some of Ursa's stew.

Despite my own displeasure, I didn't want the animal to share in my feeling of disappointment. I found a misshapen sweet cake that, apparently, had not been good enough for Actius and gave it Geb.

I slunk up to the top of the staircase and sat sulking for quite a while until I heard the door to Actius's room open. A moment later, I caught sight of Cornelia walking down the peristyle. She crossed the garden and went to the door leading to the back of the storefront and her apartment. She turned back to glance in the direction she had come from.

She wore a seductive smile, as if, despite the distance and the columns supporting the second floor, she just might still catch sight of Actius. Too many obstacles were in the way. The smile faded, and her shoulders relaxed. She was turning to reach for the door when her gaze drifted upward, onto me. Her eyes fell, and she reached for her wrap dangling off of her and tightened it as if to conceal the revealing gown she wore. Cornelia looked back to me and attempted a nonchalant smile before slipping inside the empty shop.

Zenobia was correct. I was starting to regret Actius Anicetus's presence in our home.

Chapter Nine
The Conspirators

Several of Tay's clients were dispatched with letters to Balbus, Siricus, and Proculus (the local politician, not our friendly admiral.) In them, he had asked that he might call on each man during the course of the day. The dependants were told to rush back with their replies and to give them to Corax or Ajax. This was, of course, after he had already sent a message and received a response from Valens, in which he asked that he might meet late in the morning, and Valens had welcomed him to stop by.

At a leisurely pace, we walked toward the home of Valens's son. We navigated our way past carts full of building materials and piles of debris. The deafening sounds of construction echoed from the brick and plastered surfaces. Dirt choked the air just as it had the day the city was assaulted by the gods' wrath. I was tempted to hold my cloak to my face, but I anticipated Tay snatching it away, embarrassed by my behavior.

We stopped short of the grand house belonging to the Valens family. Tay pointed toward a little open restaurant neatly tucked into the front of a midsize home sitting on the opposite side of the road.

My companion sat on a stool at the counter and aligned himself so he might keep watch on young Satrius Valens's imposing front door. He pointed me to a stool that would not obstruct his view and ordered two cups of warm mead for us.

The proprietor was a chatty fellow. He explained that he and his wife lived in the house which the café sprang from. They grew many of the fruits and vegetables that they served in their own garden. The rest came from a nearby farm that his brother ran.

Each time Tay glanced at the door across the wide, stone street, the man mimicked the action. A good, dutiful neighbor, he finally asked, "Do you have business with Satrius?"

Unperturbed, Tay responded, "With his father. I'm early, waiting for a few others to arrive."

With that, the fellow relaxed and began telling us about his daughters and who he was going to marry them off to. Each young man's family grew a local produce that he looked forward to serving.

Ajax appeared before us, out of breath from sprinting, and coughed out the words, "Proculus sent word that he is unable to meet with you today."

Tay requested a cup of mead that the young man swallowed in one long gulp after he caught his breath.

Only moments later, Corax ran to us uttering, "The messengers returned, neither Balbus nor Siricus are free to receive you today." He took the cup handed to him and drank the liquid.

The restaurateur, leaning against the counter listening to us, pointed across the street. "There's Proculus right there."

An army of slaves clustered around an ornate litter stopped in front of the Valens's home. Several servants assisted an aged man out of the curtained sedan and walked him to the door.

Tay thanked the Greeks and sent them home. Little time passed before another fellow, attended by only one hulking brute, arrived. He fidgeted at the door, glancing this way and that way, until he was ushered inside.

Tay drank the last of his mead and told me to finish up.
As if on cue; one more man, who was escorted by two
slaves, approached the house as I placed my empty cup on
the stone counter.

Tay thanked our host and wished him success on his
daughters' upcoming weddings. He then sauntered across
the street with me in tow.

My companion peered at the costly litter, nodded to the
numerous slaves waiting for their masters, and then gave
me a wink indicating that I was to knock at the massive
closed doors ahead of us.

An attentive doorman greeted us quickly. Anticipating
another rushed demand to see Valens, he smiled when Tay
treated him kindly and said, "I was curious if I might see
Valens, when he has a moment. My name is Regulus. I
don't believe he'll be surprised by my visit."

We were ushered to a nearby sitting room, and the
servant went off to the conclave that Tay had set in
motion. When the doorman returned there was no trace of
the smile he had departed with. I'm sure mention of the
name Regulus subjected him to undeserved hostility.

We were led through the large house, past one
courtyard, and into a small garden where Valens stood
among four other men. I did not recognize the eldest
fellow, but the other three had each called on Celer the
day he was killed.

"Regulus," the politician said in the form of a greeting.
His tone was neutral, but his eyes conveyed annoyance. "I
believe you've met Siricus."

The youngest of the group, perhaps in his late thirties,
responded smoothly, "We've bumped into each other
delivering bribes to Primus, although, we were not
properly introduced."

Siricus *appeared* wealthy. The tunic and sandals belonged to a prosperous man. He was perfectly groomed and manicured, yet there was a quality about him that seemed pretentious.

"As I have learned, an introduction from Primus costs one of his higher fees," Tay countered in good humor.

Valens gestured to an older man squirming in his little chair. He had stared at Tay while Siricus had spoken, but his eyes dropped to the mosaic floor at the mention of his name. "This is Balbus. Have you met?"

While Balbus gave a shudder, Tay replied, "I don't believe we have."

Balbus looked up without making eye contact with Tay and uttered, "Good day to you, citizen." His high-pitched voice cracked as he spoke.

"And good day to you," Tay responded jovially.

Valens paused and looked to the oldest of the group. He grimaced before saying, "And this is Proculus…"

The ancient fellow's milky eyes turned to Valens as he said, "What…this is the one…why would he send me a message…why does he want to see me?"

The elder man's confusion was handled by his attendant. This was the same man who had arrived at Actia's house shortly after I had last seen Celer alive. It was his raised voice that had caught my attention while I painted the bust.

"Calm down, you are worked up over *nothing*." The caretaker, a rather exotic looking fellow with pale blond hair and cold blue eyes, glared at Tay while he spoke.

Valens sighed and asked Tay, "Why indeed?" He did not offer a chair to his guest, or recline beside one of his compatriots. Instead, he crossed his arms and stared straight at the young man causing him trouble.

"Three days ago, Actius Anicetus returned to Pompeii after receiving word of his mother's death. He found that the caretaker of her affairs had been killed as well. Then, only hours after his arrival, Actius came across a list of names he found in Celer's papers." Tay paused, glancing at each man. Old Proculus's eyes drifted without focus, and the nervous Balbus did his best to stare at the ornately tiled floor. The others defiantly returned Tay's gaze. "Actius was struck on the back of the head, and when he came to, the list was gone. My good men, all of your names were on that list."

Siricus leaned forward from his chair, "That's all good and well, but what does it have to do with you?"

"My valet was in Actia's home when Celer was killed. I was concerned that he might be a suspect, only he and the old doorman were in the house when the murder took place. Not one finger was pointed at him, not the slightest hint that he was suspect. This, I found even more concerning."

"And, at that point, you should have minded your own business," Proculus's caretaker responded with an edge to his voice.

"I had every intention to, until Actius arrived at my home with questions. My tenant," he paused for effect, "Gavia—"

Proculus became momentarily alert, "Gavia – that poor girl."

Balbus muttered something under his breath, but I couldn't make any sense of what he said.

Siricus spat out the words, "Filthy bitch."

With an arched brow, Tay went on, "Gavia attacked him, thinking he was an intruder."

Siricus gave a light laugh, Valens's frown broke into a disgusted half-smile, and Balbus hunkered even lower into his chair.

"Actius is now under my roof, and I have a responsibility to protect him." Once more, he paused to let the meaning of his words sink in. "Celer sent Actius a letter that his mother had been killed in the quake. A second letter was dispatched, in which Celer indicated that he had reason to suspect that someone took advantage of the disaster and killed Actia."

I noticed that Balbus's eyes darted to Siricus. The sly man didn't return the glance but, instead, shifted in his little chair.

Tay went on, "Actius is in my home, unable to poke at you fine gentleman and ask why his mother might have been murdered. And before he can dig up the foundation of whatever past conspiracy you all are involved in, I would like to deduce who killed Actia and Celer so that Actius might know his foe and leave the past alone."

"Well said," Siricus commented before setting his gaze on Valens.

Old Proculus, who hadn't reacted to any of Tay's statements, began to snore. Valens tossed his hands into the air and suggested to the elder man's servant, "Eutychis, take him home."

Only roused momentarily, Proculus asked Valens, "The matter is solved then, no one will come pestering me?" Valens assured Proculus that he would no longer be pestered, while the old man's attendant glared at Tay.

In the commotion, Balbus stood and announced, "I want no more part of this. I should be off, too." He waited until he was sure Valens was distracted by Proculus's departure before making eye contact with Tay and giving him a strange nod and a pained smile. The nervous little man then fled.

Siricus, who had remained draped on his chair while Proculus was gathered, stood and took several strides toward Tay. "Regulus, it is important that Actius be appeased. I personally will ascertain the culprit and inform you as soon as I am certain of the guilty party." His lie was delivered with fantastic self-important arrogance. Siricus turned to his host and said, "Valens, you know where I stand on the matter."

After his pompous guest sauntered away, Valens remarked, "Lying bastard." He turned to face Tay and said, "That was almost amusing, very clever to say the least."

"I apologize, and I want to explain. I only wish to know the truth before Actius can start dredging up the past. If the killer can be identified before Actius goes to Frugi and Poppaeus or Claudia Antonia, wouldn't that be better for everyone?"

Valens appeared taken aback by Tay's knowledge of the players. Still, he hesitated. "These people have nothing to do with Actia's murder…"

"*Actia's murder*? Then you agree with Celer, she wasn't killed in the disaster?"

"Regulus, you are trying my patience."

"And you mine."

I feared Tay had not only crossed a line, but may very well have burnt an important bridge.

"My young friend," Valens's voice betrayed his anger, and he paused to find a softer pitch, "…you have much to lose if you set out to make enemies in this city."

Tay nodded in agreement. "And we all have much to lose if Actius sets out to make Nero an enemy of this city's leaders. If Actius finds himself at odds with Poppaeus, what do you think is going to come of this? Frugi will be consul next year, what secret does he keep? Whoever murdered Actia must be thrown to Actius's feet so that he has no reason to tell Nero we are undeserving of the Golden One's aid."

Tay had taken the fight out of Valens. The man dropped to a backless chair and sighed, "I understand what you are saying, give me time."

"Actius will be on his feet in a matter of days, his investigation will be far more intrusive than mine." Tay's words were not said as a threat, but as a friendly warning.

Valens actually smiled before he replied, "And yet, my young friend, I think he might just be easier to handle than you."

"I don't know, it will take a more powerful blow to the back of the head than the last one."

"I'd like to know which fool thought that violence was the answer." Valens stood from his chair and walked toward Tay. "I realize I can't deter you, but I can't protect you either. Frugi and Poppaeus are powerful men. They will not be trifled with."

"You could save me the trouble and tell me the secret?" Tay replied with a devious smile.

"Ah, but I fear their wrath as much as you should."

Valens began leading us to the entrance, and again, he said, "Actia's death has nothing to do with what happened in the past, I wish I could convince you of this."

"Considering who called on Celer before and after he was killed, it would be hard to convince me."

Valens nodded agreeably. "There is someone else who had reason to harm Actia and Celer. She could rid us all of Actius if she was asked to make a potion for the man."

Tay's brow arched uncontrollably at Valens's suggestion. "True, but I think she might enjoy seeing Actius disturb what is being hidden."

Valens paused before the door as his servant opened it. "I shouldn't have said that, I sound rather guilty of all you are accusing us of, don't I?" His unruffled politician's manners had returned to him.

"I believe it was Eros who accused you, not me." Tay was unable to contain the sarcastic remark.

"Yes, I confronted him on that matter. He apologized and claimed that Actius misunderstood him. Then, as I've been told, he departed for Baiae. I'm sure that Poppaeus has already heard Eros's version of all the lies he has said." Valens took a deep breath, and then let it out very slowly as he put his words together. "Give me time, Regulus. I hear what you are saying, and I agree with you. This will be solved."

Tay bowed his head and extended an open palm, and as Valens extended his own hand, Tay said, "I will not go out seeking more information, but I must be honest with you, I won't send anyone away who comes to me."

"Fair enough," Valens replied, shaking the hand of my clever companion.

Tay and Servia went about arranging the furniture of the formal rooms. The Greeks lit lamps while Mucia, Delia, and Gaia swept and cleaned. Tay had set his plan into motion and wanted the house to be as perfect as possible for the guests that he was sure would arrive.

While all of this work went on, I hid upstairs with Porcia and the babies. She chattered on as if I really were mute. She knew I was distracted and was too polite to inquire.

Porcia hinted that the other girls had realized Cornelia was, in fact, the Oracle of Nephthys. Of course, this was bound to happen.

Porcia went on to tell me that Sosia had snuck into Actius's room early that morning. Despite his injury, Sosia had some rather sordid details to share with the other girls that I didn't care to hear.

Once the work was done, Mucia was sent to check on Porcia and give her a reprieve from the two infants. The genderless creature informed me, "The master has been looking for you."

I found Tay in a nervous yet chipper mood. He was looking over the newly arranged drawing room and appeared rather pleased with himself.

The formal chamber, open to both the atrium and courtyard, was lavishly furnished. After the quake, Tay had bought a number of quality items from people either in need of cash, or with little desire to repair their damaged property. I realized, as Tay had transformed the nearly empty and bland home that we had inherited into a lavish showplace, that he had impeccable taste.

A set of backless chairs carved from exotic wood sat facing the garden. Between them was a small pedestal table with wrought iron legs and a marble top. A large chair, with its back to the courtyard, faced the ornate guest chairs. This seat reserved for the host had a rounded back and ivory inlaid in the wide arms. A cushion leaned against the back. The fabric was a particular shade of brown that, at first glance, appeared purple.

Pedestals sat about two corners of the room, those corners in sight of the guest chairs. A nearly life-sized statue of Fortuna was positioned to gaze over the host.

The other figure was a local favorite, a detailed marble of Hercules. His face pointed directly toward the guest's place and even tilted downward at just the right angle to give the impression that the god was watching whoever might sit across from the home's owner.

"There you are, go change. I want to see you in the blue tunic and your best silver," Tay said, waving me to the staircase. He had already traded his white tunic for a dark green chiton, with a brocaded hem and just a few pieces of gold.

Geb chased me back up the stairs and stretched out on my bed while I changed into the clothes that had been laid out for me.

As I left my room, I could hear the voice of Lutatius Gallus echo through the garden, "I don't want to meet Actius Anicetus. I must get home before Mother starts to look for me."

The misshapen man shuffled away from Sosia, as she giggled and pretended to clutch at him. "You had better be back here tomorrow to see me or I'll see to it that *Mother* finds out about your outings."

Sosia's words were said playfully, but Lutatius's reaction seemed rather panicked. "Oh, no, I'll be back. I'll see you tomorrow, before the fifth hour." He shuffled through the open gate to the alley.

I was just on the bottom step of the stairs when Sosia noticed me. She ran her fingers through her undressed blonde hair and licked her lips. "Good day, Demetrius."

The attractive girl had lost her allure to me. She was tainted by the gossip that Porcia had shared. As we looked into each other's eyes, there seemed to be something sinister behind her playful façade, almost threatening.

Catlike, Sosia was next to me in an instant. She ran a finger down my chest and whispered, "One day, when you are bored with that old woman across the street, I'll put that lame tongue of yours to work."

She mistook the unhappy expression on my face as shame rather than disgust. After a playful giggle, she slunk off to bathe.

I stood dumbly for a moment until Actius whistled at me. I turned to see him peering from his bed down the peristyle. He waved me to him.

Once I had closed the door, he said, "She's an interesting little monster." He made the pantomimes' traditional, over-exaggerated face of a man in love.

I only nodded. Actius was naturally a likeable fellow, despite my growing jealousy of him. It was hard to blame him for seducing Sosia, had she not been a prostitute by trade, I'm sure the insult would have still been put to her all the same. However, Cornelia's previous visit to his room still rankled me.

"A house full of women, must be nice?" he baited.

I shrugged in response. So far, I had yet to experience the benefits.

Actius gave up on the subject of women and said, "I'll share with you the next plate of delicacies that Ursa brings if you tell me what Regulus omitted from his meeting with Valens."

Tay had edited the story quite a bit. There was no mention of his own willingness to supply Actius with a killer and be done with the whole business. He certainly did not comment on Valens's mock suggestion of encouraging Gavia to poison the man.

"There was a little more tension than he mentioned. And he played down the risk to his relationship with the local powers that be," I told him. I knew Actius would squeeze me for some information, and it was better to leak a bit of worthless observations and appease him once the follow-up questions started.

"I have to commend him. I'm not really sure why he's helping me." Actius's eyes probed me, as if I might betray the answer.

Fearful of the gamble that Tay was making, I replied, "I can't fathom that either."

Chapter Ten
The Innocent Men

回回回回回回回回

I had just left Actius's room as the second part of the farce began. Balbus was the first to arrive, apologizing to both Ajax, who opened the door, and to Corax, who led him to the drawing room. "I'm so sorry that I didn't send a message ahead."

Once ushered past the partially opened curtains separating the spacious room from the atrium, he asked Tay, "Please, forgive my intrusion...I should have sent a note ahead ...such bad manners on my part..."

The anxious fellow nearly jumped as he caught sight of Corax pulling the curtains closed behind him.

Tay smiled and graciously said, "Think nothing of it. I am happy that you are here." He gestured to one of the lovely chairs and reclined on his own seat. The nervous man pushed the cushions aside so he might perch on the edge of the piece of furniture.

Resigned to play my part as the dutiful, silent slave, I placed a tray with water, wine, and food on the low table between the two men. Tay picked up an elegant glass cup and began to poor wine for his guest. He looked to Balbus to see when to stop. The squirming man gave no indication that he wanted room left to add water. Tay handed the man the cup, which he took with trembling hands.

"Thank you," Balbus mumbled before drinking down half of the liquid. He reached forward to place the glass on the table and then thought better. He pulled it back to just below his chin and then cleared his throat. "I must tell you, I had nothing to do with the death of Actia or the murder of Celer. I can't say that I was on friendly terms with either of them – that is to say, I had little dealings with them. Not that we were unfriendly with each other in any way." He put the cup to his lips and drank more. "I hadn't so much thought of Celer until the very morning he was killed." Balbus shuddered, lifted his right hand, and twisted his fingers into a symbol meant to ward off evil. He then gulped down the rest of the wine.

Tay reached for his guest's empty glass. At first the man waved him away until he realized his host's intentions, and then, after an excited nod, he pushed the glass toward Tay so quickly their hands almost collided.

Tay refilled the drink, and as he gave it back, he stated, "What a tragedy that you should end up at his door on the very day he died." Tay's voice was friendly and without suspicion.

"Oh, yes." Balbus took a drink of the wine and shrugged. "I suppose you would like to know why I called on him." After Tay nodded, Balbus took a deep drink and said, "Celer sent me a letter. It was a bit vague and mysterious, perhaps even threatening. He spoke of past secrets and favors and stated that he thought Actia's death was no accident. Why, I didn't even know that she was dead!" Balbus paused to take another sip of his wine. "You know, I had my own share of disaster in the calamity. My wife was injured, and my properties were damaged. I'm not a rich man, politics did me no favor, I will tell you. No, I didn't even want to be Duumvir, but Valens gave me little choice."

Tay perked up. "Why would he do such a thing?"

Balbus rested the glass to his chin and he explained, "With Gavianus and Grosphus dead, *they* needed Duumvirs with no particular political factions. We needed unity, not more division. As aedile, I served my community well, but I hadn't really made a name for myself." Balbus shrugged and sipped his wine. "All the better *they* told me. I could do what needed to be done for the city after the riot, without owing to nobles or the common man; no favors to repay while in office. I could get to doing what needed to be done," he said proudly before finishing off his second helping.

Rather playfully, Tay asked, "And what did you do as Duumvir?"

As Balbus handed his empty glass to his host, he responded, "Just what *they* told me!"

Tay and I both repressed a chuckle. After Balbus's glass was refilled, Tay asked, "Poppaeus, Valens, and Frugi?"

Balbus frowned, he wasn't so nervous sipping on his third helping. "Not Frugi, no he left town after the riot…rarely here anyway."

"So you took the advice of Valens and Poppaeus?"

Balbus ran a hand through his ruffled grey hair. "At first, but then there was a falling out. Marius and Pansa became better friends with Poppaeus, and he became less involved with Valens. I think they got wind of Nero's relationship with Poppaeus's niece and began to pay court to him."

I knew each of the names mentioned by our guest. Marius was a wealthy freedman with a prosperous shipping business and a good deal of property around the city. Pansa and his son were both leading politicians involved with the rebuilding efforts.

Balbus shrugged and went on, "Poppaeus told me to make a few decrees, to urge the council to do this or that, and then my term was over. I can tell you this, I was happy to be done. My business had suffered from neglect while I was distracted, my steward had nearly let my farm falter, and my wife had started holding court with women far too wealthy for her to be associating with."

Somewhat frazzled by his own storytelling, he had another sip of his wine. Tay gave him a moment and asked, "What part did Actia play in the aftermath of the riot?"

"I had never heard of her until someone mentioned to me what became of Gavianus's house after he killed himself." Again, he lifted his right hand and gestured. "Awful, just awful. He never should have gotten himself mixed up with Livineius Regulus!" The man's eyes opened wide, and he said, "No relation, I hope!"

"None." Tay smiled and took a sip from his own cup. "Why do you say that?"

"Livineius had the games fixed! He and Lucretius Valens were in on…" realizing he had just spoken too freely, Balbus trailed off.

"No worries, friend, I knew that already. My dear friend Popidius told me all about it."

The color began to return to Balbus's face as remarked, "Oh yes, old Popidius, he enjoyed the fixed games, too." He paused to gather his thoughts. "Well, Gavianus wanted to make a name for his son-in-law and his adopted son while they were all in office, and Livineius knew how to stage a spectacle." The little man, tipsy from his drink, snorted a bit as he spat out, "Well, by Pluto, we had one!"

I heard a distant knock on the front door. Tay ignored the slight distraction and asked, "Why would Actia end up in that house?"

"A very good question, but one I never would have had the nerve to ask." He drained the last of his glass. "I prefer to leave well enough alone!"

"Is that a piece of advice?" Tay's voice still remained jovial.

"Not at all, the preference hasn't taken me far in life." Balbus admitted.

Tay reached to refill the man's glass, but he declined. Tay asked him one last question, "What did you discuss when you met Celer?"

"I told him not to send me any more cryptic letters and to just come out with what he had to say." After observing Balbus's nervous nature I doubted that's quite how the conversation had taken place unless the man had drank a jug of wine on his way to the house. "Celer told me that he no longer needed my help, that he had resolved his problem. He told me that the man who killed Actia would be revealed as soon as Actius arrived. I left it at that; I wanted nothing more to do with the matter."

With some help, Balbus walked to his single attendant waiting for him in the vestibule. After stating his well wishes, he stumbled out over our threshold.

Ajax appeared and handed Tay a wax tablet. As my companion read the message, his devious grin told me that his plan had succeeded. Tay returned the tablet to Ajax and said, "Reset the stage for our next performance."

A short time later, Siricus arrived, trailed by his brawny slaves. He was admitted inside the house and led first to the small sitting room. Tay had quickly formed the same opinion of the man as I and decided to toy with him a bit.

When Ajax reported that the guest had impatiently asked what business was keeping his host, Tay told the Greek to bring the guest to the drawing room. And then, having only just hatched the idea, he waved at me to follow him, and we slipped into the peristyle, tugging at the curtains to conceal us. Tay held a hand over his mouth to keep from laughing.

We listened to Ajax apologize, "I thought he was in here. I'm sure he will only be a moment."

"He knew I was coming, I sent a messenger."

Tay dramatically threw the draperies open and entered the drawing room, catching his flustered guest off-guard. I trailed behind, holding my lips tightly to repress my smile.

"Ah, Siricus, welcome." Tay paused and studied the red-faced man and the puzzled Greek. "Is something the matter? You look displeased?"

Ajax slipped away as Siricus ran his hands down his costly tunic and rearranged the thick, silver bands at his wrist. "No, no, of course not."

Tay gestured to the same piece of furniture that Balbus had perched himself on. After Siricus draped himself on the chair, he remarked, "Thank you, for your hospitality."

Tay began to poor wine for the two of them. When his guest's glass was only half-full, Siricus waved a hand. Tay added an equal portion of water and handed the glass to his guest.

"How nice this place looks, Popidius had let it fall apart." He took just a sip and then looked into the glass and back to his host. "A fine Faustian, had I known, I would have taken it undiluted."

"There's more, pour that out and–"

"Waste such an expensive vintage? No, no." He took a deeper drink. "It's fine."

Tay pointed to a platter of garlic-encrusted dormice. It would seem that Ursa only had the one recipe. Greedily, Siricus grabbed two and shoved them both into his mouth. "Delicious," he commented before taking two more.

"My cook's specialty," Tay remarked benignly.

Siricus licked his fingers and let out a chuckle. "That was pretty clever this morning. Sending us all a request to meet you and then watching us scramble to our patron." He sipped at his wine and went on, "And you got what you wanted. My messenger said Balbus's freedman was pacing outside your door when he arrived, and here I am now."

"Sometimes men can be very predictable," Tay responded casually.

"And sometimes they can be very unpredictable, such as when they kill."

"Indeed. Do you have a theory on what might make a man so unpredictable?" Tay's brow arched as he spoke.

"That all depends – am I a suspect or just a scholar on the subject?" Siricus mused.

"You weren't a suspect until now. What would make you a scholar?" Tay's voice held a hint of condescension.

Siricus stretched out his legs and leaned to one side of the chair. He studied the craftsmanship of the piece of furniture as he spoke. "When I was Duumvir it was I who gave the orders to the executioner. A number of men who participated in the riot had to be dealt with."

"You were left with the task rather than the Special Prefect?" Tay attempted to sound surprised, although I knew better.

"Proculus wasn't any less senile four years ago than he is today. Why do you think Valens had the council appoint him? An old name, with old money, who wouldn't be alive too long to deal with any enemies he made while cleaning up Gavianus and Grosphus's mistake."

"Still, execution and murder are two different things…"

"Judicial murder?" Siricus said with a dramatic flair. "That's what Celer accused me of." The man took a long drink of the fine wine.

"Did he have reason to?" I could tell that Tay was biting back his typical sarcastic tone.

"I was just the instrument, Poppaeus wanted two men silenced. He arranged for a witness to claim the men had taken part in instigating the fight."

"You didn't believe him?"

"I did at the time, until the witness was found face down in the river a few days later, and the wife of one the dead men came into some money and moved off."

"What of Celer's accusation, why would that matter at this point, four years later?" Tay inquired.

"It didn't matter at all. And that's what I went to tell him. He sent me a letter telling me he needed my support, and in return he would continue to hold his tongue."

"How could he betray you and not think that Poppaeus would react?"

Siricus stiffened slightly. "He knew things that Poppaeus didn't, he was Valens's freedman, and he knew why Valens wanted to make me Duumvir." Before his host could ask, he said, "Some secrets are best kept. Anyway, Celer told me when the time came, he would announce Actia's killer. He wanted me to step forward and support him."

"Why would he need support?" Tay sounded more amused than curious.

"He told me that the man who killed Actia had a powerful patron, someone who might be able to intimidate Valens into ignoring the truth."

"What did you tell him?"

"I told him to keep the past in the past, and never to bring up that I..." he fumbled for words, "what he knew. I told him I didn't care who killed Actia, and I wanted nothing to do with it."

"And he left it at that?"

"No, he offered me a fair amount of gold to back him." The man laughed. "And I agreed to. I'm no fool. I was going to say whatever he wanted rather than risk him exposing me. Valens couldn't protect me. He doesn't hold the same weight that he used to. This disaster has been a blessing to him, giving him the opportunity to swoop in, playing the part of the city's favorite patron."

"It sounds as if you had a good reason to kill Celer." My companion's tone remained inquisitive.

"A better reason not to, was because Celer hadn't given me the coins yet." Siricus gave a sigh before finishing off his wine. He took his next helping without water. "Whoever killed him had a bigger secret than I. Celer poked the wrong scar."

"What part did Actia play in this?" Tay asked his familiar question.

"That's a mystery to me. When I was brought to meet with them after the riot, Poppaeus referred to her a few times, but when Valens heard her name, he cleared his throat and glanced at me like I was some sort of gossipy slave girl. I didn't know who she was until weeks later. I know that she was at the amphitheater, and she witnessed who started the brawl. But there was more to it than just that, there were other witnesses, too, rather than a fine house belonging to a dead Duumvir, they were disposed of."

"The two men you had executed?"

"There was one other, someone too important to just disappear."

"And what became of this person?"

"After Nero's ruling, he became pretty upset with the ten year ban on gladiatorial spectacles. He may have rethought his silence in the matter. I know he had words with Poppaeus and Frugi, and then...he died in his sleep." Siricus took a long sip of his fine wine. "Old men do that, no one thought much about it."

Tay asked, "And who was this important man?"

I knew the answer. His name was painted on the fresco in Actia's house. He'd owned an opulent home near the arena and had adopted the leading citizen of the day.

"Decimus Lucretius Valens." Siricus named the adopted father of Valens.

Tay had no response as he weighed the information.

"I was *selected* by the town council, I served the first month's term because they knew I was motivated and had the stones to order the legitimate executions of the rabble that looted and went wild, as well as removing whomever I was told to. Meek little Balbus had his turn, they had him push some taxes and dole out some honors.

"You can speculate on the cause, but after Lucretius Valens *died*, Poppaeus and Valens seemed to have a falling out. Once the crisis had passed, Balbus and I were left alone to serve out our terms. Neither of us made any friends or earned any favors other than Valens's patronage. He's been good to me when I need help, otherwise, he keeps his distance."

"And Poppaeus?"

"I keep my distance from the man, never trusted him, never will." Siricus reached for the remaining dormice and finished off the plate. He spoke as he chewed, "You may be a friend of Nero's, I guess that's why you are looking out for Actius, but that won't do you any good with Poppaeus. He's like a crocodile, relaxed on a sand bar. He doesn't seem to even notice you until your guard is down, then he's in motion, and there is nothing that you can do to get out of his way."

I hadn't much cared for the overdressed, underfunded man at first, but he had grown on me during the meeting. He said what he had to say and seemed surprisingly honest, even when admitting that he had a secret to keep.

I felt a shadow of pity for him. Like Balbus, he had thought that serving as Duumvir would enhance his career and coffers. Instead, he was used by others who knew his weaknesses, and virtually discarded once they no longer needed a puppet.

"I will take your words to heart," Tay commented, gesturing to the jug of wine.

"No, thank you. If I have more, I won't stop until I have drunk your stock."

As Tay was leading his guest to the vestibule, we heard a sound rap at the door. Siricus laughed, "That will be Eutychis on behalf of Proculus. He likes to bark, but he's just as quick to hold his tail between his legs and cower."

Ajax swung the door open, and was quickly pounced on by Eutychis, "I'm here to see Regulus. I can see that Siricus is here, but I have no time to…" he looked past Ajax to see both Regulus and Siricus striding toward him. Rudely, he pushed past Ajax and pointed a finger at Siricus, "I should have known you'd run straight here to confess to this *outsider*!" He scoffed, "Have you no shame?"

"None whatsoever, life's more fun that way. I don't have a rich old man who keeps me as a pet and lets me dictate to others, like some eastern ruler's pampered eunuch."

Eutychis made a rather crude gesture inferring that he was far from a eunuch as he spat out his rebuttal, "You took your orders rather well, if I recall, maybe you would have been more successful in the East?" He did not wait for Siricus's retort, "Regulus, I'm Eutychis. I'm here on behalf of Proculus."

Eutychis had pale blue eyes and light golden hair. His skin was darkly tanned, giving him an exotic appeal. He wasn't young but still seemed youthful. If Siricus's words weren't merely slander, I could see how the old man, if his tastes ran that way, would have been easily manipulated by his freedman.

After exchanging farewells with Siricus, Tay joined Eutychis in his study. Tay played his part well. A young noble wouldn't visit with another man's underling in his drawing room. Instead, Ajax had been instructed to see Eutychis to the less formal chamber.

Eutychis was offered a little backless chair as Tay sat behind his writing desk. He snapped his fingers at me, and I poured a cup of water and set it down before the new guest.

Eutychis did not play his part, "Water? I smelled wine on Siricus's breath." He let out an ugly laugh and told Tay, "I may be a freed catamite, but I'm still better company than that used-up cheat."

Tay allowed his devious smile to show itself. I doubted that he was immune to Eutychis's exotic appearance, and he typically enjoyed the antics of those who were outspoken. He looked to me and said, "Bring us wine, Demetrius."

I dashed from the study to the drawing room in a mere heartbeat. I poured the wine myself, missing the irony that it seemed inappropriate to me for *Regulus* to serve Proculus's servant.

"I'm here on behalf of Proculus..." Eutychis sniffed the wine that I handed him, and his lips curled at the edges. "What a fine wine to waste on Siricus." He took a delicate sip and savored the flavor. "Very nice, it dates back to Tiberius's reign." Eutychis then took a moment to survey the room as if his opinion of his host had suddenly changed. He gathered his thoughts and restarted, "I'm here on behalf of Proculus, that is to say as much as he understands what's going on. His mind isn't what it once was. He has no idea what business you want of him, or even who you are. I disregarded your request for an interview. It was Balbus who sent word to him that he should rush off to Valens's." He sipped at the wine and then added, "Nicely done. I noticed you across the street and had a premonition of what was to come. You made fools of the lot of them." He paused and then asked, "Is it true what I hear – you are friends with Nero?"

"I'm a friend of *his* friend, Petronius," Tay politely corrected.

The smile on Eutychis's face grew wider, "Ah, yes. Petronius, dear fellow. So it's guilt by association. Or should I say, lack of guilt. You can get away with such behavior relying on the assumption that you are untouchable." He nodded his head shrewdly, "Very nice."

Tay merely smiled and took a sip of his own well-watered wine.

"Well, you want to know what Proculus knows about Actia and Celer's deaths; that's rather easy, he knows nothing. The morning that Celer died, he sent a letter to Proculus. The man no longer reads correspondence. I handle that. I received Celer's strange request. It read: *"When I announce Actia's killer, you must stand behind me, we can have no division. Actius will not stand for the guilty man to go unpunished, regardless of circumstances."* Goat droppings! Proculus is too old to be drawn into some little drama. I went straight away to Celer, while your handsome valet was playing artist in the courtyard, and told him to leave my master alone."

"Was he agreeable?"

"Not at first, but I explained that Proculus couldn't tell the difference between figs and olives. He eats well and enjoys the sound of music, but the simplest question confounds him. Celer resigned himself to the facts and then asked that I might support him.

"I told him that I had no idea what he was babbling about in the first place. Besides, I wanted to be left alone. Men like Frugi and Poppaeus aren't intimidated by a pushy freedman with a nasty streak." He paused to chuckle. "Would you believe Celer offered *me* money to back up his accusation? As if my *endorsements* were for sale. Proculus's funds are already in my hands, I only need wait. Not that I'm in any hurry. When he did have his wits, he was kind to me. The favors he asked of me were no worse than what is expected of other slaves cursed with my appearance. He never passed me around to his friends, or humiliated me.

"When he realized he was becoming forgetful, he freed me and promised me his estate if I would see to his old age and keep him from harm."

"Did Celer indicate why Actia was killed?" Tay asked his forthright guest.

"No, nor did I ask. I assumed it had something to do with the riot and all that business. Perhaps she let out a secret she shouldn't have."

Tay leaned forward and asked, "What secret did she know?"

Eutychis let out his ugly laugh. "Oh, now if I knew that, I would be a little more afraid of Poppaeus and Frugi. I am happily ignorant."

"Does Proculus know?"

Another laugh was barked out by the man. "Oh, Diana, no!" he shook his tanned head "You see, Proculus was already *slipping* when he was made Special Prefect. Valens, Poppaeus, and Frugi wanted someone they could manipulate. Dear Proculus didn't fully understand what was going on. He was pleased when they told him they were bestowing an honor on him. But it all became tedious very quickly. Witnesses were dragged before him, documents were shoved in front of him to sign – they were clutching his hand, dipping his ring in wax, and stamping official reports themselves while he begged to be left alone. I gave them a copy of his signet ring and suggested that the stress he was under was bad for his health. After the executions were done, Marius sent the ring back to us, no note of thanks or concern, and it still had red wax smeared on it. What it really was soaked with was blood. I buried that cursed thing in the grove." Obviously annoyed, Eutychis drank down the rest of his wine.

In once fluid movement, he stood up and said, "There you have it, and I request that you ask me no more questions. Let Proculus be, he can tell you nothing that might shed light on who killed Actia or Celer." His tone had become somewhat hostile. He closed his eyes and took a deep breath, and when he spoke again, the edge was gone from his voice. "Some deaths are better left unexplained. They say Actia was killed in the quake, plausible enough, I would say. And Celer was killed for saying something different – why suffer the same fate, Regulus? Let Actius do what he must, why should you be ruined, or worse?"

Eutychis had asked an excellent question, which Tay had no answer for. Graciously, he replied, "I will take your words to heart."

After his guest departed, Tay removed my father's wig and ran his fingers through his own cropped hair. "Why am I digging at this?"

It was a rhetorical question, and I surmised whatever I had to say might only annoy him. I shrugged and returned the glasses and the jug of wine to the silver tray.

His devious smile slowly appeared, and he commented, "You are a much better servant than I ever was."

I considered slamming the tray back down on to the desk and leaving in a huff, instead I replied arrogantly, "Perhaps if I treat you well, you will free me and leave me all of your money!"

I returned the tray to the kitchen where I found Samson, in the disguise of the Oracle, eating the few delicious dormice that I had removed from their plate and hidden for myself.

"These are fantastic," he whispered as he popped the last one into his mouth. "If another woman asks us today if her husband is cheating, I'm afraid Cornelia is going to go mad. How many riddles can she come up with to give them an answer where she's right either way?"

Samson pulled down the golden veil that hung from his crown, adjusted his fake bosom, and passed through the doorway back into the curtained pergola. The scent of sandalwood wafted into the kitchen, removing any trace of the lingering smell of garlic, and leaving me with a bitter taste in my mouth.

Chapter Eleven
A Tranquil Melody

𝌆𝌆𝌆𝌆𝌆𝌆𝌆

Evening came at last. Samson and Cornelia stripped themselves of their costumes and darted through the garden to the back room of the empty shop just before the first of the sailors arrived.

Staphylus, sitting on his stool near the courtyard's gate, leered at Cornelia until he noticed me. His dumb smile faded, and I realize that I was scowling at the man.

I was distracted when a lumbering figure, covered in grime, burst through the gate and called out, "Gaia, I need a bath!"

Servia appeared, and after a brief inspection, she held her nose and sent Mucia to submerge the fellow in a waiting tub.

One by one, each of our girls led an amorous man to the bedrooms, all except Servia, who kept herself busy waiting for the Admiral to arrive. Tay brooded in his study, leaving Staphylus and the Greeks to chat with men who waited their turn.

After Eutychis left the house, Tay had briefed Actius on the meetings he'd held with a few of our suspects. He had abbreviated the information and removed any negative comments regarding Actia. After meeting with and listening to the first three men who called on Celer, it was hard to believe that one of them had killed the man.

Actius believed that Eros was the prime suspect. My description of his changed behavior and the spill of oil he had tracked, set him apart from the other men. Furthermore, Eros's instant appearance upon Actius's arrival to point a finger at Valens was admittedly suspicious. And what could be more damning than his departure from Pompeii after being confronted by Valens?

Despite Actius's enthusiasm, Tay's manner was subdued. I, too, felt that we were missing something – a clue before us that had yet gone unrecognized. Eros was, yes, the obvious suspect. Yet there was something anticlimactic about supposing his guilt.

Once Admiral Proculus arrived, Tay emerged from his seclusion. With the perfect mask of a delighted actor, he greeted the man. I could not help notice that Tay called him by his first name, Volusius, as if to distance himself from mention of the old Special Prefect.

"How is Actius?" the beast of a man asked, as Servia handed him a large clay cup of sweet wine.

Hobbling out of his room with Corax and Ajax each under an arm supporting his weight, Actius answered for his host, "Tired of lying on his ass."

Tay forced a smile, Servia repressed a frown, and the group moved to the nearby drawing room.

The Admiral was not privy to any details regarding Actius's belief that his mother had been killed. Both Actius and Tay feared the rough man might cause more harm than good. There was no talk of the matter. Instead, the Admiral informed us that the harbor was now able to host a few ships. New piers had been built, and the shallow areas had been dredged to be sure a vessel wouldn't get damaged by sunken debris.

Ursa, who was as fond of the Admiral as she was smitten with Actius, whispered something into Tay's ear, and after an approving nod, she returned with a tray laden with food.

The event was informal; Tay asked Ursa to join us and beckoned me to sit down next to him on the couch. He even sent Corax to invite Cornelia and Samson to join the group.

The couches that had been removed to make the drawing room's appearance more impressive were returned to accommodate the odd household.

My heart skipped a beat when Cornelia entered the room, trailing behind Samson. Always smiling, the dark-skinned man seemed giddy as he was introduced to Actius.

Cornelia's behavior was unnaturally demure. Sinking onto a couch beside her companion, she greeted everyone en masse as if we were all friends. Her voice was soft and lyrical.

While Sosia, Lucia, Delia, and Gaia entertained the men who wandered into the courtyard, we ate and listened to Proculus and Actius tell far-fetched but highly amusing stories.

I worked hard to keep from glancing in Cornelia's direction unless she spoke or laughed at one of the two men dominating the conversation. I could not, however, ignore the glances from Actius toward the beautiful woman.

Tay drank more than was his custom. I was pleased to see him relaxed, and a little embarrassed by how often I noticed Proculus and Actius glance toward us. Their curious looks caused me to notice Tay's hand draped around my shoulder or brushing against my thigh.

Did they assume that I performed the role of Eutychis in our household? I didn't care; let them think what they wanted about poor, mute Demetrius. Like Eutychis, I was treated well, and despite the absurdity of our role reversal, I had nothing to gain by fighting character.

As the night progressed, even Servia seemed to be enjoying herself. She fed the Admiral and whispered in his ear from time to time. She couldn't help herself from occasionally gazing at her master's mysterious tenants. Of course, the Admiral's eyes fell on Cornelia quite often as well.

Geb sat at my feet, and I reluctantly shared the garlic-encrusted dormice with him, along with some mullet and a bit of honey cake. His tail swung back and forth until he tired and curled up into a large, furry ball.

Samson and Cornelia were masterful at making conversation that revealed nothing about them. They asked questions and made interesting observations on the answers they were told. No doubt memorizing any valuable snippet of information that they might use while disguised as the Oracle and her acolyte.

Late in the evening, the little dark-haired advocate, Albius Varro, stumbled into the drawing room and asked, "Why wasn't I invited?"

Tay gestured for him to find a seat, and the little man eagerly nestled himself beside Cornelia. Obviously inebriated, Albius commented, "I've seen you before?"

Actius's eyes sparkled, and he redirected the man's comment, "We all have, she's the beautiful woman we dream of when we fall asleep."

Albius swung his heavy head toward Actius. "You know you snore?"

Actius shook his head. "That's Proculus, not me!" he said, then tilted his head to one side and began heaving his chest and imitating the big man's breathing. In between the deep exhales, he mumbled, "Raise the sails, drop the anchor." And to everyone's applause, he grumbled, "Admiral overboard!"

Proculus bellowed a great laugh and then wagged a thick finger at his old comrade's nephew.

Actius turned his attention back to Varro, "You are here nearly every night, why don't you buy Sosia from Regulus?"

Varro, helping himself to a cup of wine, shook his head. "No, I think not. I had a mistress and a wife, both robbed me blind." Several laughs made the man smile. He held up his hand in protest while he drained the cup and went on to say, "My wife spent half her dowry on a pearl necklace and then claimed to lose it – when we divorced, I had to pay that money back to her father. After she remarried, my sister was at a dinner party with her and saw her wearing the necklace!"

"And your mistress?" Proculus asked.

"She wanted a gift each time I visited her; after a few months, she told me we had to stop seeing each other." He paused and looked about the group with his glassy eyes. "She told me she sold every ring, necklace, and the rest that I had given her, and it all amounted enough for a respectable dowry – she was getting married!" He laughed more than the rest of the group, spilling his drink down the front of his tunic.

I noticed Mucia, who sat in the shadows of the atrium watching us, swing her head toward the vestibule. She hopped up from the bench and went to the door. After only a moment, she slipped into the room and handed her master a wax tablet.

Although curious, no one commented. All eyes fell back to Actius as he began telling a story about a stage that he accidentally caught on fire during a performance.

I watched Tay's eyes move over the words and felt his body grow rigid. He turned the tablet over and gently placed it on the floor underneath the couch we shared before reaching for his cup of wine. Tay smiled on and looked toward his guest Actius, but I could tell he didn't hear a word the man said.

Ursa's delicacies were finished off, several empty amphorae of wine leaned against the tables. The Admiral and Actius's stories were becoming disjointed and complicated. Servia, playing the part of the intoxicated hostess, realized the guests were growing tired and decided to add life to the evening. She called for Mucia, in the atrium. The little creature obliged and was then told, "Sing for us."

The group fell silent, and all eyes, dull as they were, focused on Mucia. Her cheeks flushed; she closed her eyes, and took a deep breath. She began to sing, hardly above a whisper, but her voice grew louder and slowly more powerful.

I was amazed by the beauty of her singing. It was unexpected, and I felt an odd sense of guilt for paying so little attention to her. She blossomed from an oddity into a living being with feelings, as her voice penetrated my soul.

I had never heard the song she sang, but it spoke of Pluto and his desire for Persephone to love him as he loved her. I recall that the words were haunting. Sadly, I am unable to recite a single passage.

Mucia's voice returned to a whisper as she described Persephone's submission to Pluto, and her own desire to be loved in return.

While we all clapped our hands, my eyes fell onto Cornelia. She hesitated, but bestowed upon me a brief smile.

Tay asked for another song, and she sang us a local tune with humorous lyrics. The gist of the story poked fun at the obsession with opulent private bath suites.

After another round of applause, she treated us to one more melody, involving young lovers. I could not help but notice Ajax leaning against a peristyle column mouthing the same words as Corax watched him. I rolled my eyes at myself for ever thinking that they were brothers.

Relaxed and half drunk, the Admiral was on the verge of falling asleep. Servia prodded him from the couch, signaling that the evening had come to an end.

Ajax and Corax helped Actius back to his room with much difficulty, thanks to the wine. Sosia had appeared, free from the paying guests as Mucia had sung to us. She collected the drunken advocate and led him to her room as Servia pulled a drunken Proculus to her own little cell. Ursa and Mucia went on to cleared the mess around us and disappeared.

Cornelia stifled a yawn and said, "I haven't stayed awake this late in years."

Samson nodded while he stretched his long arms.

Tay stared off into the middle distance, until Cornelia said in a very low tone of voice, "Ursa said you had a number of guests today. Did you find out anything more about Actia?"

Tay's eyes focused and fell onto the woman, "Hmm...no, or at least nothing helpful. I'm more confused now than before."

"I was thinking I could plant some seeds. I know that a woman who comes to see the Oracle fairly often is on friendly terms with Valens's wife. Perhaps–"

Tay raised a hand, and attempting to smile, he said, "I don't want to put you in harm's way." He could see that she was about to argue, "I'm beginning to regret my own efforts in the matter."

Cornelia's brow arched, but she only nodded. I could tell that Tay's statement intrigued her. "Thank you for the invitation, a rather odd gathering, but very enjoyable."

The last of our guests got to their feet and started toward the garden. Cornelia paused to look over her shoulder, "The Oracle misses you, Marcellus."

Before I could react, she slipped into the shadows.

The two groggy Greeks returned to the drawing room ready to replace the scavenged furniture to wherever it belonged. Tay waved at the items and said, "Leave it till morning, put out the lamps and get some sleep."

Tay went off to the courtyard to check on Staphylus, and no doubt collect the coins the man had been given throughout the evening. I reached for the wax tablet that had been delivered and read the brief message.

Friend Regulus, please come to my son's house at the third hour of tomorrow morning.
We have urgent business to address.
Valens

I woke with a terrible headache and the sounds of Geb's rumbling belly. The mutt stretched and lay his head back down on the bed while I contemplated rising. There was just enough pressure on my bladder to motivate me out from under the warm blanket.

Once relieved, I looked about the foot of my bed, surprised that Tay's choice of clothing hadn't been laid out for me. I opened a shuttered window to let what little light there was in and looked through my growing collection of tunics before I found a blue-green garment that reminded me of the sea midway from Alexandria to Italy. I didn't bother with any adornment and picked out the simplest of my sandals.

Geb lifted his head from the bed as I neared the door, but with a belly still full from rich food, he hesitated before leaping down and following me on our morning routine.

Ursa frowned as I entered her domain, and remarked, "You're up early." I nodded and went for some bread and honey. She reached her short, stubby arms out to pat the dog's head and said, "Baby likes Mommy's cooking." She handed Geb a stale pastry and mumbled that the stench of garlic was everywhere.

I disagreed. All that I could smell was sandalwood seeping into the house from the nearby door.

After making my morning prayers and leaving a humble offering on the household shrine, I snatched a cloak from the little sitting room and slipped out through the unattended front door.

As the gods would have it, Julia was being escorted across the street by four stout men.

"Demetrius, I was wondering where you have been." I smiled to her and then she asked, "Is it true what I have heard? Actius Anicetus is Regulus's guest?"

I replied with an unhappy nod, and she beamed. "Well, Regulus owes me an invitation."

I deliberately stood some distance from Julia after dropping a coin on the offering table. When the curtain concealing the Oracle pulled open, both the star of the show and the assistant joined us. The white veil concealing Cornelia's lovely face obscured her reaction to my presence, if she did react.

We devotees, growing in number now that we had entered the city, stood in awe of the Oracle, clad in a silver gown, with a dark blue, beaded wig. A tall silver diadem, affixed to the wig, sparkled in the pink morning sunlight.

Hymns were sung, and the prayers were chanted. The Oracle blessed each of us, calling upon Nephthys to watch over our day. With the morning rites concluded, the assembly slowly dispersed toward the ruined vineyard's gate.

Julia crossed the distance between us. I feared a flirtatious invitation to walk the woman home, while I hoped to make amends with Cornelia. Instead, she pointed a jeweled finger toward our house and said, "I expect an invitation to meet Actius, soon." There was just a hint of a suggestive smile and then she joined her escorts.

I walked back to the offering table and scattered the coins around in an attempt to gain Cornelia's attention. Instead, the curtain hanging from the front of the pergola rustled, and Samson poked his veiled head through. "Is everyone gone?" he asked before yawning.

I whispered out of habit, "Yes."

"Good, we are going back to sleep – such a late night." With that said, he let the curtain fall.

I wanted Cornelia to see that I hadn't slipped away with Julia. More so, I wanted to talk to her. I had nothing to say, but that wouldn't stop me from babbling something that might provoke an insult or a compliment.

I decided to sprint around the house, to the alley, and enter through the courtyard. If I ran fast enough, Cornelia would find me in her path. If I only received a pleased glance, or even the trace of a smile, I would be contented.

Dust flew behind me as I took off. I passed the gate, nearly falling off the sidewalk. I was picking up speed when a familiar voice called out, "You can't run fast enough to escape the angry spirits of Carthage!"

I skidded to a stop and raised my finger to my mouth.

"Ssh yourself, you little fool," Gavia snapped. "What, by Hades, are you doing out running around like a madman?"

Workmen were already making their way down the street, so I couldn't speak. I shrugged and pointed to the house.

Gavia ignored my poor pantomime and asked, "Were you tramping around that pest-ridden vineyard praying to Isis's sister? All that gibberish and screeching wakes me."

My chance to meet Cornelia had passed, so when Gavia pointed at the open door of her shop, I entered. "There, now you can talk. Tell me, what did you think of the men who took my father's office?" There was a nasty bite to her voice.

"Siricus struck me as the kind of man who would sell secondhand silver and claim that the dents and tarnish made it more valuable. Balbus is afraid of his own shadow. They were put in place to do what they were told. Neither benefited from their appointments."

"Hercules! They did too! Do you know what a campaign costs, do you know how much you spend when you are in office? Festivals, games, shows, public feasts! They didn't pay for any of that. They were given gifts from every sycophant in town. Marius and Pansa paid them off, and then once those two bastards were done with the fools, they found themselves back on your friend Valens's list of dependents!" Spittle leaped from the woman's mouth as she raged on at me.

I shrugged, she knew more than I.

"You watch out for Eutychis too, he's just pretty enough to take your place." She snapped her fingers, and her raven flew from her worktable to her shoulder. "Old Proculus didn't even know what was going on, what a travesty." She made a terrible sound with her throat and then spat on the floor. "I curse them all!"

The raven lurched on Gavia's shoulder due to her violent movement. She reached a hand up and stroked the bird's back to calm the creature.

Timidly, I asked her, "*Did* you curse them?"

"Every last one of them!" she beamed.

"Then perhaps the gods finally heard you and brought about the quake?"

The ugly smile faded from her face. Under the dirty eye patch and the stains on her pale skin, I saw a frightened young woman stare back at me.

"Don't say things like that, you fool." Gavia's lips had moved, but I didn't recognize the timid voice that spoke the concerned words.

Surprised that I had brought about such a reaction, I began to tell her, "I wouldn't say it to anyone else– "

"Something like that could get around; I've been ruined before–"

"I would never–"

"I see why Regulus keeps you silent, that mouth of yours is dangerous, best that you just keep it closed."

I hadn't meant to frighten or upset the woman. I hadn't thought that I was capable of doing either.

Gavia looked about her cluttered shop, and then reached for a few items. She slowly regained herself and mixed up a pot of some sort of liquid. "Here," she snapped. "That bastard Actius should be needing more by now."

Her hand trembled slightly as she handed me the brew. I tried to lighten the moment by joking, "You left out an ingredient."

She squinted with her single eye and replied, "My spit is too good for that man."

Gavia was already upset, so I decided to toss the dice and ask once more my accusatory question. "It's been suggested that someone with a vengeance to settle against Actia killed her, hoping that the quake would be blamed for her death. Whoever killed her, murdered Celer because he suspected the truth." I did my best impersonation of Tay, raising my brow as if to say more.

She nodded and tapped a finger to her chin, "I also heard it said that you struck your father over the head during a fight and fled Rome. People hear lots of things, don't they? You just never know how true they are, Marcellus."

She had silenced me. With the little pot of pain medicine in my shaking hands, I stumbled back out onto the street.

Sick to my stomach, I entered the house to find Tay's growing collection of clients waiting about the atrium.

Paying little attention to my steps, I entered Tay's study as he gave orders to a rather large young man.

"Remind Aelge that she missed her first payment. If I have to, I'll send someone down there to handle her money for her." Tay glanced at me while he spoke, and realized that something was wrong. "That's all. Stay at her shop, do what you can to be helpful to her."

The big man bowed his head and started to leave, and Tay called out, "Take this, stop at Paquius's bakery and buy bread for your family, tell Onesinus that I sent you."

Tay waited until his client left the room before asking me, "You look as white as bones. What happened?"

In the lowest whisper I could manage, I said, "Gavia, she knows who I am, and what I'm accused of."

Tay's eyes narrowed, and he gave a little shrug. "That doesn't surprise me, nasty little witch."

I was both disappointed and relieved that Tay seemed unmoved by my shocking news. "What are we going to do? How far can she be trusted?"

Tay waved me to him and took the tonic from my hand. "Did she just make this for Actius?"

"Yes."

He sniffed the liquid, his nostrils flared, and he pulled it away from his face. "Foul stuff. Valens was right, you know. We could solve two problems at once. The addition of a little poison would remove Actius, and this whole mystery would be forgotten. Accuse Gavia, and that would be the end of her…"

The horrified look on my face caused Tay to fall silent, and I asked, "You can't be serious?"

Tay's devious smile and arched brow disagreed with his response, "Of course not." He handed me the little pot of medicine and said, "Forget about Gavia, she has nothing to gain by exposing us. I will deal with her when the time comes. Let's concern ourselves with one problem at a time."

His words still weighed with me, and somewhat distracted, I offered, "Speaking of problems, Julia wishes that you invite her here to meet Actius."

Tay managed a little laughed. "Now, tell me, my friend, which one is the problem? Actius or Julia?"

I stuttered, unsure.

He gave me a slap on the back, "Go give that stuff to Actius." He pointed to my sandals, and remarked, "I didn't know you were leaving the house so early. I went to set out your clothes and you were gone. Change into the dark brown sandals and put your gold arm bands on." He sighed and said reluctantly, "We must go on and suffer Valens's wrath."

Chapter Twelve
Basic Politics

🁢🁢🁢🁢🁢🁢🁢🁢

Both Tay and I were surprised and concerned as we neared Valens's son's home. Body guards, slaves, and empty litters crowed the street outside of the house.

Heads turned as *Regulus* approached. A few men who recognized him gave him respectful greetings. Tay returned the salutations and quickened his step to the open door.

Inside the vestibule, we were acknowledged by the familiar doorman. He didn't respond so kindly to Tay's greeting. He wasn't daring enough to be rude, yet there was still a bit of huff in his tone.

The man snapped his fingers at an underling and pointed at me. While Tay was led in one direction, I was taken to the back of the house where the other valets and personal attendants loitered.

Most of the well-placed servants knew each other, just as Jucundus had told us. I received a few curious glances, and heard someone whisper, *"Demetrius, the mute."*

I recognized one man, who I gathered was the valet of Pansa the Elder. The servant was a large fellow, with an imposing build. He crossed the space and said, "Help yourself to some of the sweet cakes, Praestina makes the best."

The sole female in the room smiled and agreeably suggested, "Try one, and tell me if this man's a liar."

"He can't talk. Well, he can write, I guess." Pansa's man pointed at the wax tablet dangling from my neck.

I bit into the honey cake, and as it melted in my mouth, my eyes rolled up. "He speaks well enough," Praestina remarked, pleased by my reaction.

Two raised voices caught my attention as Praestina handed me another sweet cake. Pansa's valet glanced toward two men standing aloof from the others. They were arguing with each other. "Don't mind the *Julias*," he told me. "They always bicker."

The two short, stout men ceased their quarreling and glared at us. My new friend nudged my elbow and asked them, "What's the matter, ladies, did one of you drop a pearl earring at dinner last night? Stop fretting, it will turn up."

"Libanus, mind your tongue!" snapped one of the sour-faced men.

The other pointed at me. "You're the mute? Regulus's man?"

As I nodded, the two unpleasant fellows looked to each other and smiled. The sight wasn't pleasant. They reminded me of two feral beasts teaming up against a weaker creature.

"Come here, we want to talk to you!"

I looked to Pansa's servant for support, and he replied on my behalf, "The poor fellow can't *talk*, you silly ladies!"

Both men pointed at the same time towards my wax tablet, and, in unison, they barked, "He can write!" Their four hands flailed at me to join them in the corner of the kitchen.

Libanus stayed by my side as I cautiously neared the men. They alternated back and forth between frowning at Libanus and smiling at me as if I were a half-wit.

"I am Marcus Julius Phillipus Felix, steward to Julius Phillipus. This is my younger brother, Rufus. I understand that–"

Rufus nudged his older brother aside and interrupted, "I am Rufus Julius Polybius Felix, steward of Julius Polybius."

The elder brother elbowed Rufus and stepped closer to me. "Your master, Regulus, he's friends with Petronius, I understand?" he pointed at me and nodded his head. I returned the nod. The two brothers smiled to each other, and I was asked, "He is friends with...*The Golden One?*"

I knew how Tay would want me to respond, so I looked away from them, pressed my lips together, and shrugged, only to look back with a coy smile.

The two brothers beamed with excitement. "And is it true that the actor Actius Anicetus is a guest in your master's home?"

I gave a simple nod to confirm the question. The brothers glanced at one another before Marcus asked, "Regulus is friendly with Admiral Proculus, too, is he not?"

I gave them the response they wanted, and they both gave me a condescending smile. Rufus patted my wax tablet, and said, "There now, you didn't even need that. Go have yourself another honey cake."

Dismissed, I was pleased to take the portly man's suggestion, however, Libanus blocked my way. "And what of this, what does this all mean to you?"

The elder brother put his hands on his wide waist and retorted, "If Pansa doesn't inform you of what's planned to happen, it is not my place to do so either."

Libanus threw his shoulders back and took a step closer to the brothers. Rufus reacted with a little squeal and blurted out, "The council wants Regulus to travel to Rome with Polybius to petition the Emperor for aid."

Jucundus had been correct; not only did the elite's servants all know each other, they also knew everything that was going on within the city.

Libanus steered me away from the sniveling brothers and sought out an older man leaning against the work table. "Ocella, what's this about Polybius leading the delegation? I thought it was between Pansa and Maius?"

The grey-haired man answered, "The competition is at an end, neither of our masters won the honor. Polybius's father was old Tiberius's freedman; they want to remind Nero that Pompeii is nothing but loyal servants to the imperial family."

I let out a bemused sigh, and both men looked toward me. "Well, what do you have to say?" Libanus asked.

I opened my little wax tablet and carved out a few words. Libanus took the tablet and read it aloud for the benefit of Ocella. "Not a wise choice. Nero isn't fond of imperial freedmen. He ridiculed his stepfather's dependence on them."

Both men eyed me cautiously, realizing that either I wasn't the halfwit they had thought me to be, or that *Regulus* knew Nero better than they had supposed.

A page came running into the kitchen calling out, "The meeting is breaking up!"

Dumbly, I watched the other attendants scramble toward the hallway. I was about to follow when I noticed Libanus plant a firm kiss on the cook, Praestina, and tell her, "Sweeter than your honey cakes."

Libanus led me in the hall and said, "You're new to town, and things are far from normal, but if you need anything, I'll be happy to help you out."

As we entered the vestibule, he gave me a friendly warning and piece of advice, "Never trust the *Julias,* and flirt with every cook, maiden, or water girl you can bear to look at." Libanus caught sight of his master strolling towards us and quickened his step to join the man.

Near the impluvium was Tay, ensnared in the grip of two men bearing a striking resemblance to Marcus and Rufus.

Tay looked very wary of the two chubby fellows, each with a hand on his back as he tried to slip out from under them. As I neared, he saw me, and his brows arched while his eyes darted comically back and forth between the men.

The heftier of the two spoke with a charmingly fake tone of voice. "We must meet with Actius as soon as possible. Send word as soon as you can. Think nothing of his injury. He shall be carried by litter the entire Appian Way. My best men shall attend to him; what luxury is in store for him."

"And for you!" the other brother added.

Tay wiggled out from their clutches as he responded, "Yes, I'm sure. Well, I will send word to you as soon as I have spoken to Actius."

"Yes, we will be waiting," the smaller brother replied. "But we must not wait long. Our city is depending on us."

Tay forced a pained smile and pointed with his eyes toward the grand vestibule. I took his hint and started for the front door. My steps paused when I heard a voice call for my companion, "Regulus, I was hoping to have a word with you."

The grey-haired Ocella walked behind the hawkish man who had signaled to Tay. My companion did not respond, he only raised a brow at the wealthy man.

"What an honor, Regulus, I'm so pleased for you." The man's words dripped with insincerity. "And what a friend this city has in you. As surely as the sun rises, the gods have blessed us with your timely arrival."

Tay gave a polite bow of the head before responding, "Maius, the honor is mine, but surely you exaggerate."

Maius spoke in the low, throaty manner of a man suffering from a head cold. "Do I?" he asked, mirroring Tay's own raised brow. "Now, before you leave the city, do come and see me."

"Regulus," called Valens, breaking away from the two men he had been speaking with. His interruption appeared painfully deliberate as he fumbled for something to say, "Perhaps I should send one of my men back with you, so that once you've conveyed our request to Actius, he can return at once with the response."

Maius looked his host up and down and sneered before make a few departing remarks. Afterward, Tay thanked Valens for the offer of a messenger and assured him that he had ample staff.

During the entire exchange, I could not but help but notice that both the elder Pansa and his son stood with a young man I had not yet seen, but still recognized. The youthful fellow, surely no more than five years my senior, bore an uncanny resemblance to Valens. I had no doubt that he was the man's son, and the owner of the palatial residence. Like any other slave, I went unnoticed by Satrius as I watched him glare curiously at my companion.

Outside of the house, Tay fled from the dispersing group as quickly as he could. We darted down the first side street just to avoid falling into the wake of one of the many entourages. With some difficulty, I scratched out a few words into my tablet as we speedily walked along an uneven, stone sidewalk.

The message read: *I trust you have a brilliant plan to keep from going to Rome?*

Tay grabbed the tablet, read it, and then thrust it back to me. "Not yet," he mumbled.

"He isn't awake," Ursa said fretfully as Tay neared Actius's bedroom door. The look he shot her silenced any further comment. Without a knock, he stepped in, leaving me to close the door behind us.

"Actius."

The man shifted under his blanket but didn't respond.

"Actius, wake up," Tay snapped.

"Too early...too much wine..."

Tay ripped the blanket from him and demanded, "Wake up, it's late enough."

Actius glared at Tay before rubbing his eyes, "I'm awake. What's the matter?"

"Are you sure that you are awake?" Tay paused before he told Actius, "The town council has decided on whom to send in its delegation to beg Nero for aid. *You!*"

If the actor hadn't been fully awake, Tay's comment remedied that.

"Julius Phillipus and a handful of sycophants will be headed off to Rome. I have been asked to attend, and the good elected officials beg that you will lend your voice."

Actius rubbed his head and stuck out his tongue before yawning. "Why me?"

"Officially, to bear witness to Pompeii's need; obviously to get both of us out of town. When we get back, no doubt a scapegoat will be waiting, blamed for Actia and Celer's murder."

"That's ridiculous…"

Tay shook his head, "No, that's politics."

"You have to get out of this." I might have been whispering, but my words were clearly said as a demand.

"Yes, I realize that!" Tay snapped as he sat behind his writing table with his head held in his hands. "I should have sent Actius on his way after that damned woman attacked him."

"When do they plan on leaving?"

"Five days from the Kalends." Tay's voice sounded unusually resigned.

I counted the days and blurted out, "That's four days from now!"

Tay looked up at me. "Yes! Thank you, I am aware of that!" Irritation brought back a bit of his normal bravado.

I looked toward the strong box and pointed, "How much coin do we have? We could leave, disappear as mysteriously as we came."

Regardless of how preposterous our situation had become, Tay had no desire to abandon *Octavius Regulus* and his possessions. "Be sensible. Just let me think."

"Make your excuses. Let them take Actius—let Valens find a scapegoat—what does it matter to us who killed Actia and Celer?"

"Enough!" Tay pointed toward the door, "Leave me be, I need to think."

Always the well-bred aristocrat, I did as my servant told me. Perhaps his solitary brooding would lead him to reason.

I was headed down the peristyle when I heard a knock at the door. I speculated that Julius Phillipus had already sent a slave to see if Actius had agreed to join the delegation.

I retraced my steps toward the atrium as Ajax opened the door. I recognized the silhouette as he spoke in a gentle voice to the Greek, "I'm Fannius, from the house of Anicetus. I came to check on Actius."

Ajax pointed toward a bench in the atrium. "Please wait."

Fannius spotted me and nodded his head in recognition. I waved Ajax away from the entrance to the study and gave him a maniacal frown, indicating what was in store if he disturbed his master. I then waved for Fannius to follow me and led him down the peristyle to Actius's borrowed room.

"What?" Actius called out in response to my knock.

I opened the door and slipped back so that Fannius could enter the little cell.

Actius's brow drew together, and his head tilted to one side. "Fannius, is something the matter?"

The big man looked over the actor and replied, "No. I just came to check on you. I thought you would have returned by now." He pointed at the man's leg. "Are you healing?"

"Slowly," Actius responded cautiously.

"Can I send anything that you need?" I heard true concern in the man's voice.

"No, I'm being taken care of." Actius's tone was somewhat defensive.

Fannius looked over his shoulder at me, clearly wishing I would leave. I was about to take the hint when Actius remarked, "The *artist* has been good company. He can't talk, but he is entertaining all the same."

Fannius gave me the polite smile of someone who had just heard a false compliment but felt obliged to agree. He turned back to Actius and lowered his tone, "Xeus told me that the woman who lives in a shop connected with this house had a grudge against your mother."

Jovially, Actius rebutted the statement, "Oh, no, we've made fast friends of each other."

Fannius cocked his head and sighed. The man wasn't prone to lying. "Good. That's good to hear," he replied stiffly and took a deep breath. Realizing that his visit had not been appreciated, Fannius let out a deep exhalation and concluded by saying, "If there is anything that you need, please let me know."

Actius gave the big man his actor's smile of insincere gratitude and told him, "I'll do just that."

I was reaching to open the door when Actius made one last comment, "Fannius, I suppose Celer's remains should be dealt with."

Fannius hesitated before he replied, "Valens had the undertaker burn the body this morning. I hadn't realized he'd done so without making you aware."

"Was there a funeral?" Actuis inquired, his voice full of curiosity.

Fannius hesitated once more. "A small one, attended by the household."

"And you?" Actuis asked the question skeptically, though he seemed to know the answer.

"No." Fannius glanced at me, my presence unwelcome.

"Thank you for checking on me," Actius said, politely ending the visit.

Silently, I escorted Fannius to the door. He stopped and told me, "Please, give your master my thanks for taking care of Anicetus. If there is anything needed for him, please send word." With obvious disappointment, the man went on his way.

When I returned to Actius's room, Ursa was setting a tray of food on a little table for the guest. When she noticed me eyeing the honey-coated dates, she warned me, "You had your morning meal, this if for Actius!" After frowning at me, she smiled at the actor.

I shut the door with a bit of force after the plump cook departed. Somewhat bravely, and unconcerned with pretense, I grabbed a date and popped it into my mouth.

"You treated him as if he stole your signet ring and gave it back to you as a Saturnalia gift," I commented as I helped myself to another date.

"He's so familiar – I think I remember him from my childhood?"

My brow shot up like Tay's. "He was a servant of Agrippina's." And then I corrected myself, "No, one of Lollia Paullina's?"

Actius grabbed for the same date that I was reaching for, and replied, "Yes – I think?" After eating the date he reached for the pot of tonic and took a sip with a grimace. "I'm going to need a lot more of this if I'm headed to Rome."

"You are going?"

"What choice do I have?" He shrugged. "If I refuse the request, it would tarnish my reputation. I would be seen as turning my back on the city my mother lived in. Besides, why shouldn't I?"

"What about your mother's killer?"

Actius looked into my eyes and said, "If I leave for a while, someone will let their guard down." His tone was rather sinister.

After I exited Actius's room, I heard voices from the atrium. Curious, I walked down the peristyle in time to see Ajax entering the study with a rolled scroll.

Corax caught sight of me and whispered "Another summons."

Once Tay regained his temper, for the second time that day, we set out to cross the city. Maius lived on the west side of town toward the bay, only a few insulas away from Satrius's magnificent home.

When we arrived at our destination, we found the place shrouded in scaffolding. Dust-covered men swarmed every surface. I could not tell if they were dismantling or rebuilding. Assuring us that it was safe to enter, a young slave standing on the uneven sidewalk waved us to the entrance.

"The master is expecting you, welcome, welcome. Mind your step."

The residence was close in scale to Satrius Valens's home. Standing at the entrance, I could see that the house was a perfect example of architecture. Past the vestibule was a spacious atrium, then the opened drawing room looking on to a sizable courtyard, past this was another sitting room that appeared to overlook a second garden.

We were ushered into the grand home, where the interior echoed with sounds of hammering, chiseling, and the rough voices of craftsmen. Several of these men recognized my companion and greeted him. A few added friendly inquiries about the girls of their preference.

We were led through the bare atrium, a dismantled drawing room, and into a large peristyle and then left to wait under a portico facing an ornate garden.

The peristyle consisted of sixteen beautiful Ionic columns supporting the portico. Painted yellow on the lower portion and then white above, they stood out brightly from evergreens planted systematically about the garden.

Slaves appeared with two chairs and a little table. Moments later, another servant arrived with a tray of food and drink. With their tasks complete, we were once again left alone.

Maius kept Tay waiting just long enough to remind his guest that the host was a man of significance, without stretching out the period so long that an insult might be perceived.

Trailed by his freedman, Ocella, Maius emerged under the portico. The lean man raised his hands and sighed, "May Jove bless this silence." The echo of construction still seeped into the lush, green space, but compared to the rest of the house, it was relatively peaceful.

"Regulus, thank you for accepting my invitation." Maius waved to a chair as he sat in the other.

Playing my part as the silent valet, I passed from notice as Tay reclined in the finely-carved wooden chair that had been provided.

Maius offered his guest a drink. Ocella poured each man a cup and served them while Maius proceeded to his point. I had to strain to hear his low, guttural voice over the sounds emanating from the house. Had he not spoke so slowly, it would have been a challenge to understand him. However, the man did, in fact, mean to be clearly understood.

"I am sure that Petronius will be pleased to see you upon your arrival in Rome. I take it that he is your patron?" Maius lifted his delicate, silver cup to his hawkish face, but did not take so much as a sip of the drink.

Tay gave a little shrug. "I consider him a friend, not a patron."

Maius gave a well-rehearsed grunt that might have passed for a chuckle. He seemed to be the embodiment of *the villain* from every farce I had ever seen at the theater.

"A good friend indeed then, I understand that only a few days after the quake, a weighted chest was delivered to you. I believe the men bearing the gift were here in the service of Petronius. As I heard it, they were collecting the remains of some runaway criminal. Perhaps I am wrong, but a heavy chest is often filled with coin?" Maius's rasping voice was positively irritating.

"My friend was kind enough to arrange for my own assets to be turned to coin and delivered. Under the circumstances, and being new to the city, I doubted that I could lay my hands on the sum with merely a promissory note to the local treasury." Tay did his best to sound unperturbed by his host's line of questioning.

Maius drew out the single word, "Yes," while he contemplated his next choice of words. "It seems to me that you are no longer *passing through* our city, you might be here to stay now?"

"I believe that I am. I have no desire or need to return to Alexandria at this point."

"I am pleased to hear this. And in light of your decision to stay, I must offer you my hope to be of service to you."

Tay had kept a friendly air about him, however, his brow began to rise. "Of service?"

"Well, Regulus, if Petronius is not your patron, then perhaps..."

Tay smiled and shook his head. "How very kind, but I'm not in need of a patron."

Maius's sharp features formed the most frightening grin that I had ever seen. Drawing his words out, he responded,

"Come now, a young man such as yourself, allied with me, you would be well-protected."

Tay appeared puzzled and asked, "Protected? Am I in danger now?"

Maius was straining to continue the play-acting. "You've been reaching far into the wasp's nest, so I hear. Men like Poppaea and Valens are sure to react." The old man leaned toward his guest. "I don't know their secret. I don't know what went on that drove the two to turn on each other. You seem to be on the verge of discovery. Siricus, Balbus, Eutychis, not much help to you, were they? No. But you are a cunning one, you'll sort this out." Maius sat back and nodded his head, "And when you do, I want to know their secret."

"I see," Tay said from behind his cup of wine. "And for this information, you would become my patron?"

The nasty grin returned to Maius's face. "Oh, yes."

Tay set his cup down on the little table, and losing the pleasant air in his voice, he replied, "It's a shame I'm have no need for one then."

Maius's grin ever so easily turned into a scowl. "Don't you? Not only to protect you from the trouble you are stirring up for yourself, but to provide for your own coffers. Just how heavy was that box brought to you? How quickly will those coins be gone, and where will you be getting more? As I've heard, your father has crossed the river of life, and you have no ties to his assets." Maius pointed a talon-like finger at his prey, and spoke with a quickened pace, "You have that caterpillar-ridden vineyard, nothing more than dry ground now, a few tenants, and a handful of whores. Oh, and I hear you've tried your hand at being a small-time money lender; mostly women and old men in need. Well, son, it takes a mean streak to make money in that market. Where will you be when the sailors move on and the craftsmen are gone? What will those used-up women be worth to you then, when your favors and generosity catches up to you? When you no longer have the funds to insure that the politicians keep smiling at you, what will you do? You need a man like me watching out for you, someone who has the means to keep you from ending up like your old friend Popidius."

"I see..." Tay replied, quizzically.

Maius relaxed the muscles in his face and attempted to slow his speech, "Now, I mean no offense, I'm just stating my thoughts. I'm making a sincere offer, and all I ask for is loyalty."

Tay flashed a devious smile and nodded thoughtfully, his tone was very even when he responded, "Yes, I do see. I understand." His brow lowered and he asked, "But what if I am unable to discover the truth to this secret?"

Maius let out a long exhale. "My offer never depended on such a condition," the man lied.

Tay nodded again and took a long drink from his cup. He looked at Maius very thoughtfully, and suggested, "Perhaps you can help towards the resolution we both seek. A man in your position must know much more about the riot and the aftermath than what I've so far been privy to?"

Maius's lips turned up, slightly. He wasn't so sure he wanted to trust his guest, but on the other hand, if his knowledge could prove helpful, he wasn't about to stifle the pursuit. After a lengthy hesitation, he said, "We all know there was some sort of fight, and it fueled the tempers in the air. Violence broke out inside the arena, and spilled out around the grounds." He paused to choose his words before continuing, "When the fighting had stopped, Valens and the old man who adopted him had Actia in their possession. Both Frugi and Poppaeus were holed up with them. The next day, Livineius Regulus and Gavianus got pulled in. Regulus left that very night for Sicily, happy to take his fair share of guilt, and then some, so long as a ship with some gold in it wasn't far behind. Gavianus went home and opened a vein; regardless of what really happened, he was done for. His son and son-in-law were killed trying to stop the riot, and he just wasn't a strong enough man to see past the moment." Once more he paused to reflect on the events. "Valens, Poppaeus and Frugi agreed to appoint Balbus and Siricus as replacement duumvirs. Puppets, that's all they were. Next, Valens and a little delegation headed to Rome to defend the town from the Nucerians' accusations. As I heard it, Actia bore witness that she saw one of the Nucerians shove a Pompeian as they both were coming up the tunnel from their seats. They started fighting, and the Pompeians ganged up on the man. His own friends joined the fight, but in the scuffle, he got killed. Then things got out of hand...and so the tale goes."

"And?" Tay simply asked.

"More people were questioned, the Senate sent officials to seek out more witnesses..."

"After they had already been executed for participating in the riot?"

"*Yes*, indeed. So a decree is made, the city is heavily fined." Maius's ugly grin reappeared. "And then the worst, Nero bans the city from hosting gladiatorial events for ten years."

"And the elder Valens, who owned a troupe of fighters, wasn't so pleased?"

"He got so mad and worked up, he became sick. He claimed that he was going to go to Nero himself and have the ban overturned. He died the next day."

Tay couldn't help but ask, "And was his death at all suspicious?"

Maius shrugged, "He was very old, and in poor health. Besides, I'm not sure who to point a finger to if I thought otherwise."

"When did the break between Valens and Poppaeus take place?"

"Right after the old man died, Valens went from wealthy to just whatever it is you call *beyond* wealthy. It upset the balance of power, and Poppaeus stewed over it. Not long after, rumor spread that Poppaeus niece was Nero's lover. I imagine he leaked the information, just to grab at the implication of favor." Maius emitted his ugly laugh, "Did him little good, he was petitioned with favors to ask of his niece. As it turns out, they loathed each other!"

While I had a fair inkling as to why, Tay wasn't as well-informed. "How is that?"

"Poppaea was married to Rufrius Crispinus, formerly the commander of the Praetorian Guard, and a willing accomplice to the demise of Poppaea's mother. The woman ran afoul with old Claudius's wife, Messalina.

"Poppaeus never believed that his niece was incapable of helping her mother; he blames her for the death of his sister as surely as if she had thrust a dagger into her heart." Maius reacted as if the words flowing slowly from his mouth were delicious.

"I see. Can you tell me then, is it true that Claudia Antonia had been staying in the family's villa and departed the very morning of the riot?"

With his ugly grin spread wide, our host nodded, "Yes, Antonia resided there frequently. She was on good terms with Zenobia.

"My own men were at the harbor and witnessed Antonia's departure just after daybreak. Zenobia was yelling at the sailors who tended to a small ship belonging to the household. I'll tell you this, they were fleeing. While Zenobia returned the next day, Antonia hasn't set foot in the house, or this town since." Maius looked very pleased with himself.

"It would seem that Actia witnessed something that perhaps she knew was going to happen?" suggested Tay.

Maius only nodded.

"What do you think they are hiding?"

"I have thought up a hundred ideas, I just don't know. Right now, they are all protecting each other – it's just a matter of time before one of them turns on the rest." He obviously relished the thought. "Frugi will be Consul next year; Poppaeus is now the uncle to Nero's firstborn, and Valens and his son seem to be on good terms again. What might happen next?"

"Valens and his son?"

Maius was savoring the moment, "Well, after Lucretius died and left Valens everything, for some reason, it was the son who remained in the old, grand house. Valens lived up to the agreement and kept the old man's name, even moved into his family home, near you. All seemed well, but they were rarely seen together. Pansa's boy and Satrius are quite close, he's indicated some *break* between father and son. Ah, but young Pansa enjoys being the center of attention, and he's rather jealous of his friend's wealth and apparent *freedom* from his father."

"I see…" Tay noticed that his host was looking past him. I could see that Maius was being signaled by a servant in the adjoining drawing room.

"Well, now," Maius spoke rather quickly, "you will be off to Rome soon. Contemplate my offer with great care."

The same slave waiting in the shadows was beckoned forth to direct us back through the house after Maius uttered several pleasant and insincere blessings and well-wishes.

Once deposited on the street as quickly as a stinking pot of yesterday's mid-day meal, Tay mumbled, "That man has all the charm of a lizard."

It turned out to be an interesting choice of words. Only moments later, Ajax caught his master by the elbow and forced a scroll into his hands. "It's from Zenobia!" the young man whispered, as if merely saying the woman's name was a curse. "It just arrived by messenger, I ran all the way here."

And so he had. Despite the cool breeze, Ajax was short of breath and perspiring heavily.

"Thank you," Tay said absently as he inspected the parchment. "Good of you to get this to me. Head home, and be safe along the way."

The loyal servant, far more fit than I, gave his master a bow, and after pivoting on one heel, he took off sprinting toward our home.

I wanted to ask, *What does it say,* and Tay seemed to read my mind. He handed me the scroll. I unfurled the piece of parchment and found that it was completely blank.

"You know the way," Tay remarked and ushered me to lead him to the imperial villa.

Chapter Thirteen
Prophecy

𝄢𝄢𝄢𝄢𝄢𝄢𝄢

To My Dear Appian:

May this letter find you well, as am I. Only in the most poorly written Roman plays do two fugitives do anything other than attempt to blend into the place of their escape. Our farce most certainly defied convention.

Tay had meant to help his position, by proving to be a friend to Actius and a shield from him to Pompeii. Instead, he had trodden into marshy land, which the bottom had quickly fallen out from. Tay had not considered that while he was scrutinizing the conspirators, he was opening us up to too much unneeded attention.

I believe this was one of the few times that my perspective was more cautious than my companion's. I was concerned with Gavia's knowledge of my identity; and that Actius and Julia were both vaguely aware that some deception on our part was being carried out. Tay seemed unconcerned, or at least distracted. He dismissed Gavia as a trifling nuisance. As to Actius, his intentions were to have the man indebted to him. Julia, well, perhaps he supposed that I was taking care of that problem.

As to the intended trip to Rome, the thought was complete madness, which was why I feared he would actually join the delegation. I had enough to worry with, so I did my best to cast out the notion.

As I have described, our efforts had uncovered quite a bit of information. And nothing that we had learned simplified the pursuit of our query. However, as you can imagine, that was soon to change. We were on the verge of finding out exactly what we did not want to know.

Gavia had directed me to Zenobia via the roads and paths running along the city wall. However, Maius's home was very near the Herculaneum Gate, which would lead us to the villa.

With Vesuvius looming northwest of the city, navigation was rather easy, I merely had to look to the horizon to determine our direction. A forked road split by a lifeless fountain led to our intended gate.

After passing the archway and leaving the boundaries of the city, we were immediately surrounded by the funerary monuments of the town's wealthy elite. I directed Tay past a wall to our right and pointed toward the new marble tomb that Gavia had shown me.

The perplexed expression on his face transformed into a frown. "The late Titus," he remarked with a bit of scorn.

I did not show Tay the crude grave of Gavia's husband. She had opened up to me, not to him. As I hoped that she would keep my secrets, I chose to maintain her privacy.

We moved on, past the tombs, the arcade of shops, and the few homes overlooking the bay. Down the path and past the meadow, we came to the open gate of the imperial villa.

A different man guarded the way this time. He was an obese fellow, dressed in the costume of a Praetorian Guard. His brass helmet fit so tightly that his jowls pushed out over the chinstrap. His leather breastplate lay on top of him, like an apron. The cords that should have tied it around his waist hung to his sides. A billowing tunic, that did not appear to be standard military attire, hung to his knees. While he possessed a pair of fine soldier's boots, he did not wear them, instead they lay on the cobbled road beside him. On the massive man's feet were red felt slippers that appeared very well worn.

Standing on a stool was one of the little pygmy girls. She was tossing grapes at the guard's mouth until she noticed us. She gently placed one last piece of fruit into his open mouth before handing him the bowl containing the rest.

"Zenobia is waiting for you." She jumped off the stool and ran ahead of us toward the villa.

We followed at our own pace and arrived at the open entrance a few moments later. The albino doorman waved to us from the shadows of the vestibule.

Tay started to speak to the man, "I am Octavius Regulus, I am here to—"

"The mistress shall see *you.*" The pale-skinned man pointed at me, then to Tay, he said, "Wait there." His pale finger veered toward a small bench in the vestibule.

I could see Tay's jaw tighten, but he fell silent. I was led directly through the peristyle and then past a large atrium, a specious drawing room, and ended my journey within a semicircular room looking out to the sea, to either side the chamber opened to a garden terrace. A single couch sat in the middle of the room, and Zenobia reclined, facing the magnificent view.

I did not speak, but waited to be spoken to. The singular lady continued gazing at the bay while I studied her. She wore little more than she had when I first met her. A sheer, vibrant orange silk scarf concealed parts of her decorated body. The orange-brown henna covered her grey-brown skin, creating the illusion that another semi-transparent material was draped under the silk scarf.

As if coming out of a trance, the woman spoke in her low, sultry tone, "Few people are permitted within this dwelling, and fewer are seen by me. Those who seek me, favor me with obedience."

I stood silently, contemplating her words, as she had intended. The sound of waves rolling toward the jagged shoreline below us was pierced by the ominous cry from an unseen falcon.

"Actius remains in your home, and you have sought out old Proculus, Siricus, and Balbus. Perhaps, rather than masquerading as a mute, you should present yourself as deaf." Finally, her gaze fell on me. "All you have done is made the water murky. You've gained no knowledge to aid you in the discovery of Actia's murderer."

Fumbling for words, I said, "I am sorry–"

"It's not your doing, it's the Egyptian's." She paused, her light brown eyes seeing through me. "Perhaps, now he will see the power I have. I dispatched a blank scroll to you, not even a wax pressing to identify its authenticity, and what happens? You come running."

Once more, her eyes fell to the sea. "I told you that I would discover the murderer, and I am very close." She let out a long breath, and her smile indicated satisfaction. "Balbus, Siricus, and Eutychis all came running to me after calling on your Egyptian. They told me what they would not tell him–"

From the other side of the sprawling home, I heard a familiar voice making an unfamiliar sound. I took off and dashed toward the direction of Tay's shout. I found the albino with a broom in the peristyle directing the Komodo dragon toward the corner. The poor man was nearly blinded by the bright sun above.

The beast lumbered toward a row of shrubs. I could see a swath of yellow material dangling from the creature's mouth. Oddly, the dragon almost appeared to be smiling.

Tay stood rigid in the vestibule, defensively holding a single sandal in one hand, and inspecting his torn tunic with the other.

At a slow, undaunted pace, Zenobia appeared and barked at her servant, "Get out of the sun! *He's* subdued, let him be."

Tay's eyes shifted from the monstrous lizard to the exotic sight of Zenobia. Her long, orange scarf only covered part of her painted body.

"If you've been bitten, you will become ill," Zenobia said, with little concern.

At first, Tay was at a loss for words, which was rare for him. "No, just my tunic was caught when it lurched–"

"*He!* Not, *it,*" she snapped.

Tay looked to the creature, now basking in the sun and asked, "How do you know the sex?"

He fed her just the line she wanted. "I am Zenobia. I am all-knowing." The woman's tone was playfully condescending.

Tay appeared to concede to her and bowed his head, although, perhaps, he was merely concealing his wry smile.

"You should find a way to prevent Actius from traveling to Rome with the delegation. And *this one* mustn't leave the city." Obviously, she meant me. "Stop asking about the riot; as I told Marcellus, I shall tell you who killed Actia when the time is right." Zenobia snapped her fingers, and the albino proceeded to lead us to the door.

Tay leaned against the threshold and attempted to put his sandal back on. Zenobia's servant commented, "You broke the straps." He considered the options for a moment. I thought, perhaps, he would offer to loan Tay a pair, instead he told us, "Wait here, I'll have a litter prepared."

Once in front of our home, eight brawny men lowered the most elegant sedan I had ever ridden in, so that it was level with the sidewalk. Tay stepped out easily as if he were completely accustomed to the form of conveyance. I tumbled out as if I had stepped backward on a curb.

It would seem that Julia Felix had stationed a slave outside of her home to watch for Tay. I heard her steward's voice call out from across the street as the empty litter was hoisted up and moved away.

"Regulus!" The man's voice called a second time. Julia stood beside the fellow, too proper to shout at her neighbor from across the avenue.

Tay obliged the summons, and we went to Julia. She was dressed in an ornate, light green gown, with a pale yellow shawl draped over her shoulders. Emeralds dangled from a gold necklace, and her small earlobes. She appeared somewhat overdressed for the hour of the day.

"Why, Julia, so good to see you."

"And you." She looked toward the litter moving away from our home. "Just returning?" she asked, curious to find out why we had been in the recognizable conveyance. The purple and gold curtains enclosing the interior would not be found on any other litter than one belonging to the imperial family.

"Yes," he replied and declined to explain where we had come from. Instead, he held up his sandal and told her,

"As you can see, my footwear has suffered a catastrophe." With the sandal in hand, he pointed to our door. "I feel a fool and need to get inside, would you care to join me? I would be pleased to introduce you to my guest, Actius Anicetus."

Without a glance at me, the delighted woman agreed and followed us across the street.

Ajax opened the door, and seeing that we had a visitor, Corax leaped from a nearby bench and darted toward the kitchen.

Ever the gracious host, Tay suggested, "Demetrius, take Julia to the drawing room."

I did as I was told. Julia followed me, and once inside the rather public room, she whispered, "You must pay me a visit, *soon*."

I blushed and bowed my head before slipping through the billowing sheers into the peristyle. Tay was standing at Actius's open door, and he turned back and waved me forward.

With both his host and myself supporting him, his arms over our shoulders, Actius hopped on one foot to where Julia awaited.

The elegant woman rose from the couch as we lowered Actius to his own seat. I propped his leg up, and, lacking any grace, shoved a pillow under it. He winced with pain. Julia cupped her mouth with her little manicured hands, unable to repress a sneer at my deliberate mistreatment of the actor.

Once both parties had a moment to relax, Tay introduced the two. "Actius Anicetus, I would like to present my dear friend and neighbor, Julia Felix."

Julia burst out, "You are a marvel on stage. I've seen you perform here, in Herculaneum, and Baiae."

Actius, all charming, thanked her, adding, "How could I not have seen a woman of your beauty in the audience?" He sighed expressively. "Thank Venus I hadn't or I would have been too distracted to perform."

I let out a low groan that Julia seemed not to hear, instead, she put a hand to her bosom and batted her eyes. "Now, Actius, you exaggerate."

"Well, if you think so than I suggest you have your mirrors polished, for they aren't doing you justice," he said, ever so smoothly.

Forgetting my place, I rolled my eyes and shook my head. Tay nodded in full agreement that the performance was more than a bit much.

"Well now, already it would seem that you two are old friends," Tay remarked, as Corax slipped into the room with wine and a dish of cheeses and olives.

I studied the tray and heard Maius's words in my head. How quickly were our funds flowing out the door? Wine, food, hungry clients, small loans, surely the sum was adding up. Each amorous fellow arriving and departing might leave four or five bronze coins behind, but what could that amount to?

As pleasant conversation was made, I wasn't able to look at Actius, who was charming the woman whom I enjoyed being seduced by. Their chat consisted of nothing more than flattery and nonsense, until Julia commented, "I was so sorry to hear about your mother's death. She was a kind woman, I shall miss her."

Tay's brow lifted, and Actius cocked his head.

"You knew my mother? I didn't realize that."

"Oh yes, we met several years back. Claudia Antonia introduced her to me, not that I knew Antonia well. After Actia took up residence in the city, we saw each other regularly, at the women's bathhouse, the temple of Isis, and we even shared the same jeweler. She had such refined taste. I suppose she inherited that from Lollia Paulina."

Actius's piercing eyes fixed onto Julia, "Her death, what do you know about it?"

The well-concealed lines on Julia's face appeared, and her smile faded. "I didn't attend the sacrifice on the day of the calamity. The Oracle of Nephthys advised me to distance myself from the rites," she said rather distantly, recalling the prophetic warning. "Alas, I mentioned the Oracle's words to your mother, but she did not pay heed to them."

Julia let out a sad sigh and said, "She had planned on seeing Valens after the sacrifice, she had something of importance to tell him that couldn't wait."

Carefully, Tay asked, "What business did she have with him?"

"I didn't ask, it really wasn't the topic of our conversation..." her words trailed off, and the mask she wore returned. "I do hope that you are healing," she added rather suggestively, "Please, let me know if there is *anything* that I might be able to do for you."

After a short exchange of more pleasant small talk, Julia departed. I followed the woman to the vestibule.

Stated as an afterthought, Julia looked over her shoulder as she crossed our threshold and said to me, "Perhaps I shall see you at the evening rituals?"

I forced a smile that gave no indication of my intentions.

Starved, I ate all of the untouched food set out for Julia's benefit while Tay explained to Actius that Maius knew little more than we did in regards to the alleged conspiracy. He did not mention the man's offer of serving as his patron, the suggestion of betraying Valens, or the speculation that a rift had occurred between Valens and his son. And while Actius's eyes focused on the rip of Tay's tunic more than once, there was no mention of our trip to see Zenobia. I contemplated that the Greeks, seemingly susceptible to Actius's charms, might have mentioned the summons to the man while we were away. If they had, he didn't ask his host a single question regarding the topic.

Not long after we assisted Actius back to his room, I noticed Ursa stationed in front of the gate leading from the alley into the courtyard. She played the part of the look-out while Samson and their mistress emerged from their quarters intending on slipping through the kitchen where they would enter the vineyard.

Sitting on the top step of the upper floor, I went unnoticed. Like the peacock in the garden, my head tilted and followed the two as they gracefully, but quickly, walked under the portico and disappeared. While Cornelia's eyes never turned upward toward mine, I saw that she glanced in the direction of Actius's room.

I dropped a coin on the Oracle's offering table. One more coin taken from the strong box that Petronius had sent us. Perhaps it would return in the form of rent, but I had to ask what worth the offering really served. Was I there to see Cornelia, shrouded by her costume, perhaps thinking of the actor in my home? Had I come to see Julia? She had made a clear invitation, with ample innuendo. But was it I whom she wanted, or would I merely do? No doubt her thoughts were on Actius.

As the physical embodiment of Ra lowered toward the horizon, the other devotees arrived for the evening ritual. As was her custom, Julia was the last to arrive. We exchanged glances that only further confused my youthful heart.

The Oracle appeared in *her* usual splendor. Samson was hidden behind an elaborate, golden gown. Almost unnoticed, Cornelia trailed beside her accomplice clad in her simple, forgettable attire.

The veiled form of Cornelia was merely an extension of what I had briefly shared with her, something yet unseen, or understood. After so many days, Cornelia's kiss lingered on my mind, even if it was Julia's more recent advances that lingered on my lips.

The sky over the bay was a deep red, and creeping darkness behind us was the hue of purple reserved for the imperial family. The last chant ended, and the loyal followers of Nephthys began to disperse.

Rather clumsily, I made my way closer to Julia, foolishly intent on keeping her attention. I would like to blame my behavior on my youth, but this might not be just.

Cornelia and Samson went on to wait behind the heavy drapes of their new shrine. Once we had all left, they would come out to collect the offerings like pigeons descending on spilled grain.

Julia led me to her bedroom. With the door closed, she turned and embraced me, and our lips met. She was hungry for what I had to offer, which was very pleasing to me. I had a score to settle with Actius, and Julia would serve the purpose. I pushed aside the notion that while I held Julia in my arms and thought of Cornelia, perhaps it was Actius that Julia was fantasying about.

Once we were done with each other, Julia wrapped herself in a pale pink shawl. I was left alone on the bed, while she sat at her cosmetics table. Julia frowned as she studied her mature, yet still lovely, face in the mirror. With a sorrowful sigh she told me, "I was once beautiful."

I didn't bother to whisper when I replied, "If you were any more beautiful in the past than you are now, then you *would* have disrupted Actius's performances."

The compliment did not please her. "I thought men didn't feel the need to lie to a woman, once they had gotten what they wanted," Julia snapped. She stood and tossed my tunic toward me, "I'm sure Regulus is looking for you by now, you should leave."

The vigor I briefly felt vanished, and I scrambled out of the woman's bed and quickly redressed. She saw the hurt expression on my face and reached out to me. Her fingers brushed my chin, and softly she said, "Come now, I haven't the power to hurt your feelings. What could I mean to you, you strange enigma?"

I had no response. I wasn't sure what feelings I possessed for the woman. It was her passive and carnal interest in me that created any relationship we felt. What I wanted from her was limited to a physical nature. My jealousy over her attraction to Actius was not an indication of love, only pettiness on my part at not being the sole object of the woman's interest.

Unsure how to respond, I clutched the hand that had touched my chin and kissed it. She did not pull back, but rather, leaned into me. With little grace, I struggled back out of my tunic, as the shawl that had been wrapped around Julia fell to the floor.

"Ah, there you are!" Tay remarked when he found me in the kitchen. Geb watched me dance around Ursa attempting to remove a few pickled eggs from a plate destined for Actius. She swatted at my hand, and I swatted back at her. Tay intervened, "Ursa, let him have what he wants." And to me he said, "I'll be in my study."

With Tay's back turned, I took several eggs and a handful of olives. The stout woman gave me an ugly glare, and I believe that she was already contemplating her revenge as she watched me hand Geb a whole egg.

I stood outside of the study, cramming the food into my mouth. Other than winning the fight with Ursa, I took no enjoyment in the delicacies. As I finished my last bite, I joined Tay.

"Well, I don't think that I shall ask what it is that has kept you busy for the past hour." Tay looked at me rather grimly and added, "You always preferred the mature women. A houseful of girls here and you are courting danger across the street." He pointed to a wax tablet on his writing table. "The good brothers Phillipus and Polybius are planning to pay a visit tomorrow morning. They want to see for themselves that *Actius is in good hands.*"

The day had been long and eventful. As was the routine, the house filled with tradesmen and sailors once the sun set. I spent the few waning hours of the evening with Porcia.

As I suspected, the arrival of Zenobia's messenger was well-known. The ginger-haired woman, cradling her drowsy son, while I held little Regula, asked me what the feared woman was like. I described her as best as I might, which could in no way convey the true exotic nature of the

Zenobia. The strange, grey-brown hue of her skin, covered in henna, and her metallic, copper-tinged hair were simply indescribable. The woman's detached manner could not be explained. The description of Zenobia's giant lizard and bizarre servants sounded far-fetched even to me, despite my having witnessed them all. Numerous times, Porcia asked me, "You're teasing, aren't you?"

Much later that night, alone in my room with Geb nestled at my side, as I dreamed, it was not of Cornelia or of Julia, but instead, I was immersed in a rather exotic nightmare involving Zenobia.

Chapter Fourteen
Revelations

𝕫𝕫𝕫𝕫𝕫𝕫𝕫

Morning came all too soon. I had no desire to endure
Nephthys's morning blessings so I stayed in bed until Tay
came to rouse me.

"It is time to wake, or you will miss the good brothers."

I shrugged, unconcerned. Tay began to pick out what he
wanted me to wear for the day. When he set my silver
armbands on the stand beside my bed, I asked, "Have you
already dealt with your clients?" I had left the subject
unaddressed as yet.

Paying little attention to my attempt to start a quarrel, he
replied simply, "I have."

"I know better than to expect a straight answer from
you, but Maius made a statement that has stuck with me."

"And that was?" Tay laid a light blue tunic at the foot of
my bed as he made his reply.

"How full, or how empty, is our strong box?"

"Our funds are fine," he responded cheerfully.

"Why did you buy the vineyard?" I inquired.

"Because it was available at a highly discounted price."
Tay's response sounded like a tutor answering a child's
question.

"Who owned it?"

"Popidius was *forced* to sell it to the city. As it turned
out, Primus, who machinated the sale hadn't the approval
of the city council. He was rather eager to remake the
funds he put out for the land when the council started

asking what plots were owned by the city now that they may have to pay for rebuilding or demolishing."

Primus was the town's slave, in charge of the city records, taxes, and bribes. To listen to Tay, he sounded like the most corrupt fellow in Italy.

"So it was cheap, and you did him a favor?" I nodded thoughtfully, as if I were in agreement of the disbursement of our funds, before asking, "What about all the wine we serve to the sailors and tradesmen?"

Tay shrugged, "The Admiral pays well before he departs in the mornings."

I was surprised by how agreeable my companion was behaving while I questioned him.

"What about the clients you've collected?"

"When I send them off to work at a grain mill or a bakery, the favor is returned in trade. If they labor with a craftsman, then a favor is owed, it works itself out."

One last question, "Maius was correct, you've become a money lender, too?"

Tay's devious grin appeared. "Oh yes, I have. As of this morning, I have made back ten percent what I've loaned out."

I wished that I understood a bit about finances, but I had to rely on Tay's lopsided smile as an indication that we did, indeed, have a fair income supporting us.

"Besides…" Tay started to say as he opened the door to my room, "after I return from Rome, I will be showered with gifts and favors in gratitude for persuading Nero to finance the rebuilding of the Forum." He pulled the door closed behind him before I could react.

As I neared the last step of the staircase, I heard Gavia's voice from Actius's room.

"You can't drink it like Egyptian beer! That pot should have lasted you for days, fool."

Actius's plaintive voice responded, "I'm in pain."

"You don't know pain!" she snapped.

Hesitantly, I joined the pair. While Actius gave a smile of relief, the little witch groaned when she saw me.

"Please, make him more, I'll see to it that he drinks a smaller portion," I whispered.

"You'll do that, will you?" she responded sarcastically.

There was nothing that I could say that wouldn't irritate the woman. "Fine, don't make more for him!" I wasn't whispering any longer. "You aren't the only person who can spit in tonic."

I looked to Actius. "Corax or Ajax must know where another healer can be found, we'll send one of them– "

"He's my patient, just be still, you little fool." Her words were no more kind than before, but the sharp edge was gone from her voice.

I had nothing more to say. I was just opening the door to abandon Actius to his fate when Ajax and Corax pulled the door from my grip and excitedly told me, "Phillipus and Polybius are here to see Actius!"

The Greeks helped our injured guest to the drawing room as Gavia trailed behind and complained, "No wonder you're in pain, and you deserve to be. Hopping around like that, with those two pretty boys dragging you like they found you passed out in a tavern."

I walked ahead and parted the sheer drapes that were attempting to shield the room from the morning chill.

The two middle-aged brothers nervously sat side by side while Tay made small talk. When the brothers caught sight of Actius, they rose and began fawning over the man. Then they saw Gavia and fell silent.

The one-eyed woman looked to Phillipus. "Look at you, getting plump again. Remember what happened last spring? Too much salty food."

The portly man looked utterly afraid of the woman as he nodded his double chin. "Yes, I haven't been feeling well, perhaps you could mix a purge for me."

"I'll do just that, but you must go a week without the fish sauce."

He was more fearful of the prescription than Gavia. "A week? Oh, but that won't do. I'm leaving for Rome in just days."

"And you'll eat like the last rat on a sinking grain ship," Gavia remarked with light scorn.

Polybius couldn't help but chuckle, and Gavia swung her head toward the younger brother, "Don't laugh friend." She pointed at his foot, "I can tell that the gout is already coming back."

With a surprisingly delighted smile, Polybius concurred, "You know, I think you are right. Oh, how I hate the taste of that foul stuff you made for me."

"Then follow the diet I gave you," she snapped as she patted the man's large stomach.

"Come by my shop before you leave."

Both men bobbed their heads up and down. Once Gavia was away, Phillipus remarked, "She can cure anything. Polybius's wife had the most terrible wart on the tip of her nose. Gavia was able to get rid of it."

Polybius appeared rather embarrassed as he disagreed with the statement, "It wasn't a wart, just some sort of blemish."

Phillipus waved a hand in front of his younger brother's face, "It was more than a *blemish*, she had it for a year!" The elder brother fell silent and cleared his throat, signifying that the topic was finished. "Well, now that she's gone, Actius, tell us, you are well enough to travel to Rome, aren't you?"

"Of course, if you need more time, we might be able to wait It is Valens who wants us to rush off," Polybius remarked.

"Is that so?" Tay asked, "I thought the decision had been made by the town council?"

Phillipus spoke before his younger brother could, "The council elected me to lead the delegation, but the quick departure is at Valens's insistence.

"From what I understand, Ianvarius received a letter from Frugi that suggested Actius join us. Genius, wouldn't you say? Who better to express the devastation that surrounds us than the finest pantomime actor of our day?"

Tay and Actius both repeated the single word, *genius* at the same time. It would seem that neither brother was aware of the concern that both men were generating among their fellow elite. The brothers babbled on, interrupting each other, for some time. They described the planned trip in nauseating detail; from the color of the curtains on the litters to the number of wagons needed to follow with supplies. They even mentioned the choice of courtesans selected to attend the journey as neither man had planned to bring his wife.

Tay and Actius listened politely while I stifled several yawns. Once the men had run out of details and began to repeat themselves, Tay suggested that if they were to depart in just a matter of days, Actius needed his rest.

Frightened that a missed nap might ruin the voyage, they leapt from the couch and said their farewells before paying a call on Gavia.

Once I had finished helping the Greeks deposit Actius onto his bed, I found Tay in his study. Unable to remove the smirk on my face, I asked, "Four days, maybe longer, up the Appian Way with the two of them talking incessantly? Still planning on going to Rome?"

Tay ignored my question; however, I could tell by his furrowed brow, the thought of spending unlimited time with the two brothers was taxing. Instead, he suggested, "I think that it is time we meet Ianvarius."

"But you promised Valens you wouldn't seek out anyone else involved in the riot."

Tay gave me an unconvincing innocent look. "I merely want to present myself and have him send thanks to his master for the recommendation that I should be so honored as to be made part of the delegation to represent the city."

"Frugi recommended Actius…"

"Then I'll apologize for my misunderstanding of the facts as told to me by Phillipus and his brother." Tay concluded his comment with a rather amusing grin.

Unsure of how to string together my words, I began, "Perhaps I shouldn't accompany you – Frugi's younger brother and I…"

"Yes, I know, *were invited to the palace to be tutored with Britannicus,*" he mocked.

It did seem rather absurd that I had shared the education of the potential heir to imperial monarchy. That was a different existence, the life of Marcellus. Not the day-to-day farce of *Demetrius.*

"I doubt the brothers have shared servants, and besides, the last time they saw you, you were just a boy," Tay rationalized.

The residence belonging to the absent Frugi family was a short distance from our own home. The large house was quite close to the Temple of Isis and the town's two theaters. The bulk of Pompeii seemed to rest on a high plateau, with the southern ridge of the city clinging to a steep slope toward the river plain. Frugi's home faced a long avenue leading to the Stabia Gate, just at the end of the plateau.

The home had apparently weathered the quake with little or no damage. It stood quietly, almost ambiguously, amid the other dwellings. Blending in with the street, nothing about the structure spoke of the power or wealth the Piso family held. This particular house was just one of many that belonged to the family. Their line stretched back to the days when Rome was ruled by a king; over the centuries they acquired houses, villas, and farms in every part of Italy.

Tay had made a tactical decision to disregard proper form; he did not send a messenger ahead to seek an audience with Frugi's freedman. Instead, we showed up unexpectedly.

An iron gate before the two solid wooden doors stood open. I climbed two steps, clasped a brass ring, and knocked it against the door. Within an instant, we were shown in by a non-descript doorman. He listened to my companion's introduction with a blank face, made no reply, and led us both to a large sitting room open to the garden.

We had not been escorted to the bright spot to wait for the freedman to be found, instead; he was sitting on a comfortable looking chair reading a scroll.

Ianvarius was in his middle thirties; he had thick black hair, wide but neat dark eyebrows, and a plain, almost unmemorable, face.

As he carefully rolled his scroll together, he looked to a nearby chair and suggested, "Please, relax." The faintest hint of a smile remained on the man's mouth as he spoke with an elegant, evenly-pitched voice.

"Thank you," Tay replied stiffly. Ianvarius was not what my companion had expected. He wasn't a pompous ex-slave, or the typical, nervous minion that we had so far encountered. "I take it that introductions are not required." Ianvarius gave a little bow of his head, "I am Ianvarius Frugi Piso Felix, freedman of the Piso family. You, are Octavius Regulus, of Alexandria."

Showing less grace than normal, Tay nodded. "I apologize for calling without sending a message ahead. I found myself in the area and stopped in."

Our host's brows rose. "My servant, who's been following you, indicated that you seemed to be headed directly here, that's why he broke off and passed ahead of you to alert me." The tracing of a smile remained on Ianvarius's lips.

Tay was unsure how to respond, but after a moment, he had decided on his line, "I'm flattered that I warrant such attention from this fine house. In fact, the reason I came was to ask that you might thank your master on my behalf for the suggestion that I take part in the delegation to Rome."

While Tay had spoken, Ianvarius narrowed his eyes and pressed his lips together. "It was, in fact, my suggestion. I thought removing you from the city was imperative."

Tay lost full control of his right eyebrow as it arched dramatically. "I am being followed, and *removed from the city?"*

Our host's gentle voice gave no indication of hostility, "Yes, you've presented a problem to a number of men whom my patron would prefer left alone and forgotten." Ianvarius clasped his hands together and took a deep breath before continuing, "Let us be honest with each other, I shall not toy with you, and I ask the same."

Tay gave a flourish with both hands. "That sounds rather refreshing."

"Good." The well-mannered freedman caught the eye of a hovering slave, who went on to beckon a nearby serving girl. Even as he spoke, a little table was arranged with food and drink. "Your man and his little wax tablet," he pointed to me standing just several steps to Tay's left, "can he be trusted?" Tay merely nodded, and our host went on, "He was at Actia's home the second time I came by on the day Celer was killed. I presume his presence there is why you have involved yourself in the matter."

"Yes," Tay responded as he studied a plump, garlic-encrusted dormouse. "He was never treated as a possible suspect, my first indication that something was amiss."

"Ah, clumsy," Ianvarius agreed.

"And then Actius appeared at my home, wanting to confirm with Demetrius who had been at the house before Celer was found dead." Tay gently placed one of the dormice on his tongue. He chewed slowly, contemplating his next statement. "As I am sure that you know, Actius is convalescing in my home. He shared with me some information. It would seem that Celer suspected Actia had been murdered, rather than killed by the quake. Actius was in the process of going through Celer's desk, and he was struck on the back of the head. He had just found a list of names, which was taken from him."

"Suspicious, yes," Ianvarius agreed, and then asked, "How did his ankle become injured?"

"My tenant thought he was up to no good, sneaking around my house."

"Would this be the beautiful woman attended by a Nubian servant, or poor Gavia?" The man's smooth voice held just a hint of humor.

"Gavia," Tay responded before he popped an olive in his mouth.

"Ironic justice then." Ianvarius took a long drink and dabbed his lips with a napkin. "So you took it upon yourself to deduce the reason Actia and Celer died? May I ask why you felt this obligation?" The words were not spoken with any ill-will, just curiosity.

"The whole affair struck me as strange. Valens isn't a man all that comfortable with lying, his attempt to prohibit my interest in what happened was, as you said, *clumsy*. Furthermore, the sad story that my tenant told me of her eviction was rather curious. But what really motivated me, were the names on the list that Actius found. All of the names either could be connected to the riot, or to Nero. I thought perhaps the truth about Actia was best left unknown by her son. Something was hidden, and for good reason, I'm sure. I doubted that Actius would use the same discretion that I intended. Of course, I wasn't nearly as discreet as I had planned."

"Yes, the impromptu arrival of the small fish at Valens's home after you alarmed them with an invitation." Ianvarius gave just a light chuckle.

"Which I thought might prove who the big fish was."

"Valens?"

"That's what I thought, at first. But Valens seems to only be the one left tossing crumbs into the pond. The big fish are all done with them, done with Pompeii it would seem as well."

"Appropriately said."

Tay took a deep breath, exhaled, and then said, "Frugi and Poppaeus were the ones directing the aftermath. Your master was formerly the brother-in-law of Claudia Antonia, and at the time Poppaeus's niece had begun her affair with Nero. I know that Actia knew in advance that something was going to happen the day of the riot. She warned the Emperor's stepsister. Actia then arrived at the arena to witness what she had removed Antonia from. That's what I am missing, what *was* to happen?"

Ianvarius spread his hands and replied, "You have been very forthright, and please believe me when I tell you that I am not privy to the story in its entirety. I shall share with you what I know, and have deduced." He paused and placed his thoughts into order, "Poppaea had visited the imperial villa on several occasions, I dare say in an attempt to make friends with Claudia Antonia. I'm not sure of her success, but I do know that she had ensnared Actia with her charm and cunning." He paused again, choosing his words. "I believe that Poppaea was successful in turning Actia into her spy. With that in mind, I propose that Poppaea, still the secret lover of Nero, set in motion a plan to incriminate or ruin Claudia Antonia. Perhaps Actia, as Poppaea's agent, had second thoughts, or had always been loyal to Claudia Antonia. However the case, the Emperor's stepsister left town without anyone's knowledge, and oddly, on the same day the riot occurs. Then we have Actia embroiled in the events as they unfolded. Furthermore, my patron and Poppaea's uncle take a heavy hand at placing blame and cleaning up what has happened. Both men were in attendance of the spectacle. As well, both are on an unsure footing. Poppaea and her uncle were on poor terms, and Frugi lives under a perpetual cloud of suspicion from Nero."

"What would have happened if Antonia had been there?" Tay asked.

"I can't say… other than, the riot might have been quelled rather quickly if the six lictors and the numerous strongmen who trailed the woman had been present."

Tay nodded thoughtfully, "But that theory only plays out if a riot were the intention."

"Poppaea was one step closer to marriage with Nero. The Lady Agrippina had been killed four months before. Claudia Antonia's husband had recently been exiled, no one was left to look out for her, no one had any use for her. What if she was meant die in the riot; one less heir to old Claudius, and one less obstacle for Poppaea," suggested Ianvarius.

"Plausible," Tay conceded. "And why the scramble to hide the truth?"

"Why bring shame on Poppaea; perhaps she had even taken a *hint* from her lover?"

"Perhaps." Tay picked up a cup of wine and wet his lips. "You wanted me out of town so that I wouldn't stir up any more of this, and here you add kindle to the fire?"

Ianvarius let his slight smile blossom into a happy grin. "That's because Actia and Celer's death have nothing to do with the conspiracy."

Tay slowly set his cup down on the little table between the men. "Of this you are sure?"

"Oh yes, quite."

"Would you care to share the reason with me?"

"That depends. If I tell you the truth, will you convince Actius that his mother was killed in the quake, and Celer was using her death to remind those involved in the conspiracy that he still had something over them?"

"Is that what happened?" Tay asked.

"I believe that it is *very close* to what happened. Besides, you've stated that for the interest of Pompeii, you were willing to misdirect the man."

"There is the matter of justice," Tay said cautiously.

Ianvarius gave a deep nod of the head, and replied, "I believe when you hear what I have to say, you will see justice has served itself."

Skeptically, Tay responded, "I can tell Actius what you suggest, yet I have no power to see that he lets the matter go."

Ianvarius pressed his lips together and nodded. "I understand, I think you will help *direct* the man better once you've heard what I have to say."

Tay waited a moment before asking, "Is there a particular god you wish me to make an oath to…"

"No, not at all. We agreed to speak honestly, and we have. I ask no binding oath, just a continuation of our conversation. If you tell me you will trade the truth, at least what I have deduced as the truth, in return for telling Actius that his mother's death was not meted out by those involved in covering up whatever caused the riot, then I am satisfied."

Tay had little choice but to agree with the convincing man. "So be it."

Ianvarius took a sip of his drink before he began, "Let me start by telling you who Fannius once belonged to – Publius Memmius Regulus."

I'm not sure if Tay would have realized the connection, the man mentioned was both the father of that year's Consul as well as the first husband to Lollia Paulina.

Ianvarius went on, "The old man died last summer, a terrible toothache turned into an infection of the blood. Fannius found himself freed, and for a short time, resided with Regulus's son. Now, just a few months ago, Fannius comes to Pompeii and, however it happened, took up residence in the house of Actia. I'm not sure if you are aware of this, but before Actia was a member of Lady Agrippina's court, she was a freedwoman to Lollia."

Tay nodded that he did, indeed, know this information.

"Actia took Fannius, her fellow former slave, into her home. According to Celer, Fannius seduced her. More, however, that he was trying to lull her into a false sense of security. Celer didn't trust the man; of course, Celer had certain feelings for Actia, too. As Valens's man, placed in the house to watch over the woman and see to the funds she had been generously given, it was his duty to be vigilant. Celer warned Valens that Fannius was trouble, and he even suspected that the man might discover where Actia's wealth had come from.

"Valens and Actia were to meet, after the sacrifice to Augustus and the city founders. That meeting never happened. She left the house, insisting on Fannius escorting her rather than Celer. She did not return." Our host paused to let his words sink in. "Do you know why Actia was invited to become one of Agrippina's entourage?"

Tay shook his head; he did not. I had been grasping at a particular notion and wished to blurt it out. Instead, I held my tongue.

"Agrippina was jealous of Lollia for a number of reasons. Lollia had been married to Agrippina's brother, while it's rumored that the practice of incest was taking place. Agrippina and her sister were both accused of plotting against their brother and exiled. She may very well have had some suspicions that her *sister-in-law* might have been whispering these plots into Caligula's ear. And many years later, it is well stated that Claudius had considered marriage with Lollia.

"Agrippina was the old man's fourth wife, what's to keep him from reconsidering Lollia as a possible fifth? However it happened, Lollia was accused of sorcery and exiled. There was no trial, Claudius listened to a single witness produced by Agrippina and sent poor Lollia away. She was later forced to suicide, mere exile did not pacify Agrippina." The man's thick, dark brow rose.

After a moment of silence, Tay remarked, "Actia was the witness."

"That she was." Confirmed Ianvarius.

I wondered, then, if this was why Actia feared the afterlife. Might Lollia be waiting on the other side of the river, with a vengeance?

"Celer sent a letter to Frugi the morning that he died. I intercepted the document. It read..." Ianvarius picked up the scroll that had been in his hands when we arrived. In his polished voice, he began: "*My Dearest M. L. Crassus Frugi, May this letter find you under Jove and Juno's protection. My fears have been realized, Actia has been killed. I gave clear warning to my former master, Valens, and he did not act. While the blame might be laid on myself for not removing the threat sooner, or Valens for not taking my earnest warnings, the sinister hand of fate belongs to a freedman named Fannius. The wretched creature served Lollia Paulina before her divorce from Publius Memmius Regulus. Freed by the old man at his death, Fannius arrived with a single desire – vengeance.*

"I had arranged for Valens to meet with my mistress, fearful that she was in danger. She was blind to my warnings, due to her kind and sentimental ways. I trusted that Valens would help her to see the truth. But the meeting never happened. As you know, disaster struck the city. Actia was found near the house. Respectful citizens, recognizing Actia's lifeless body, brought her home. I had believed that her death was caused by the quake. Yet in the following days, I heard that she had been seen running from the site of the disaster, and Fannius was with her.

"It is clear to me that Fannius saw the opportunity that he had sought and avenged his former mistress, Lollia Paulina. And more, I fear that the man learned the truth of what happened at the arena. It is imperative that Fannius be dealt with, and soon. I fear that with time, his knowledge might be shared with the son of his late master, the current consul. If this were to happen then I would have failed at my mandate of keeping Actia from exposing the truth.

"My words fall on deaf ears, Valens ignores my concerns. I pray that your voice might improve the man's hearing…" Ianvarius dropped the scroll to the table in exchange for his wine.

"Fannius?"

"Fannius, and *fate*." Our host cocked his head and suggested, "A crime for a crime. Actia betrayed her mistress. It took fourteen years, but vengeance was served."

"And Celer…"

"The letter was sent here, to be added to my next dispatch to Frugi. I saw Celer's seal and opened it, wishing to spare my patron from anything tedious. When I read the letter, I went straight away to Celer." He shook his head, the faint smile was gone. "I told him that letter writing would do little good. He should kill Fannius outright and be done with it." Ianvarius sighed. "But I should have known he didn't have the stomach for it."

"Or he tried but Fannius struck back, harder..."

"As it seems, yes. After the incident, I realized that I had forced the letter back on Celer. I decided I wanted to hold onto it. That's why I returned later in the day..." Ianvarius pointed to me, "when he was there, playing the part of the painter, a break from his pursuits with the lovely Julia Felix." He gave me a rueful expression, and then went on with more enlightenment. "Celer was dead. Well, I had no intention of bringing that to anyone's attention. I personally didn't care to rifle through Celer's desk with his body crumpled on the floor." Ianvarius paused, considering his next statement, and went on to say, "The following day, I sent the fellow who's been keeping an eye on you to retrieve the letter from Celer's desk. My apologies for the use of force, but I made it clear that the letter needed to be obtained. He struck Actius, and along with the letter, he also took this."

The collection of names that Actius had found was handed to Tay. My companion held the parchment so that I might catch a glimpse. The name on the top of the list was Actia's, the *A* was large and written ornately. Under Celer's name, a bold, flourishing line had been inked. The rest of the names were printed in small, rolling letters, and I could not make them out despite knowing them. Tay placed the scroll back in Ianvarius's outstretched hand.

Unable to remove the sound of frustration from his voice, Tay asked, "And why must we keep this truth from Actius?"

"Nero will make all the flowery speeches this city wants to hear, and promise gold and men alike. And then he will grow bored and forget his promises." Ianvarius shook his head. "We must depend on the senate and our current Consuls, one of which is the son of Lollia Paulina." Ianvarius let out a disappointed groan. "We must ask ourselves, did Fannius avenge his former mistress on his own accord or perhaps...for the pleasure of someone else?"

The simple question was rather thought-provoking. Both Tay and I clearly understood why Actius could not be told the truth.

Ianvarius stood from his chair, indicating the meeting was concluded. "I would, of course, appreciate knowing the outcome, once you've told Actius *our version* of what took place."

Tay assured him that he would send word. We were just turning to be led back to the entrance by a waiting servant when Ianvarius made one final statement, "Oh, and Regulus, in the spirit of friendship, I must tell you this – my man hasn't been the only person following you."

My companion attempted to act unsurprised, however, I knew that his carefree tone was employed most often when he was concerned. "Can you tell me whose minion is making repetition of your shadow?"

Ianvarius responded with disappointment. "He hasn't been recognized; although, he and my own servant have tripped over each other in pursuit of you."

Unable to control his wicked grin, Tay asked his new *friend* for a favor.

Ianvarius followed four slaves carrying a curtained litter out of his patron's home. As the brawn stepped onto the road, he told the lead man, "Take Regulus back home and return as quickly as possible." The servant nodded, and as one, they moved onward.

Emerging from the alley beside Frugi's home, Ianvarius's young spy set out in pursuit of the litter. And shortly afterward, another fellow slipped out of the shadow of a nearby doorway.

Of course, we were not in the litter. We were standing just inside the Frugi's vestibule.

Believing that his quarry was on the move ahead of him, we left the residence to slink behind the unknown tail.

Keeping the litter in his sight, the dark-haired man strolled at an even pace. Watching the farce before us, I must admit that I was a bit embarrassed to think that these two young men had been trailing after us for days, unnoticed. I could only imagine Tay's indignation that he had not been aware of them.

Once we were only a few blocks from our home, the dark-haired man slowed. He must have thought *our* destination was obvious. Ianvarius's man went on past our house as if innocently walking by, while the litter was set down at the front entrance. The leader of the bearers opened the curtains concealing the passenger. One of Ianvarius's pages climbed out of the litter and proceeded to our door.

The man we had been following did a double take and spun around towards us. He was either about to run back to Frugi's house to see if he might find us, or more likely, return to his master. Instead, he caught sight of us and froze where he stood. We rushed him, and as easily as a hawk might scoop up a field mouse, we grabbed him.

Within an instant, the slaves that had served as our decoy rushed to our aid. The man was carried with great ease down the street and deposited in our atrium.

"I would like to know who has put you up to spying on me," Tay asked with his most menacing tone.

The man attempted to squirm, but his movements were restricted by the four big men holding him in place. He realized that he had no alternative, and mumbled the name, "Valens."

Tay looked to the leader of the men who had been so helpful and asked politely, "I would like to speak to Valens without interruption. Do you think you could place him in the litter and take him for a tour of the city, just long enough for me to get to my destination?"

I was distracted from the reply as I watched the door at the end of the peristyle open. Cornelia emerged from Actius's room. Her makeup was smeared, and her dark, wavy hair was uncoiled. My eyes fell to Cornelia's shoulders, the left strap of the woman's gown was ripped, forcing her to hold the garment in place.

Our eyes met, and her pink skin began to burn red.

"Demetrius," Tay called, waiting for me in the vestibule.

Dumbly, I looked back down the portico toward Cornelia, who no longer returned my gaze. Tay misunderstood my reaction and said, "This isn't the time to tell Actius…besides, I'm not quite sure what I'm going to tell him. Come along."

Numb, I did what I was told.

Chapter Fifteen
Truth Be Told

〔리〕〔리〕〔리〕〔리〕〔리〕〔리〕〔리〕〔리〕

Valens greeted his guest with an odd smile as we were ushered into a large office. "Regulus, I had hoped to see you soon." He gestured to a chair, and stepped over to an oddly-placed, wooden chest.

"Did you? Well, here I am." There was nothing friendly about my companion's tone of voice.

Valens sensed his guest's displeasure. He reached over to the chest and opened it. I could see an abundance of silver and gold coins. "I had never considered that you might be in need of a patron. I will also add that Maius is incorrect, I *am* a loyal patron to those who trust me."

Tay lifted his head back and drew his brow together while remaining silent.

Valens went on, "I have ears in Maius's house, as I'm sure he does mine."

I thought of Ocella, standing nearby while his master attempted to buy *Regulus*. Had he told a member of Valens's household himself, or had the conversation been repeated by one servant to another? The secrets might very well have been a sort of currency, with freedmen like Ianvarius and Eutychis growing rich from them.

"I know that Maius presented himself as your best choice to ally with, and he discounted my abilities. I would like the opportunity to prove him wrong."

Tay took a deep breath and let it out very slowly while he stared at the coins in the chest. He raised his head and looked Valens square in the eye. "I'm afraid that *your ears* didn't hear everything. I am not looking for a patron. Nor am I allying with Maius. I don't mean to make enemies with the man any more than I wish to betray you. I left him without answer, only because *no* would have set me down a path that I wished to avoid just as much as telling him *yes.*"

Valens shrugged, unconvinced. "Well, men have second thoughts after being offered a fortune and refusing it…they look at their own coffers and reconsider their ideals and what they are worth."

Tay stood up and stepped toward Valens in one quick, fluid moment. He kicked the lid of the strong box closed and said, "It would seem that mine are worth more."

A look of shame descended upon Valens's face. He had misjudged the young man. "I meant no offense…"

Tay nodded slowly before replying, "I wasn't offended by Maius's manipulations. I quickly surmised that he had few scruples. You can't blame a buzzard for eating carrion. But I do take offense to how you have treated me. You have misled me, you've arranged to distract me, you've spied on me, and now, you are trying to buy me like I am one of the whores I inherited from Popidius."

I felt a bead of sweat run down my forehead as I listened to Tay's stinging words.

Valens swallowed hard and backpedaled to a nearby chair. I wasn't sure if the man would lash out at Tay or attempt to apologize. He stared at his guest for several moments before saying, "It's been a long time since someone took that tone of voice to me." He considered his words and suggested, "Perhaps I should tell you the truth, I suspect you know most of it already."

Tay let out a sigh. "The truth would be worth far more than that chest. And the debt I owed you would be paid with my silence."

Valens nodded, and a weak smile appeared on his face. After a little sigh, he remarked, "Well said." The man paused, mentally putting his facts in order. "Actia, having been a member of Lady Agrippina's court, found herself without an *official* patron after our Emperor had his mother killed. She was in Misenum at the time and fled here. Zenobia, a collector of misfits, welcomed her at the local imperial villa. From time to time, Claudia Antonia had frequented the villa, otherwise the place was rarely used by the family.

"Actia and Antonia found themselves on friendly terms. By this time, Poppaea was waiting for Nero to abandon his wife, Octavia, and marry her. Of course, Poppaea knew how easily Nero was influenced. She realized that Nero's marriage to his stepsister had political ramifications. If he succeeded in discrediting her, his advisors might urge him to marry the other daughter of Claudius. Poppaea wanted her removed from the list of women who might stand in her way.

"Poppaea flattered and charmed Actia any time she was in Pompeii. Little gifts were sent, that type of thing. She never overtly attempted to turn Actia against Antonia, but she subtly worked to claim favor.

"Poppaea's plan was simple but effective. She merely asked Actia to deliver a letter to Frugi while he was leaving the games. What Poppaea hadn't planned on was that Actia would break the seal and read it. The letter was written, as if from Claudia Antonia to Frugi, *her former brother-in-law.* The letter alluded to previous conversations and stated that Claudia Antonia agreed to marry Frugi and help him usurp Nero's position. A date was suggested for the deed, along with a few details of how it might be done.

"Actia shared the information with Claudia Antonia. They surmised that the letter was of no value unless intercepted. They suspected that either Antonia or Frugi would be seized at the arena, and the damning message would be found and revealed. Zenobia removed Antonia from the city after frightening Actia into following a new plan. The three women knew Nero would be displeased if they accused his mistress of any ill, let alone such a scheme.

"They abandoned Frugi to his fate, and Actia went on to hand off *a* letter to the man. One that, if recovered, would be unworthy of the emperor's notice. Actia realized that her life was in danger, but she also knew Zenobia would readily kill her if she did not continue the scheme.

"Actia did as she was told and found Frugi leaving the arena just before the executions, as was his custom. She forced a letter into his grip. She saw the men who were staged, watching for the hand off, and she panicked. Frugi's own strongmen reacted to her shrieking and were already alert when Poppaea's Nucerian strongmen rushed in. Frugi made away as the skirmish turned into a brawl. Once a few Nucerians saw their own men cut down, they retaliated.

"Frugi summoned me to his home, even before the riot was quelled. He explained how, after being handed a benign letter from his former sister-in-law, the female messenger became hysterical. Men were sent to search for her, once someone recognized her description. Actia was found, fleeing toward the villa, and brought to us. She didn't waste any time telling us the whole story.

"Frugi called for Poppaeus, and Actia was forced to retell the scheme. Poppaeus broke down with shame, by the gods, the man had no control over his niece…"

Valens gave a great sigh. "The rest is rather obvious. We couldn't blame Poppaea, that much was certain. Grosphus and his brother-in-law were dead, Gavianus was nearly mad—and then he killed himself—Livineius Regulus was already emptying his house when we sent for him, blame seemed easily placed."

"There were a few more witnesses, they came forward to defend the city and say that the Nucerians started the fight." Tay managed to say this neutrally.

"Yes, they were *detained*, and then once Frugi, Poppaeus, and I convinced the council to let us appoint a Special Prefect and new Duumvir…they were silenced." He closed his eyes and did not speak for a moment, "I'm not proud of that, but it was done for the needs of the city."

"The greater good," Tay said softly, without scorn.

"The greater good," Valens repeated. "We went off to tell Nero we were not at fault, but Actia's description of *the revised events* damned us. She told him what she saw, subtracting Frugi's presences and her panicking, two Nucerian men were attacked by several Pompeians." He held his palms out and shrugged. "Gladiatorial events were banned from the city, and we were fined." He forced a sad laugh. "But we escaped telling him that his secret lover had meant to destroy his stepsister and one of our most noble citizens, then failed and we all knew about the plot."

"And if he had any part of it, he was saved the embarrassment," Tay muttered.

Valens said nothing, but closed his eyes.

Tay commented, "As a *reward,* you gave Actia the home of one of the disgraced duumvirs, and you put your own man in the household to watch out for her."

"Yes, she had nowhere to go. We didn't want her to fall into Poppaea's hands and expose that several of us knew the truth. She couldn't go back to Zenobia, she still feared the woman. I had her right where I wanted her, where I had someone keeping an eye on her." He ran his hands through his greying hair. "Then Fannius arrives and everything began to fall apart. Actia toyed with Celer, there had been something between them. I should have known that would eventually cause a problem. Celer became jealous of Fannius, who found not only an invitation into Actia's home, but also her bed. Celer was distrustful of the man. He warned me that Fannius couldn't be trusted and that Actia might reveal our secret to him.

"By Pluto, Actia had contacted me the day before the disaster. We were to meet after the ceremonies. I had planned on telling her to send Fannius on his way. But the Gods had a different plan, didn't they?"

Tay repeated what had already been pieced together for us by Ianvarius, "Celer suspected Fannius of killing Actia, disguising her murder as a result of the calamity. Fannius had reason, he had also served Actia's former mistress's household…"

"Oh yes, Celer explained it all quite clearly. Again, I did nothing. Nothing but give Fannius time to kill Celer." Valens stared at that strongbox with a forlorn expression.

"And Fannius, related as he is to the Consul Memmius Regulus, cannot be punished." Tay added.

"You understand," Valens said with some relief.

"The greater good," Tay quipped, this time with a hint of scorn.

"Actius can't retaliate, he must be misled." Valens's word, while said as if a command, sounded more like a plea.

"I understand," Tay remarked somewhat hollowly.

Valens attempted to apologize to his guest. My companion stopped him and quoted Aesop, *"A doubtful friend is worse than a certain enemy. Let the man be one thing or the other, and then we know how to meet him."*

Valens assured Tay of his true friendship and then we departed rather abruptly.

Tay and I walked home at a brisk pace. I kept turning back to see if we were still being followed. There was no longer any point in keeping track of us, yet I had the feeling that there were at least one set of eyes still on my back.

Actius surprised me when we entered his room to check on him. He gave me a slight, nervous smile and then avoided eye contact. He had seemed more the type of man who would ignore his wrongdoing, perhaps even gloat that he had stolen the affections of a woman that an acquaintance desired.

Tay sat down near Actius's bed and told him a convincing story of more failed audiences and then asked, "Is it possible that Celer was mistaken? Could your mother have been killed by the gods' design when the ground turned on us?"

"That wouldn't explain Celer's death, would it?" Actius said, his voice giving away his concern that his host had turned on him.

"Perhaps the deaths are mutually exclusive…"

Actius's eyes narrowed.

"Hear me out. Yes, your mother was, indeed, part of some dark secret, and Celer as well. But all involved were better off to leave the matter as it had been concluded. What good would come of eliminating one conspirator? However, Celer lives under a guilty cloud. He sees shadows where there aren't any. Your mother is killed in the quake, but he can't accept this; he convinces himself otherwise. Then, he starts pointing fingers, and the men who had shared the secret with your mother were cornered into silencing him before he could expose them all."

Actius shook his head vigorously, "No, you see, while that sounds plausible, my mother had written me a letter telling me she needed to see me. She had something that she wanted to tell me, something that couldn't be communicated through a letter. I knew whatever it was had to have been important." He leaned back in his bed, his dark eyes focused on something far away. "Celer didn't even know that I had already made plans to leave Athens when he sent me his letters."

Tay's shoulders slumped, he would not be able to convince the man of the lie. "You believe she was going to tell you the secret, after all these years of silence?"

"I do, and that's why she was killed," Actius said with a sorrowful voice.

Tay cupped his hand to his chin and stated, "I see, and my sympathies are with you." He paused and said with true regret, "But I don't know what more I can find out."

Actius placed a hand on Tay's arm and said, "You've done what you could, and at peril to yourself. I can ask no more of you." The statement was said kindly, while in truth, he knew that his host had taken the side of the conspirators.

As the sun set, the house filled with the familiar men. I was surprised by how casually Tay behaved. It was as if we'd spent the day frivolously. He made small talk and laughed with his guests as they waited for their turn with one of the women.

When the Admiral arrived, Actius was hauled to the drawing room, and the three drank from some of Tay's best vintage. Mucia was asked to sing again, and she entertained the odd group until the night grew late.

I had hidden in Tay's study, pretending to read, while I sulked. Despite my relief that the mystery was solved, I had no desire to share the company of Actius.

I woke the next morning with a terrible headache. I had drunk my fair share of wine, even though I had not joined the guests on the evening before.

In addition to the discomfort that I felt, I could hear the sounds of two wailing children coming from Porcia's room. I wanted to fall back to sleep, but once Geb felt me stir, he leapt from the bed and pawed at the door.

A bite to eat, and some distance from the disgruntled infants seemed a good start to cure my headache.

I found the kitchen blessedly abandoned and helped myself to a honey cake. In fact, I took three, one for me, one for Geb, and I tore the other one into a few pieces and offered them to the crude bronze idols in the household shrine. The peacock, strutting through the garden, was fortunate enough to snare some of Geb's.

I heard movement from the nearby room where the bathtub was housed and quickly headed for Tay's study. As the curtain closing off the room from the courtyard fell closed behind me, I heard Ursa's unhappy voice call out from the kitchen, "Who's been in here?"

Geb was at my side, and I was fearful that the peacock, with honey and crumbs on his beak, might get the blame.

"Ah, you are up early considering the amount of wine you drank last night," Tay remarked. I noticed his eyes were bloodshot. He had drunk more than he was accustomed too before collecting me from the study and ushering me to bed.

"The wailing of the babies woke me," I replied in a hoarse whisper.

Tay shuddered, "Poor woman, I should buy her a helper."

"You should get another slave for the chores you have Mucia do and let her help Porcia. She seems to like the children, and she and Porcia get on well."

Tay was nodding at my suggestion approvingly when a rapid knock on the study door surprised us both. "Yes?" Tay called out.

A rather disheveled Ajax opened the door and blurted out, "Zenobia's messenger is here."

A moment later, a tall, lanky young man with a shaved head entered the room. He was dressed in a flowing robe of emerald and bejeweled like an eastern king. Ajax carefully led the man toward us, and I realized that the messenger was blind.

"You have a message?" Tay asked, perplexed.

In a deep, lyrical voice we were told, "My mistress seeks the master and his servant of this house."

I wasn't thrilled with returning to Zenobia's domain, but I was pleased at the notion that even without names, I was being referred to, for a change, as the master.

"It is early, I have clients to see." Tay's tone was rather testy, but he had little choice in the matter.

"Zenobia beckons, all the same." The blind man replied, knowing that his mistress's wishes were seldom refused.

The purple and gold trimmed litter sat awaiting us outside the front doors. We climbed in, and the conveyance was hoisted upward. Tay pulled the curtain aside and told the blind man, "There's room for you."

"I will walk," he replied and followed behind, listening to the footfalls of the men carrying us away.

Tay leaned in to me and scoffed in a whisper, "This is pointless, we know the whole story now."

This time it was I who cast the devilish smile on my companion. I had the distinct feeling that the gods were about to prove him wrong.

The familiar albino ushered us inside the imperial villa and took us straight away to his mistress.

Zenobia reclined on a large couch, strewn with silk pillows, in an ornately painted room overlooking the bay. The artful depiction, set against a dark red backdrop, portrayed an initiate being led through a religious rite. The participants, painted rather majestically, were life-sized. Each face bore unique character, their robes almost looked as if they were in movement. As fanciful as Zenobia kept her surroundings, I would not have been surprised if the figures had stepped out of the wall.

"You do not take instruction well," Zenobia said, her sultry tone giving no hint at amusement or displeasure.

Tay's voice held a hostile edge. "I do not–

"I suppose that is why *he* makes for the better slave." She let her eyes slowly skim over me. I suddenly felt naked before her. "It is of no matter. I shall end your poking and questioning. *As I told you,"* Those few words had a bite to them. "Actia's murder had nothing to do with the riot."

Tay puffed up his chest and proudly said, "Yes, I know. Fannius killed her, and Celer."

Zenobia gave a great laugh, but Tay ignored her and went on, "Fannius had also served Lollia Paulina, he avenged her and then silenced Celer…"

She laughed again, "Fannius was Actia's lover. Both in the past and again after he was freed. Fannius wasn't loyal to poor, dead Lollia, he was loyal to the mother of his son."

"Actius?" I blurted out.

"Actius," Zenobia concurred. Her voice dripped with condescension as she explained, "She had planned to meet with Valens to ask that he remove Celer from her house; the man had grown jealous," she looked into my eyes, "as forgotten lovers do when faced with a rival." Her gaze fell back to Tay. I could see that she enjoyed his blank expression.

"Celer…he killed Actia?" Tay sounded more like me than himself.

"She and Fannius were together at the sacrifice, they became separated. Like the two of you, he dug through the rubble to assist as he could. Actia went back to her house. She and Celer had one last fight, and he murdered her. When Fannius returned, Celer gave his own explanation.

She had been killed in the quake, and her body had been found and brought back to the house. Honest men tend to hear the truth even when it isn't, they have no reason to suspect lies."

"Then who killed Celer?" Tay asked.

"Fannius!" I exclaimed.

Zenobia continued, "Celer changed the story that she had been accidentally killed, to murdered. He had to cover for himself once he found out that Actia had been seen alive after the quake. Celer sent Actius three letters. The first was his original lie, and then an ambiguous accusation. It would seem the last letter naming Fannius as the killer arrived in Athens after Actius departed." She paused to let her words sink in. "How better to avenge himself on the man who caused his troubles than blame Fannius for the crime? Fannius deduced this as the men who Celer sought to support his acquisition called on him. Fannius realized Celer's guilt, and as you mistakenly said before, took vengeance. Not for Lollia–"

"For Actia." I finished.

Zenobia extended her arm, covered in interlocking patterns, and pointed a finger at us as she said, "The next time I give you a piece of advice, do as I say."

Tay shrank a bit and asked, "How do you know this?"

She winked at me before answering my companion's question, "I am Zenobia, I am all-knowing."

Chapter Sixteen
The Miracle

🔲🔲🔲🔲🔲🔲🔲

The litter was hoisted atop the bearer's shoulders as Tay let out a load huff. "Well, that was all highly unnecessary. You and your damned *elven arches*! It was nothing but a lover's triangle, and we end up tangled in all of the muck that was put to rest four years ago!"

This wasn't the first time that we had solved a puzzle completely unrelated to the question at hand. I couldn't help but give a little laugh.

Tay snapped, "There is nothing amusing about this."

I shrugged and gave Tay a grin that said I disagreed. "Yes, but your dilemma is solved. You can tell Actius the truth, the *actual* truth. Celer killed his mother, Fannius avenged her."

Tay made no reply other than to let out a long sigh of relief.

Once standing on the cobbled sidewalk before our home, Tay began to brace me as I climbed out of the luxurious litter. He was then distracted. I managed to fall out and trip on the curb as Julia's voice surprised me.

"Thank Juno you've arrived! Actius is very upset – he's just left – I'm worried…"

"What's happened?"" Tay asked, placing his arms on the woman to still her.

From our open door, Ajax appeared and frantically waved an unrolled scroll at his master. "This arrived while the lady visited Actius..." he blushed, and looked away from Julia. "Mucia took the message to him, she didn't know that he...had company."

I looked to Julia, in a lovely yet rumpled stola. Her hair hung down, unbraided, and the dark red stain on her lips was smeared.

Tay stared at the scroll; on the outside was written the name Actius. I recognized the bold line inked beneath the familiar handwriting, the line curled at both ends, the flourish was mimicked with the last stroke of the oversized *A*.

He opened it and read the note aloud, "Dear Actius, The entire household prays to Apollo for your recovery. This message arrived by courier to you, it has come from Athens. If I might be of service to you, please send for me – Fannius." Tay looked to Ajax and demanded, "Where is the message?"

"Actius has it. It was crumpled into a wad of parchment in his hand. Whatever the message contained, made him furious," Julia informed us.

Tay looked down the sidewalk leading away, "Where is he, he can't be far hobbling along–"

Julia pointed toward the distance, "He's in my litter!"

We took off running, hoping to catch up with the man before he arrived at his mother's house. Julia's litter wasn't as flamboyant as the imperial livery or as elegant as Frugi's, but I recognized it and its bearers as we neared them. Wheezing, I stopped for a moment to catch my breath, sure that we would catch up.

"You're on the move early this morning," came a voice from behind me. I felt an arm slip over my shoulder and the point of something hard against my ribs.

Tay, several paces ahead of me, turned back to urge me on. He stopped in his tracks when he saw that I had been overtaken. "What's the meaning of this?" he demanded.

The dark-haired man who had been following us on behalf of Valens replied, "I have a score to settle with you. The way I see it, you owe me what Satrius Valens should have paid me for following you all over this forsaken town."

I recognized the minute changes in Tay's expression as he realized we had assumed incorrectly that it was the elder Valens who'd wanted us followed. My companion retraced his steps until he was within reaching distance.

"Well then, I suppose we should return to my home, I haven't any funds on me at the moment." Tay began walking alongside us, and just as we started to move with the same rhythm, he shoved himself into our menacing companion and pushed me away. From the fold of his own tunic, he pulled a small knife and indiscriminately stabbed at the man.

This commotion caused those on the street around us to take notice. They stopped working and moved toward us as our stalker fell to his knees clutching his stomach.

We were very near the unoccupied home of the elder Valens, which was swarming with craftsmen and the man's slaves. A thug, who should have been keeping the block safe, stepped over, looked at the pain-stricken face of the bleeding man and said, "You've caused enough trouble." The hulk stretched out a large, grubby hand to clutch Tay.

"I can explain!" Tay said, knowing better than to argue with the giant. He looked to me and said, "Stop Actius!"

Confident that Tay would solve his own problem, I took off toward Actia's house.

I ran as fast as I could. When I arrived, I found Julia's men leaning about the façade of the home. The litter sat on the sidewalk, empty.

I kicked at the door, and the men watched me with idle curiosity until Xeus responded. I pushed past the old man, after forcing the squeaky door open. Once in the house, I saw several slaves cowering and heard the cook, Martha, screaming, "Stop him!"

Just past the atrium, I saw Actius struggling with Fannius in the drawing room. Despite the twenty year age difference, Fannius had the upper hand, due to Actius's injury. The older man held Actius by his shoulders, attempting to push him away. Actius was relentless, as he forced the weight of his body onto Fannius and knocked him over.

Fannius began to rise and then abruptly stopped, instead he remained vulnerable on the floor. "Listen to me! I didn't kill your mother…"

Actius glanced at the nearby bust of Actia; the pedestal was just within his reach. He picked up the stone creation and raised it over Fannius. By this time, Julia's litter bearers stood around the atrium and stared at the spectacle just as the household slaves did. No one would go to Fannius's rescue.

Actius grimaced in pain as he held the bust over his head. Fannius did nothing, he wouldn't fight the man anymore. He wouldn't harm his son. Actius braced his weight with his good leg and prepared to cast the bust down onto Fannius.

I looked around the room, praying someone would take action. They all stood as mute as I.

"Actius, stop! *He* is your father! Celer killed your mother, not him!"

Actius froze; then staggered back several steps away from Fannius, and then he dropped the beautiful bust of his mother. It crashed and broke into hundreds of fragments. The shards scattered, and a cloud of dust fanned out and slowly disappeared into the air.

All eyes were pointed toward the man who had prevented Actius from killing Fannius. And I glanced around to each person, with a rather astonished look on my face, which matched theirs. For the mute had spoken.

Tay entered the unattended, open door of the house to find whispering servants, a large mess of shattered stone, and me and Fannius lifting Actius to a bench. Tay looked very relieved; of course, he didn't know that I had just shouted in front of a large group of witnesses.

"It would appear that I am too late to stop the confrontation," Tay remarked surveying the damage.

"And too late to see the miracle," Actius quipped.

Tay's brow rose.

Fannius enlightened my companion, "Your slave stopped my son from trying to kill me. He shouted out that I am Actius's father." The man was both pleased and proud.

Tay's face lost all color as he responded, "A miracle, indeed."

Actius looked to Fannius and asked, "Why didn't you tell me?"

Fannius shrugged and explained, "I never had the chance. Eros interrupted me, when you first arrived. Then you were in his house." The mild-mannered man pointed to Tay, "We were never alone.

"That's what my mother wanted to tell me? That you were my father?" Actius understood why the woman had wished him to visit.

"That and we had planned to marry." Fannius's eyes grew red. "Actia shouldn't have confronted Celer. All she had to do was assure Valens that his son's secret was safe."

I watched Tay's brow arch, I knew that he had a question to ask of Fannius.

Actius realized the sequence of events. "You killed Celer, realizing that he was attempting to blame you?"

Fannius responded rather honestly, "I killed Celer the moment it dawned on me that he killed your mother."

We left Actius with his newfound parent. Tay was in as much of a rush to remove me from the house as to pay a visit to Valens, Satrius Valens to be specific.

Julia's men obliged us and carried us straightaway to the impressive house with the bronze faun overlooking the impluvium.

Tay and I were both bruised, disheveled, and frowning when the doorman led us to the elder politician.

Valens was opening his mouth to repeat some standard salutation when his eyes focused on his guest and he instead blurted out, "Dear Isis, what's happened to you?"

"Your son hired a bit of brawn to follow me. I caught the man the other day and got a name out of him. I should have asked for the full name. I gather he reported back to Satrius what happened and your son refused to pay him. The brute came to me for what he thought he was owed." The next statement was said with considerable menace, "I want an explanation."

Valens raised his palms. Now, with so much of the truth out, there was no reason to lie. "My adopted father knew we had manipulated the events, following the riot. Over a lifetime Lucretius made a fortune with his troupes of gladiators. When Nero banned gladiatorial combats from the city, he decided that Nero should know the truth. Poppaeus and Frugi both tried to reason with him, but he wouldn't listen to reason. He was an old, unhappy man who only cared about his own interests. They came to me; they wanted me to discourage him. They went to my son when they realized I wouldn't do what needed to be done."

Tay sounded rather astonished as he asked, "Your son killed your benefactor?"

Valens nodded his head. "Actia was a rather convincing woman, she knew what effect tears had on men. Lucretius refused to listen to us, so my son suggested that we let Actia try to reason with him." Our host's eyes lost their focus as he recalled what had taken place. "He was in his bed, sick and weak from all of the agitation. My son showed Actia to his room. Satrius remained just inside the door after presenting her. Actia begged him not to expose the truth, she tried to appeal to him, flatter him – shame him even. The old man didn't care, he grew tired of her and berated her for her own flaws. Satrius decided to end the threat. He pulled the pillow from underneath the old man's head and smothered him."

Tay said what I had wanted to, "Actia did nothing?"

Valens's voice was almost a whisper, "More than nothing, she bore witness."

Tay nodded with understanding. "With so many other deaths, Actia couldn't be silenced too. She kept your son's secret in exchange for a house, servants and an income."

Valens only nodded.

From behind us, a soft voice spoke. "I lost my wits–" Satrius broke off and rethought his words, "I couldn't listen to him any more, the threats and the accusations. He would have ruined my father."

Tay and I both turned to see the young man standing in the wide doorway.

"Removed the threat and then you received this fine home as a reward." Tay's words were laced with scorn.

"No, this house is my punishment. I am surrounded by what I have done. My act is inescapable. The slaves, who suspect me of wrongdoing, watch me each day, as does his shade."

The young man spoke with such sincerity that I thought even I could feel the dead man's presence lingering in the room.

The elder Valens asked his son, "You had Regulus followed?"

With just a hint of defiance, the young man replied, "Despite your assurances to the contrary, I couldn't believe that he wouldn't find out what we've been hiding. I hired Aemilius to follow him. I wanted to know who he spoke with. Little good it did."

"Regulus...I am so very sorry..."

Tay waved a hand to silence the older man as he fumbled for words. "It's over, in fact, it is all over. Actius knows the truth about his mother's death."

The older politician's mouth went slack.

"Fannius murdered Celer, but not Actia. It was Celer who killed her." Tay handed Valens the crumpled up letter he'd taken from Actius.

Celer's third letter indicated that Fannius had killed Actia, vengeance served for her past crimes against their former mistress.

Tay explained, "Celer wanted you and the other conspirators to turn on Fannius before Fannius or Actius could meet. Fannius would have told him, not only that he and Actius's mother were lovers, but that they were father and son. Fannius never had a moment alone with Actius— if Eros hadn't shown up accusing you of wrongdoing this all would have be settled days ago…" Tay's words trailed off.

Valens remained silent for some time, he glanced toward the strong box that remained in the room, but thought better of suggesting what surely was going through his mind.

Tay eased his thoughts, "The matter is over. I'll repeat nothing that I have learned."

Satrius hung his head and stepped aside. As we passed, he mumbled, "I am sorry."

Tay did not pause his step as he repeated another of Aesop's clichés, *"The injuries we do and those we suffer are seldom weighed in the same scales."*

The following morning, I walked down the steps and glanced at Actius's empty room. A line from one of Plautus's plays came to mind, *No guest is so welcome in a friend's house that he does not become a nuisance after three days.*

As I stared at the darkened doorway, Geb looked up to me. I wondered if the dog sensed the pettiness of my thoughts. I led him to the kitchen, a distraction for both of us.

After sharing my morning bread, I heard the Admiral's voice in Tay's study and slipped inside the room. With his back to me, I listened to the brawny man speaking, "I thought you ought to know, a man named Maius has been loitering at the harbor. He's asked me some questions about you, and Actius. He's certainly interested in your business."

Tay shrugged and replied, "I think he will soon lose interest. Besides, I'm off to Rome in another day."

"Actius banged himself up pretty good wrestling with Fannius, he's sent word to that Phillipus fellow that he's not fit for travel," Proculus remarked.

"Perhaps they will choose to postpone the voyage after all." Tay's voice gave no indication of relief.

"They shouldn't, our work at the dock is almost done. My boys are happy to stay and lend a hand with the bridges and the aqueduct, but someone's got to tell Nero or the Consuls to give the orders."

Tay's eyes drifted to mine, as the man's words resonated with Ianvarius's.

Proculus took notice that I'd entered the room and scooted his chair, to better face me. The delicate piece of furniture gave a little creak, and I quickly stepped closer before he could strain the chair any more. "Ah, I hear you found your tongue, the gods wanted you to save Fannius!"

Tay generously said, "The credit goes to Gavia. The woman's been giving him some sort of tonic; it's finally restored his speech."

"Well, let's hear you speak?" said the benign brute.

Feigning hoarseness, as though not in the habit of speaking, I told him the truth, "I haven't anything to say."

Proculus gave a hearty laugh, pointed at me, and then quipped, "At least not in front of your master!"

We both politely chuckled at the man, neither all that amused with his statement.

After the Admiral departed Tay tapped three letters on his desk. "A short summary of events."

I nodded.

"I think that Balbus, Siricus and Eutychis will be pleased to know that both Actia and Celer's deaths have been resolved."

I shrugged in response.

"*Gavia cured you*, you don't have to just bob your head any more."

"It was easier when I couldn't speak," I admitted.

Tay's devious grin appeared before he replied, "It was certainly *safer* when you couldn't speak."

Once Tay had dispatched the three letters, he made ready to set off and tell Ianvarius the story, face-to-face. With my newfound voice, I declined his *invitation* to accompany him. I was prepared for a short argument and even curious as to which of us might prevail.

Instead, Tay shrugged and told me, "Better that you don't come along, I intend on visiting with Ptolemy. I need to find out just how well he knows *Octavius Regulus's* stepmother."

"And if he is a dear friend?" I arched my brow in imitation of my friend.

"Then I will have to explain where I have been for the past six years." Tay remarked in a condescending tone.

"Six years?"

"That is when *I* disappeared." Tay brushed by me, headed toward the door.

"What happened to him? How do you know that's when Octavius Regulus disappeared?" I questioned, highly perplexed.

Tay waited until he was several steps into the atrium and called back to me, "I should know; that's when I ran away from home."

I took a single step, intent to chase after him and demand the truth. But I got no farther; I broke into a strange, nervous laughter. Perhaps I didn't want to know the truth just yet.

Despite the early hour, Gavia had already removed the shutters from her little shop. I could hear her whistling a disjointed tune in the back room, and her bird jabbered on unseen. I stepped inside and timidly called out, "Hello?"

Gavia called back, "What do you want, fool?"

I went to the back room and found her mixing up a tonic.

"I wanted to apologize—"

Gavia didn't lift her head from her work, "I don't like apologies. They do nothing to help the injured person. They just make the one who is in the wrong feel better."

"I suppose so…"

"You are talking now, that's a pumpkin-headed idea." She eyed the mixture in her hand and sniffed it.

"I agree. Regulus is giving you full credit, I hope it's good for your business."

She scoffed, "So I heard. Now I'll be blamed for the idiotic words that tumble out of your mouth."

Ignoring the insult, I told her, "I know what happened; the secret about the riot."

Gavia's single eye focused on me, but she said nothing.

I elaborated, "Nero's wife, Poppaea, set the events into motion, she meant to ruin Claudia Antonia and Frugi."

"She failed," Gavia commented in monotone.

"The men who knew the truth scrambled to control the information, fearful of what might happen next. All the same, what they did to you was wrong." I paused, giving her a chance to snap at me for my understatement. She remained silent, so I went on, "Regulus is owed some favors, and he earned the trust of the right people. I think that he could probably arrange to have your family's home returned to you, perhaps an income too."

Gavia hissed at me and then led me to a tiny alcove behind the storeroom. She opened a large strong box and pointed at an impressive heap of gold, silver, and bronze coins. "I don't want that house, and I don't want their money." She gave me a gentle push back to her work room. "I'll never have *my* life back. Of all people, you have to understand me, Marcellus."

I did.

After a moment of silence, she pushed the pot of liquid that she had mixed together toward me. "Actius caused you some grief – told you he would. *That's* a love potion. You just have to decide if it's for Cornelia or Julia."

I stared at the little clay pot, wondering if the liquid could work. I pushed it back toward her and replied, "I don't want either of them to love me." That might not have been entirely the truth, but at the moment, it was how I felt.

Her voice softened, and I saw through the menacing façade to a fragile young woman, "Drink it yourself then, it will help take the taste of betrayal out of your mouth." Her more familiar tone returned as she added, "Perhaps it will cure that curse of yours."

Taking the route that Gavia had shown me, I set out past the city walls. A cool wind whipped at me as I skirted along the stone fortification around the city.

Following the path toward Vesuvius, which towered beyond Pompeii, I was captivated by how inescapable the mountain appeared. It was as if the gods had painted a backdrop for the entire city. It was a strangely beautiful sight, an image that haunts my thoughts even still.

As I neared the villa, I felt an odd pang of excitement that I could not quantify. One mystery was left, and I was confident that it would soon be answered.

The slightly-built man dressed in the oversized Praetorian Guard's uniform ignored me as I passed through the gate he perched beside.

I walked up the path toward the imperial villa with far less trepidation than I had on my previous visits.

The entrance was open, and the albino waved me in from the shadow he sat in. "I would like to speak with your mistress, if I may."

I was directed through the house and past the dragon. The frightening creature, with its probing tongue, raised its head in my direction but made no other movement.

The doorman announced me, and I was ushered into Zenobia's spacious bedroom. She reclined on her oversized couch, and watched the pigmy girls preform some simple, yet awkward acrobatics.

The exotic lady applauded when the little women had finished. They bowed, and then their mistress motioned for them to disappear.

"Congratulations, Marcellus, I understand that you may now be heard," Zenobia said in her sultry voice.

"Yes, I had no choice but to call out and tell Actius the truth in order to save Fannius. ."

"The *truth*, what an ugly word," she whispered.

"It can be a thing of beauty. If the truth were known, I could have my life back," I retorted, rather bravely.

"There are perhaps too many *truths;* one might serve you, the next might ruin you."

I had not come to hear her speak in riddles and innuendo. "How did you find out that Fannius was

Actius's father? How did you learn that Celer killed his mistress?"

She shifted under the orange silk sheet that concealed little of her exotic body art. "If I tell you, I might lose my reputation as *all-knowing.*"

"Your secret is safe with me."

We shared a conspirator's laugh, and she enlightened me, "I had vaguely recalled Actia telling me who the father of her child was when she was staying here. I thought that Fannius was the man she mentioned.

"The idiots who came calling on your companion told him what they felt safe to share, when I sent for them, they told me everything they knew. I realized that Celer was attempting to lay blame on Fannius, and I suspected why.

"It was Porpurio who told me what I needed to know. As people disregarded you, *the mute*, Porpurio is undervalued because of his childlike mentality. I asked him to describe what happened the day of the quake. He told me every detail, from the moment he woke up, until the sunset when Celer told him to go to sleep. Most people don't have patience. Like your clever man, they want a simple answer immediately. They discard the progression before the fruit becomes sweet.

"Porpurio observed that Valens had sent a messenger to Celer, wanting to know why Actia wished to meet him so urgently. Celer had been unaware of the meeting beforehand. With Porpurio only a room away, Celer confronted her, and asked the nature of the meeting. She told him she wished him out of the house and was going to have him removed. She left with Fannius to attend the festival.

"Porpurio said that Celer was cross and mean to him. Then the quake struck. Celer told Porpurio to go to the forum and search for the mistress. He was told by someone who recognized him that Actia had been seen and was headed back toward her house. When he returned, Celer needed his help. They moved the body from her bedroom to the atrium. He told me more, but that was the piece of information I needed to be sure of Celer's guilt. It was obvious that Fannius, too, discovered the truth and killed Celer. I'm sure, had Actius spent more time in the house, Fannius would have told him the truth. Instead, he was under your roof."

Zenobia was no more mystical than Cornelia. Threading information together, she was impressive with her insight, but it was all a sham. The Oracle used religion, to distract. Zenobia used the folklore whispered about her to intimidate.

The strange creature read my mind. "You see through me now. I've lost my *mysterious allure*."

Her accusation wasn't entirely true.

I was in the courtyard, painting gallant rebel slaves, when Tay returned home. He sauntered out and inspected the work. "It's a bit garish," he quipped.

"I like it, it speaks of freedmen, the denial of Fate, and the force of the strong-willed," I said plainly, no longer whispering.

Tay nodded. "Yes," he paused for effect, "paint over it with something pleasant. A nice garden scene, perhaps Persephone picking flowers near the River Styx."

I would not be baited into a mock quarrel. I said nothing and continued painting. Tay realized that I had made up my mind to ignore him and began to walk toward Geb, who basked in the sunlit garden. Tay paused and pointed at a fresh scab on my calf. His brow rose, and he asked, "What happened to you, where have you been today?"

I didn't turn to face him, but kept my gaze on my rendition of Spartacus. "I went to see Zenobia. I wanted to know how she came to the truth."

Concerned, he crouched and ran a finger over the reddened bite. He exclaimed, "That creature bit you!"

"I'm fine, it didn't hurt." I didn't correct him in regards to which *creature* bit me or what we had been doing.

For the time being, I was content. Neither Cornelia nor Julia plagued my mind. To add to that, I didn't quite feel the plight of the powerless slave. Indeed, I was feeling a bit rebellious. I picked up my paintbrush and began to paint another fearless rebel on the slope of Vesuvius.

To My Dear Appian:

I pray this letter finds you well, as I am. I have just read your letter, commenting on the end of my story. You are correct, we had foolishly risked our safety in Pompeii. Yet, in the end, Tay's actions were to his benefit, and mine. Tay was respected for his valor and duty to the city. He had kept the secrets shared with him and exposed Celer as Actia's killer. To the delight of the city leaders, he had even appeased Actius and the trusted freedman of the year's Consul.

Of course, I knew the truth, what were perceived as attributes were actually Tay's weaknesses; bullheadedness and contempt of authority.

As to your query in regard to Julia and Cornelia, I do not know if either visited Actius before his departure. And these many years later, I think I would prefer not to know. I was a foolish young man, and while one moment, I might have been disenchanted with either woman, that moment was soon to pass.

Tay avoided any details on his meeting with Ptolemy. I assumed that either the man wasn't a threat or he was susceptible to bribery. It would be some time before I found out the truth as to where the name Octavius Regulus came from. Therefore, I think I should keep you in some suspense as well.

I shall wait to answer your last questions in my next letter. The tale of the delegation's trip to Rome is too lengthy to begin now, with the messenger waiting to take this dispatch.

One last thought, Tay did not repeat his request that I paint over my Spartacus scene, instead, he hired a professional painter and commissioned a rather lovely fresco depicting the bay. Oddly though, the view was reminiscent of the vantage point afforded from the imperial villa. Perhaps Tay realized the true source of the bite on my calf.

Rightfully my dear friend could make the same claim as Zenobia – in the end, it would seem that he was all-knowing.

May Janus bless your travels and Jove protect you.

All of my love, Gaius Sempronius Gracchus Marcellus

Author's notes:

The Fresco that captivated Marcellus was removed from a house in Region One of Pompeii. It can be seen in the Naples Museum.

As they say, a picture is worth a thousand words. While Tacitus relays the story in his Annals (XIV. 17) a nameless artist created a fascinating piece of art depicting the riot. However, it is not an accurate retelling, but a characterized account with much artistic license. (This could be said of Marcellus's story as well.)

The amphitheater has two large staircases on the west side of the structure. Both are supported by six archways, not eleven as painted in the fresco. There may not have been a hidden meaning in the fresco's inaccuracy. But who is to say?

Actius Anicetus's name was found on the graffiti outside of the house in question. He is known to have operated pantomime troupes in Pompeii and Herculaneum.

There is no recorded link between the actor and the man who killed Nero's mother. That is an invention on my part for the purpose of storytelling.

Gavianus and his adopted son were city officials at the time of the riot and there is no trace of them after the event indicating either death or exile. Livineius Regulus, who did, in fact, sponsor those games, was exiled.

The name Gavia can be found on numerous containers that held lotions and various products. Once more, I've created the link between this woman and the politicians for the purpose of the story, however, that isn't to say she wasn't the daughter of poor Gavianus.

For more information on Pompeii please visit my website: www.robertcolton.com

Of a more personal nature, I would like to thank Tammy McNaughton, who knows Tay and Marcellus almost as well as I. While reading the drafts of this story, several times she asked, "Would Tay really have done that?" She was always right, he wouldn't have, and I made the revisions.

I am indebted to Seth Warner for his assistance on the technical side of book writing. Without his help I would be forced to learn the more tedious aspects of publishing.

I would like to thank Melissa Gray for her proofreading and editing. Without her help this would have been a fiendish collection of misplaced commas and strange wording.

Robert W. M. Greaves graciously read the final work and pointed out many needed changes. I can't thank him enough for his help. Mr. Greaves pointed out the unlikelihood that Zenobia would have a Komodo dragon. However if Robert Graves can give one to Tiberius, I hope I will be forgiven for taking the same liberties.

I also appreciate the support of my family, and the encouragement of my dear friend Audrey Pichair McCarron, who is like family to me.

A special thanks to Dana Fulton, who has found living in Ancient Pompeii a fact of life.

For more information:
www.robertcolton.com

Twitter @GaiusMarcellus

Facebook: Marcellus Sempronius Gracchus